Praise for the Outremer series:

The Books of Outremer

Visit the series' website at
www.outremer.co.uk

FEAST OF THE KING'S SHADOW

The Fourth Book of Outremer

CHAZ BRENCHLEY

ACE BOOKS, NEW YORK

FEAST OF THE KING'S SHADOW

An Ace Book / published by arrangement with the author

PRINTING HISTORY
Originally published as part of *The Feast of the King's Shadow*, Orbit / 2000
Ace mass-market edition / September 2003

For information address: Orbit,
a division of Little, Brown and Company (UK),
Brettenham House, Lancaster Place, London WC2E 7EN.

ISBN: 0-441-01098-9

ACE®
Ace Books are published by The Berkley Publishing Group,
a division of Penguin Group (USA) Inc.,
375 Hudson Street, New York, New York 10014.
ACE and the "A" design
are trademarks belonging to Penguin Group (USA) Inc.

PRINTED IN THE UNITED STATES OF AMERICA

10 9 8 7 6 5 4 3 2 1

Big hearts are big houses,
with a spare room for friends.
This one's for Richard and Jane.

I seek refuge in the Lord of mankind,
The King of mankind,
The God of mankind,
From the mischief of the sneaking whisperer
Who whispers in the hearts of mankind,
Of the djinn and of mankind.

—THE HOLY QUR'AN, 114, MANKIND, 1–6

ONE

A Dark Way to Glory

"THERE'S ONLY ONE way to see Rhabat for the first time," Elisande muttered, "and this is emphatically not it."

"No?" Julianne countered, sweet as a nutmeat, hard as the shell around it. "What shall we do, ride down with our eyes closed until you say we can open them?"

Elisande just snorted; Jemel said nothing at all, either to the girls or to Marron on his other side.

Marron himself could find nothing to say. Which he knew was not unusual, was indeed what they would expect. What they couldn't know was that his silence this evening had little to do with the Daughter in his blood, or with his own internal conflicts. He was simply overwhelmed by what he was seeing, as Jemel had meant them all to be, as Elisande was so perversely determined not to be.

It was two days since he'd fetched Hasan to the battle by the well: two days of travel, his friends riding with the Sharai and he walking easily before or behind them, keep ing his distance both for the camels' sake and to avoid the stares and whispers of the tribesmen. The staring and the whispering had gone on regardless, he knew that, though he hid his eyes beneath the hood of a new robe; he knew also that there would be a great deal more of it in days to come, and that he couldn't avoid it all. For these two days, though, he had clung to what separation he could. He'd led when the trail was obvious, followed when it was doubtful; when they had camped last night he'd held himself apart, with only Jemel for company.

The party had kept its own distance from the Dead Waters, following the line of the shore but staying always some little way inland, where the sea was just a glimmer of light on their left and the wide and trackless Sands stretched to the horizon on their right to blend at last invisibly with the pale rim of the sky. This was Beni Rus land and they patrolled regularly, Hasan had said, to know who moved at Rhabat's back, and also to watch that no evil arose from the Waters. The duty was shared, between the tribe's commanders; he had refused to discount himself, despite his council's slow assembly and the urgency of the times. And so he had led the squadron out, and so Marron had found him . . .

Though she seemed to hate to touch her father, Elisande's magic touch worked as well on Rudel as it had on Marron; he was riding with the others, when he truly ought not to have been breathing any more. The healing had brought no sign of reconciliation between father and daughter, though; if anything it had aggravated the tensions they felt around each other, that they had been forced to come so close.

Around noon today the ground had begun to rise steeply, as the party approached a ridge of high hills, almost mountains; they'd found a path then, a narrow way that wound to and fro across the face of the climb until it disappeared into a cleft in a sheer escarpment that showed rose-red to other eyes than Marron's, so that he knew the colour was true.

They'd passed from fierce light into black shadow, and then out into light again as the path brought them ever higher. That had set the pattern for the afternoon; the hills had risen in a series of steps which the path alternately ran over and cut through, always seeking a way that was gentle enough for the camels. Some of the gorges were smooth-walled to a point higher than Marron could reach, as though worn by torrents of water; others seemed freshly torn in the living rock, so sharp and harsh the walls were, though the path under his feet told of ages.

At last there had been one easy stretch, out in the open once again, and nothing but sky to be seen beyond, all the great desert behind and below. Marron had heard a boy's shout at his back, and the sounds of a galloping camel; he'd trotted quickly off the path, to let Jemel pass without pan-icking his mount.

Jemel had ridden to the top of the rise, hobbled his camel and walked off to the north, where the slope was cut away in a sharp cliff-edge. He'd beckoned urgently to Marron, and to the girls behind him.

The other Sharai must have seen this before, many times; they stayed by the path, waiting in a tolerant group while their guests were given this first sight of Rhabat.

AN EXTRAORDINARY SIGHT it was, though Elisande dis-paraged it. Marron thought she might be doing that for a purpose: to give herself an excuse to stand a little way back from the drop where Julianne could stand with her, hand in hand and unexposed to shame, here where courage counted above all.

Certainly the view did not deserve the girl's scorn. The desert lay spread out below them like a wrinkled sheet of linen, yellow and dun with age; far to the west was the ridge of mountains that closed off Outremer. To the north, Marron thought that he could just make out a jutting nail on the skyline that might be the Dancers' Pillar of Lives. By their feet, the cliff dropped sheer to cast its shadow like a mantle of mourning black across the Dead Waters far below. And, here, across more than water: for the cliff was bitten back into a wide bay, and where the sea lapped at the back wall of the bay it lapped at rock that had been shaped by more than its own tongue's lapping.

Still daylight up here, with perhaps another hour's company to be kept with the sun before it left them; down there it was dusk already, the last of the sunlight gone some time ago, though the sky would still show blue overhead and beyond the mouth of the bay.

Deep shadow couldn't deceive Marron's alien eyes. He saw how that back cliff had been worked for perhaps half its height, how natural caves had been widened and new ones cut, how steps had been carved in the cliff-face leading down to what was almost a wharf, a man-made pavement of stone to hold the waters back a little from those open caves.

It should have been a wharf, he thought, a quayside; there should have been boats tied up, ships perhaps moored out in the bay. Ropes and barrels and all the noise and chaos of a port, and those caves used for storage, for chandlery, for drinking-dens and worse . . .

But the Sharai did not drink, of course, or not in dens; and it seemed they did not sail either, or not this sea. There were no boats on the water, not a skiff, not a raft; nor was there any sign of habitation in those caves. No hint of lamplight in the darkest recesses, no whisper of sound beyond the whisper of the water on the stone.

There was a breach in the face of the cliff, though, a steep-walled gully where once a river might have run if ever there were rivers here, if ever they'd been needed to feed the sea. That would get little enough light at midday; even Marron could make nothing out within its cleft. He imagined shadows growing there like creepers, utterly undisturbed, feeding on the night-dark and blossoming by day, tangling together into dense mats of black that even his eyes couldn't pick apart . . .

Neither could he hear anything from the gully, this high up and far away. And yet this was Rhabat. Elisande had said so, and Hasan had promised they would reach it today. It took small intelligence to determine that there must be life below them somewhere, or that it must lie along that gully.

Footfalls from behind, one of the riders walking over. Hasan: Marron knew him by his breathing as much as by his step, as by Jemel's sudden stiffening beside him.

"Well, Julianne? This is the back gate into a place of splendour, and I suppose I should apologise for its shabbiness; but I never have, and by your grace I'll not do so now. God has lent it ornament enough, by laying out the whole world as a doorstep."

"It is a very far view," Julianne replied gravely, if a little faintly, "though not perhaps the whole of the world. I cannot see back all the way to Marasson."

"This is all the world that matters," Hasan said, "at least to me. Perhaps I will persuade you that you need no more. For now, though, we must go down; which I regret means that you must turn your back on distant hopes and ride in shadow for a while. I hope you do not mind enclosed spaces?"

For a moment, Marron thought she was going to laugh aloud. Her mouth did twitch, he thought, behind her veil, before she had control of it; and her voice bubbled a little as she said, "No, Hasan, I do not mind enclosed spaces. Not at all. Though if you mean to shut me in a box and lower me on ropes, then . . ."

"No, lady; I said you would ride, and you shall. The way is hidden, though, and long, and the roof is low; some find it disturbing."

"I think I can promise not to be disturbed by a low roof. I can't speak for my camel, mind . . ."

"Not many can. If she objects, we will blindfold her and I shall lead her down myself. I will not be forsworn in this, Julianne; you will ride into Rhabat as befits you, even if you must come by a tiresome road."

"Yes—will you tell us more of this road? I had heard that there was only one way in or out of Rhabat."

"Many people have heard that," he said, smiling. "Just as I have heard that there is only one way in or out of the Roq."

"That at least is true, or would seem to be. For the moment. We left that castle as we arrived, through the main gate." Not for want of trying another exit, Marron remembered, with a touch of chill. They should have gone through the Tower of the King's Daughter and into the land of the djinn; the way had been blocked, and all Rudel's art and understanding had not been enough to open it. Indeed, the man hadn't even tried. A minute's thought, and he had turned back. To lead them instead to the stables where he had killed Fra' Piet, where Marron had killed Aldo and others, so many others . . .

Marron remembered little of their time in the Tower, he had been in too much pain; but he did remember a great wall of blackness, barring their path through.

"Mmm. I cannot say how you will leave Rhabat, Julianne: no doubt in your own way and unannounced, as you have arrived. But when next you come, send me due word and I will meet you before the siq and lead you through, while my people throw palms before your camel's feet . . ."

"I think Sildana would like that," she said lightly. "For now, though, you say we must go another way. For the second time, will you tell us more?"

"Better; I will show you. Come back and mount. Sildana is her name? She is a majestic beast; white camels are said to be lucky, though I should say that it is she who has the luck, to carry you . . ."

"Would you speak to her, on that? I don't believe she sees it your way . . ."

THEY MOVED OFF, with Elisande behind; Marron watched them go, then glanced questioningly at Jemel, who had made no move to follow.

"I will walk down, with you. Someone will lead my camel."

"There's no need, Jemel. Ride with your brothers."

"I have no brothers here; I am tribeless now, and they would not acknowledge me. Besides, I am a Dancer, in my fashion," and he showed his maimed hand, which Marron ached for.

"So?"

"So I ought not to ride."

"You've been riding all day. You've been riding every day since you lost your finger. Haven't you?"

"Yes, of course," smiling. "I am not a Dancer like Morakh; where it is useful or convenient, I will ride. But you heard him," Hasan he meant, but would not speak his name, "the ceilings are low. Better to walk."

"Jemel . . ."

"Marron, I am sworn to your service, and should attend you. You are the Ghost Walker, and you will not walk into Rhabat alone."

AND SO HE did not. He and Jemel followed the camels at a distance, over the brow of the hill. Nestled on a shelf just below they found a small temple with a domed roof, hewn crudely as it seemed from the living rock; in the cliff face behind it was a crack, barely wide enough for a laden camel to pass through.

A Sharai in the robes of an imam was waiting for them there, with a lit torch in his hand. He gave that to Jemel, though it was Marron he was staring at; then he waved them through.

They'd gone barely a dozen paces inside before the dim daylight was cut off, with a soft thud as though a door had closed at their back.

Marron paused, and glanced behind him. The torchlight showed only bare rock closing the passage, with no sign of a doorway. Neither any sign of the Sharai; he must be the keeper of the temple, as well as of Rhabat's secret gateway.

The tunnel they stood in was wider than its entrance had been, though not by much. The ceiling was low indeed, and more roughly cut even than the walls. The camel-party had already disappeared around a bend ahead, but the sounds of its passage came back clearly; Marron heard Julianne's soft curse, and guessed that she had just learned to stoop in the saddle.

The tunnel sloped steeply downward and turned constantly as it fell within the massive escarpment, like a long and coiling hair caught within a crystal. Jemel held the torch at Marron's side, and said nothing; Marron looked about him, and found nothing to say. Walls, ceiling, floor all the same, endlessly curving, and themselves endlessly pacing with a steady, unchanging rhythm; it felt almost as though they were motionless, walking in place while the tunnel wound itself up around them.

The only relief was the girls' conversation ahead, rising to meet them:

"Elisande, how long have the Sharai been here? It must have taken decades to cut such a passage; and if what I have heard of Rhabat is true, this would have been the least of their work . . ."

"Nothing you have heard could come near the truth of Rhabat, sweet—but the Sharai did not make the least little fragment of it. The Sharai do not build. They found it, stole it, were given it."

"Well, which?"

"All three."

"I hope you're going to explain that."

"No one knows truly who made it. The Sharai discovered it, centuries ago; but it wasn't empty at the time, there were people living here, occupying a little of its immensity. They might have been descendants of the original builders; some of the stories claim as much. The Sharai drove them out, and took possession."

"As we were meant to," Hasan's voice cut in abruptly. "It was a gift from God, provided at a crucial time. Our tribes are disputatious, Julianne; we needed a place that belonged to none and would be accessible to all, where our leaders could meet in peace and speak to all our peoples with one voice. Rhabat is a symbol, and more. Elisande says that the Sharai do not build, and that is true; but I mean to build a nation of the Sharai, and Rhabat will be the focus of it."

"You see?" Elisande again, cheerfully, almost laughing. "I said, all three . . ."

AT LENGTH, THEY heard the party ahead stop to light fresh torches. Jemel glanced uncertainly up at his own, where the flame was guttering and weakening; he said, "I could run ahead and fetch another, bring it back . . ."

"No need," Marron said. "So long as there's an ember's glow to that, I can see well enough for the pair of us. Take my sleeve, if you think you'll lose me . . ."

Jemel snorted, as though there were no chance of his losing Marron, even in the uttermost dark; but he took a grip on the offered sleeve regardless.

Their light faded quickly, and even the embers died before that long march was over. But Marron could see the faintest reflection on the walls, coming back from their companions' torches, though Jemel swore that they were walking in total darkness; and he could feel the movement of the air around him, he thought he could hear its touch on the enclosing rock. He thought he could find his way down now with his eyes closed, and still hold constantly to the centre of the passage.

He told Jemel to discard the dead torch and walk with one hand brushing the wall, if he were unnerved by the dark. His friend laughed harshly and said that there were stories to frighten children, that might also frighten men of other tribes, of any tribe; the Sharai were not used to night without stars, and did not like it even in legend. But he, Jemel, would not be made afraid by a simple lack of light . . .

His other hand, though, the one that had taken a tuck of Marron's sleeve: already that hand had slipped down to fold itself around Marron's fingers. The skin was cold, but the hand was slick with sweat. Marron allowed himself a smile that Jemel would never see, and gripped tightly.

*　　*　　*

THAT WEARY WALK went on and on, but had to end at last. The first sign of its ending was when the quality of the light changed, that faintest hint that Marron's eyes had been following so long. It seemed to lose colour, to become not brighter but more grey than yellow against the rose-red walls.

Then he heard the girls' voices again, which had fallen silent some time since, oppressed by all that weight of rock above and the dreary monotony of their turning path. Julianne said, "Is that . . . ?"

"I think it is," Elisande replied. "I'll race you to it."

"Do not," Hasan said swiftly. "That is the end of this road; but where it comes out is no place for foolishness, and you have another road to ride before your beasts can rest."

Julianne groaned slightly, but offered no protest; to Elisande, it seemed, this was not news.

Neither to Jemel: he clearly knew exactly where they were, and what they were coming to.

Marron murmured, "Do all the Sharai know of this way, and where it leads?"

"Not all; few. Very few, I think, beyond those few who live here. The tribes seldom come to Rhabat; and when they do, only their leaders venture far within its walls. It is said in the Sands that there is only the one way, in or out, that the Dead Waters guard where the mountains don't. Most believe that; why would they not? I know I did, until I came. We were privileged, we who rode with Hasan against the Roq; we gathered here for the blessing of an imam that he had sent for, and it was weeks before that man arrived. Weeks to wait, and a legend to explore—we went everywhere, Jazra and I, of course we did, how not?

"A child of the city showed us this, though he took us only a little way up. If the children know, then so must everyone who lives here, or who stays for any time. But it is a secret, it's hidden, that much is clear. I would not have spoken of it, outside the city."

*   *   *

THE LIGHT GREW slowly, dimly: better than walking suddenly into hard sun, Marron thought, for Jemel's eyes that had been bathing in darkness for so long. His own eyes he thought could take any change, from black to furnace-bright, and not blink now.

The light grew, and the path turned—and stopped turning, stopped altogether at a simple square doorway that must have had the party ahead ducking low indeed. If this road had been meant for camels and their riders, then those who built it must have smiled as they worked . . .

No priest to watch over this door: one of the mounted Sharai did that duty here. Marron wondered how much of an imam he was, the man above, and how much of a gardian; Hasan had wanted another, to bless his adventure.

Jemel slid his hand free, a moment too late, perhaps, and walked out into the open. Marron followed, stepping wide to avoid the restless camel and breathing deeply to rid his lungs of the dry musty feel of the tunnel—and almost choked as they filled instead with warm wet sour air. He tasted salty bitterness on his tongue and wanted to spit, barely restrained the impulse; and so forgot to look behind him until it was too late, until he'd heard again the quiet, firm sound of a door being closed. He glanced back anyway, and saw only the Sharai on his camel sidling sideways along a wall of what seemed virgin rock, that held no sign of any doorway.

Pointless to stare, or to go closer and search: Jemel knew the secret, and so did the children here. Marron could learn it, if he were here long enough. He'd have liked to know now, to have the opportunity to slip away quietly and alone if ever he needed to, but he'd missed the chance. Instead he turned again and looked about him, and saw immediately why the air was so rank here.

He was standing on that broad flat area of pavement they'd seen from above, between the cliff-face with its workings, its natural and man-made caves and steps, and the sea. The water lapped the rock only ten or a dozen paces from him. In this enclosed bay, it tainted the atmo-

sphere as it had not in the open Sands. There he had
smelled the salt and the stagnation of it; here its nature was
tangible, and there was more to it than simple sterility.
There was a foulness that caught at his throat, a threat inherent, as though something utterly evil dwelt there and
permeated all its breadth and depth; he understood now
why the Sharai watched it so closely, why they were so reluctant to approach it too nearly.

Why these caves were empty, uninhabited, unused; why
there were no boats, although this surely must have been
meant once as a quayside. There were steps along the rim
of the ledge, leading down into the water; but they were
deeply, darkly stained, as though that evil he could sense
had saturated the pale rock they were cut from and was rising still higher, seeking slowly to invade the land.

Even now the Sharai and their camels both were visibly
uneasy, shifting restlessly and casting sidelong glances at
the water. Hasan was less nervous or simply more in control of himself, as befitted his rank and reputation; he was
sweating, though, Marron could see and smell it on him,
and there was an urgency in more than his words as he said,
"We should move on, quickly, before we lose the light here.
We have no more torches . . ."

The sun was setting invisibly, behind the cliffs; far out
beyond the bay, the waters were tinged with red to mark it.
Where they stood was deep in shadow, must be all but dark
already to those with merely mortal eyes. Hasan waited,
though, for Julianne to sign that she was ready, before he
led the party off.

Their route lay along the gully that Marron had noted
from on high; there it would be dark indeed, and the riders
must trust to their knowledge and their camels' better sight.
Even the girls seemed to prefer that, though, to the water's
edge; Marron heard Elisande's voice, straining to be cheerful, "Not far now, Julianne, and just wait till you see . . ."

Jemel still chose to walk, at Marron's side. He too was
full of promise, for the wonders to come. He said, "This is
not what they meant, perhaps, but the imams have always

taught that the Sharai must walk in darkness for a while, for a little way, before they can come to light and joy. The Dancers say the same—we Dancers do—though we surely do not mean Rhabat."

"Jemel," Marron said carefully, "you are not a Dancer."

"Why not?" He was laughing suddenly, light-headed, bouncing on his feet as they entered the cleft and the dark of it folded itself around them. "I have placed a stone on the Pillar, and made my oath to serve you; I have given my finger for you, in witness. How am I not a Dancer?"

You are not like Morakh, who would kill me if he could; but that was not an answer. "I do not want your service. Only your friendship."

"You will have to endure both. I would kill for you, Marron; I will kill, for you."

Which was the closest he had ever come, and likely the closest he ever would, to saying that he had more reasons than the one for that public oath he had sworn, against the life of Sieur Anton. His hand said the rest, coming back to seek Marron's again and touching fingers to wrist, then knuckles to knuckles in a gesture that was both cryptic and immediate.

Marron renewed his own private oath, that he would not permit Jemel to harm Sieur Anton, nor the knight to harm the Sharai. Jemel thought that Marron would bring the two men together eventually, face to face; Marron meant never to do that, never to risk the chance. If it meant losing the one as he had lost the other already, if it meant that he must run from both, so be it. Again he regretted the loss of knowledge, that hidden gateway by the water; but drew comfort from what was certain, that Sieur Anton was a month's travel, a whole desert's width from Jemel's eager sword. The chance of war, what they both sought so keenly might yet act against him; but for now, both were safe from each other. He could only live each day, each night as it came . . .

This night came in a hurry, in a cloud of stars like a banner flung across the narrow strip of sky above the gorge; he

glanced up and laughed at them, snatched for Jemel's hand
and held it tight. If his friend must walk in darkness for a
while, at least Marron could be his guide, though Jemel
knew better than he what waited for them on the further
side.

WHAT WAITED WAS more and greater than he had imagined, almost greater than he would have believed possible,
though he had seen extraordinary things.

It began quietly, unexpectedly, with trees and water: gentle water, fresh and clear and still as a glass, reflecting the
night and the blaze of stars overhead. The gorge had
widened abruptly, as though to make room for this long,
narrow pool and its attendant trees, tall palms whose giant
fronds drooped over the water's margin like hands stretching down for some touch of its purity.

There was a clear path now, more worn by use than laid
out by design, though the imprint of the camels' pads suggested that it was little used these days. Marron could see
barefoot tracks but few of them, and those small, to suggest
that it was bold children mostly who came this far, this
close to danger.

The path led between the trees and the water, to the
pool's end. There the walls of the gully closed in briefly,
before they opened like a tremendous gateway onto a broad
valley. Here again there was water, wide and shallow, studded with boulders; to one side the land was terraced and
farmed, all the way back to the louring shadow of a tremendous scarp.

Marron spared that barely a look, only to assure himself
that the wonder of this place was not reflected both sides
of the water. On its nearer bank, the pool pressed hard
against the cliffs that hid this valley from the world
around; there was a ledge of rock wide enough perhaps for
five to walk abreast, no more, before the wall rose sheer.

This wall was no cliff-face, though—or no longer. As
down at the abandoned waterfront, the rock had been

worked by industrious hands, so long ago that even here, protected against sandstorms and rarely seeing rain, that work was so weathered that it seemed almost natural. But what had been done at the waterfront had been simple, practical; what had been done here was grandiose, extravagant, exultant almost.

See what we can do, Marron thought briefly, *we can rival the gods . . .*

Then his cynicism was overwhelmed, crushed by the brutal scale of what he was looking at; for a while he stopped thinking at all, he only stood and gaped.

From base to high crest, this entire wall of rock had been carved and hollowed into the semblance of a city. It might almost have been the work of a god, the original that man's buildings merely mocked. Unless this had been meant itself to mock those who built with common stuff, stone and brick and wood. There were separate faces here, divided by deep recesses, as though it were a street of separate houses; each had its arches, windows, pediments and pillars, all manner of decoration and ornament.

There were lights, too: great torches and braziers burned beside open doorways, lamplight showed in many of the windows.

There were people, too. Shadows moving in the lit windows, men on guard beside the braziers; men bringing more torches now, and boys running to the camels' heads, waiting while their riders dismounted and then leading the beasts away through an ornate archway. Lights there, too, and beyond it, but Marron didn't need light to tell him that the city's stables lay that way; his nose picked out the odours of stall and manger and dungheap, his ears the sounds of restive animals.

He felt a pang for other stable-lads, one he could name and had named a friend, dead now in pain and terror; but shook it off with an effort in response to Jemel's gentle nudge.

"You should hide your eyes, perhaps . . . ?"

Perhaps he should. His coming would be common

knowledge soon enough, but the news should reach the tribal leaders first. He flung up his hood and lowered his head, then let Jemel draw him forward to join the rest of their party.

Elisande appeared quickly at his other side, slipping her arm through his. He might have been surprised that she'd left Julianne at such a time, at the fulfilment of her promise; he'd have expected her to be basking in it. But he stole a glimpse ahead and saw the other girl walking with Hasan, the Sharai's head almost on a level with hers while his arm gestured high and wide, pointing out this decoration or that.

"Isn't it wonderful?" Elisande breathed, for all the world as if he were not second-best. "I spent the best part of a year here, and thought I was living in a dream the whole time. Wait till daylight, when you can see it properly, all the colours . . ."

Marron could see colours enough already, a red stain to everything, like an omen of blood to come; but he didn't want to taint her enthusiasm, or Jemel's. He tried again to dispel that sense of sorrow for what had gone, of foreboding for what was yet to be; and failed, and held instead to silence, hoping that they would think only that he was awestruck. As he was: but his awe had turned inward, now that they were here at last. He knew himself to be crucial, potentially a pivot to the world; and he felt himself to be weak, impotent almost, only a weapon for someone else's use. Even these two, gripping either arm—they would tug him this way and that, each trying to draw or persuade or force him in opposite directions. And he would inevitably go one way or the other, he would have to; and whichever way he turned there would be war and death. War would come in any case, with or without him, but he had the power to make it so much worse. And he had no power for peace, that he could see. Even his friends contended for him; they would wrestle over his bones, he thought, and over his memory when his bones were dust.

*   *   *

THE ONE AMONG his companions whom he still thought would welcome such a sight, Marron dead and a danger taken from the world, Rudel should have been walking alone—rejected by his daughter, abandoned by Julianne and discounted by Jemel. Typically, though, he wouldn't allow them to put him in that position; instead he'd made himself one among Hasan's tribesmen, laughing raucously with them, telling jokes in a Catari that matched their own for idiom and accent. Well, if his daughter had spent time here, so no doubt had he, though doubtless not the same time. Rudel had shown no signs of building bridges to the Sharai on the journey here, indeed he'd held himself quiet and apart, much like Marron, though for different reasons. He had his recovering wound to excuse himself for that, though; and now he was using all his jongleur's skills to win himself a welcome. That it was a lesson to Elisande was certain; Marron hoped it would prove to be more. Rudel had skills that Marron lacked, and for sure he had reasons to use them: a land and a people that he loved, an inheritance, a family and a position in the world. All of which Marron lacked.

THAT ROWDY GROUP that Rudel was so much a part of moved on along this spectacular frontage, passing the guards at some doorways with ribald jests, others in ostentatious silence. Hasan followed with Julianne, and so perforce did Marron with his two companions. He noticed that Hasan had quiet words for all the guards, and more perhaps for those whom his fellow tribesmen had ignored.

Hasan drew Julianne to a halt, though, before one particular doorway that was not only guarded but screened with an intricate lattice of wood, as were the windows above. Elisande pulled a face, and sighed loudly.

"Women's quarters," she said. "It's the only drawback to this place: we're supposed to know our place, and keep to it. I was young enough to get away with a lot before, but probably not now. Especially keeping company with a married woman . . ."

That was aimed at Julianne, and sharper perhaps than it was meant; she flinched, at any rate. And glanced at Hasan, and said, "Well, if we must, we must."

"I regret that you must," he said. "There are compensations, though."

"Oh? How would you know? Prince?"

He smiled. "I am not without women in my life, lady. I have told you that; and they tell me that there are indeed compensations. You will be well cared for."

"To be sure," Elisande grumbled, though without a great deal of heart to it. "We will be fed and groomed, and cosseted even better than the camels are, though not perhaps the horses."

"Are there horses?" Julianne demanded, so eagerly that even Elisande had to laugh at her.

"There are indeed, sweet—and yes, I'm sure that you may ride them. With a suitable escort, of course."

"Of course." Again, she looked to Hasan; he bowed.

"It would be a pleasure, lady. Tomorrow?"

"If you may. If you are at liberty, I would like that exceedingly. I have learned to love Sildana, but a camel is still a camel; a horse is . . ." Words seemed to fail her.

"A horse?" Hasan suggested.

"Exactly so. There is a difference."

"Indeed there is. Hooves, a mane, no hump . . ."

"And a temperament, rather than a temper. Prince, you're mocking me, but I can endure it, if I am promised two things. No, three."

"And they are—?"

"A ride with you in the morning, early, for which I already have your word; a meeting with my father tonight, if he can be found; and a bath. Immediately. Please?"

"The first I am sworn to, as you say. The second—well, I would never like to speak for the movements or choices of the King's Shadow, but I will move the stars in their courses to discover him, if I must. The third, though, that is beyond my powers. Alas, I dare not cross this threshold; and if I did, my orders would be so much wasted air. I have no authority among the women."

"Julianne, he's teasing you. There will be a bath, I promise."

"Oh, bless you. I haven't felt clean since we left Bar'ath Tazore."

"Sweet, you haven't *been* clean since we left Bar'ath Tazore. But the Sultan's hammam is a bowl of cold water and no tent for shelter, next to the baths of Rhabat. Come on, if you're so urgent. Can't you smell the steam?"

Marron could; there was warmth and fragrance waiting in the shadows beyond the screen, aromatics and unguents and oils. Food, too, a great deal of food, and cooling drinks. It was the bath he envied, though. His own skin was parched and roughened by too many days of sand and wind. He could smell himself and the others of his party, more strongly even than the sweet and spicy remedies that awaited the girls.

A shadow moved behind the screen, a woman appeared, robed and veiled as the girls were; she beckoned, and as they went to her Hasan called after them, "Tell Sherett that I send you to her with a strict command from her lord, that she take particular care of you . . ."

"Prince," Julianne returned smartly, "I thought that you had no authority among the women?"

"Lady, I do not. She will snort at it, and bring you thorns to scrub your backs . . ."

STILL LAUGHING TO himself, Hasan beckoned the others on. He brought them past one doorway, past another and to a third, where the fat pillars that held up an elaborate pediment were only half-cut from the rock behind, and that had been left natural and rough. Unless it had been deliberately roughened, the art of looking natural . . .

"You read the message, Rudel?" Hasan said, suddenly sober. "Unfinished, but yet strong."

"I have read it before, Hasan. Believe me, I never doubted it."

"You are a wise man. And my guest, for tonight at least. As are you all," and he turned to face Marron and Jemel, throwing his arms wide. "This is our house, the house of my tribe, when we are here; and you are welcome to it. I must apologise, that we do not pamper ourselves as the women do; we keep desert customs, and live simply. But what we have is yours to share. Come in and wash, and eat . . ."

Rudel bowed, and led the way inside. Marron moved to follow, but checked himself when Jemel paused.

"Will you welcome a tribeless man?" his friend asked stiffly.

"Of course—if that man will accept my welcome." There was a moment where they simply gazed at each other, where Marron could not read the expression of either one. Then Hasan added in a softer voice, "Such a thing could happen to any of us, Jemel. As other things can happen: the death of a friend, a strong man's arm to keep you from dying at his side. Enter. I cannot give you peace, but the peace of my roof I can; I know you will not violate it. Besides, how could I refuse hospitality to the chosen companion of the Ghost Walker? You do me honour."

Oh, it was complex, the look on Jemel's face as he nodded and stepped forward. Marron went with him, wondering more simply whether there had ever been a choice, and if so, whether it had been he who had made it.

A BATH WOULD have been welcome, but a ewer of cool water in a warm room was plenty enough for Marron; it was what he'd been accustomed to, life-long. Even the Ransomers' cold plunges had seemed a luxury.

He stripped and splashed, dunked his whole head in the ewer and came up gasping, pushed away Jemel's fussing over the savage scar on his shoulder—and was startled to be pushed back in his turn.

The shock of a wet head seemed to have numbed his earlier depression, if not washed it away entirely. He reacted
forcefully, wrestling the spare, lithe Sharai back into a corner. It was hard to use only his own strength, and not the
Daughter's; but he made the effort, straining against his
squirming friend and laughing with him, until Rudel's
voice called them sternly to order.

"Boys, this again is neither the time nor the place for
horseplay. If you don't understand that, be still, and listen
to those who do . . ."

Jemel pulled a face, and straightened slowly. The arm
that had been tight around Marron's throat relaxed, but
stayed hanging loosely around his shoulders; when he
made to move away, it tightened just a little, just enough to
hold him.

Marron turned to face Rudel, who was washing himself
briskly; the older man went on, "There is a council of grave
importance met here; this you know. It could mean full war
between our peoples, Jemel, yours and mine." His eyes and
voice and meaning all slid over Marron, awarding him no
place, no loyalty. "It likely will, though I will do my utmost
to prevent it. Hasan knows why I am come; that is important to the council, and they will send for me soon, if only
to welcome me here. They can do no less, when he of all
men has already given me guest-rights. It was a lucky
chance that had you finding him, Marron; other captains
might have been less accommodating. However, Hasan will
also have told the council of you. That is more important
yet. They might simply have tolerated my presence here,
allowed me my say and ignored it. They cannot do that
with you. They will want to see you, immediately by my
guess; which means that you must be ready. Calm, and controlled—Sharai elders give no respect to wild youth. You
are a changeling, your very existence defies their prophets;
they will want to ask you where you stand in this conflict,
and you must have an answer prepared."

"I stand with my friends," Marron said simply.

"That is good—but not good enough. You have friends in both camps, and—"

What more he would have said was interrupted, as Hasan came into the room. He had washed elsewhere, there was still water in his beard; he had also changed into clean robes, and he carried three more across his arm.

"We can offer you no softness," he said, "but comfort at least lies in our gift. Comfort against the skin," and his eyes barely touched on Marron, on his two visible wounds, the one well healed and the other never to be let heal, "and comfort within it too. If you are ready, will you come to eat?"

Jemel seemed to startle for an instant; Rudel ignored him, somehow assuming a dignity that belied his nakedness. "Our thanks, Hasan. We are quite ready, and will be with you immediately."

He took the robes, and distributed them; as soon as Hasan was gone, he added, "I *told* you, Jemel—the situation here overrides all common custom. Hurrying a guest is nothing; be grateful that the council is granting us time to eat. Though that is a double-edged gift. They will be using the time to debate between themselves, which we cannot. Come, dress yourselves; and remember that you will be the focus of all eyes tonight, Marron. You wear their clothes, you carry their prophecy in your blood, but you are not one of them; they will be confused, and tense. Jemel will not mind it, if I say that the Sharai are a hot-headed people, and quick to take offence. Some will find you an offence however you act, but do your best. Above all, eat, even if you have no appetite for it; to refuse, or just to make a pretence at eating, would insult Hasan and all his tribe. That we cannot afford."

Marron might have taken offence himself, at being addressed as though he were a child; he decided it was too much trouble. Instead, he simply made a point of allowing Jemel to act the servant for once: to help him into a robe and tie it properly, to ensure that he wore sword and knife as he ought, even to push his fingers through Marron's wet and tangled hair in an effort to persuade it into some semblance of neatness. They had been given no time to shave, but among these people beards were commonplace, a sign of manhood; the soft stubble on his chin would be if anything a point in his favour.

Jemel himself took a little extra time over his own robe, cutting off those small knots and tassles that bespoke Hasan's tribe. "It is a compliment for you, for both of you, to wear their dress; from me, it would be an insult."

Rudel didn't dispute that. Indeed, his patient waiting seemed to applaud Jemel's caution, if caution it were. Marron thought that actually, it was pride; he might be Saren no longer, but he would still not appear by choice in the insignia of any other tribe.

He was ready, though, as swiftly as he might be. Rudel gathered them together with his eyes, nodded once with a wary satisfaction that was yet a reminder and a warning, repeated it unnecessarily in words, "Be very careful tonight, in words and manners; more than your own lives hang on this," and led them out.

THE OUTER WALLS were bare rock that bore the illusion of a palace; inside it was plain that the Sharai at least did not deal in illusion, even if their predecessors did. The rooms were high and square, the doorways arched and graceful, but the occupants truly did inhabit them as though they were deep in the Sands, and in their tents.

There was no decoration on the walls, only rough patches and signs of breakage to show where there might have been once, before the imams came to purify the place. Marron and his companions walked barefoot as their hosts did, on sandy stone; they followed a lad with a lamp across a broad hall and up a turning flight of stairs, into a long room with windows looking out across the valley.

In the centre of the room the floor at least was covered, in layers of patterned rugs. There sat Hasan, the men of his patrol and perhaps a dozen more; they were grouped in a circle around bowls of boiled meat and platters of bread, but none of them was eating. Jemel sucked air through his teeth, as though to say that things were not done such a way among the Saren, that no guest should be made to feel his hosts were waiting for him.

Space was made for them, to Hasan's either side; the place of honour, on his right, he might perhaps have meant for Marron by his smile, but Rudel took it. Hasan's face didn't twitch; Rudel was the elder, after all, and should ordinarily take precedence. A hand beckoned Marron to the left instead. As he settled himself on soft wool over hard rock, Jemel slid in between him and the next tribesman, another kind of padding altogether: even more kindly meant, just as unnecessary. Marron could have sat on stone all day and all night, and never felt a moment's cramp; he could have sat all day and all night next that man and never had a word of speech from him, desert manners and a guest's welcome notwithstanding. Hasan was still the only one of these who'd broken his silence with Marron, or Marron's with him. Deliberate isolation had played a part in that, but only a part; the tribesmen were equally complicit. Marron supposed that in his days as a Ransomer, he might have felt as tongue-tied or simply as wary in the presence of a Church Father, or perhaps of a saint. It was hard to picture himself as either one, but the comparison came close: a saint reborn, perhaps, might be closer yet. A Patric saint in a Catari body, now that was almost exact, except that no saint he'd ever heard of had had anything like the powers that he possessed . . .

Hasan made an open-handed gesture, politely to his right and then to his left; Rudel reached for a piece of meat, and Marron copied him.

They might keep desert customs in this house, but it was no stringy desert goat that they were served. It was mutton, pink and tender and flavoured with the salty herbs the sheep had fed on. The bread was soft and fresh, the water that was passed around had a pleasant mineral tang to it; for a wonder, eating was no effort. Even Jemel stopped watching him, after a minute or two.

*   *   *

CHEWED BONES WERE flung onto a platter that had held bread; the meat-bowl emptied quickly, and was not refilled. Even Hasan seemed a little embarrassed about that, breaking off his easy talk of life in Rhabat and life in the Sands to dip crusts into the juices that remained and pass them to his guests, right and left and further left. Jemel hesitated only a moment, before he took his portion.

Rudel was first to sit back, to wipe his fingers and beard on a linen napkin that Hasan handed to him; then he gave that across to Marron, a clear signal, not to be declined. The meal was over, and Marron could almost regret it for its own sake, let alone his dread of what would follow.

Jemel took the napkin from him, cleaned hands and mouth and passed it on around the circle. Hasan used it last, tossed it into the empty bowl and stood up.

"If you will come," he said, again to all three of them, "there are sheikhs and elders here who would be glad to meet with you. This haste is not of my choosing, believe me, but . . ."

"The time dictates its own urgency," Rudel replied. "If there were never any other lesson to be learned in the Sands, they would teach us that. And I too am impatient to speak with your council."

"Ah, Rudel, you are too late to deflect my disgrace; I will not blame my guests for my own discourtesy. But thank you for the attempt. This way, then. They are waiting in the Chamber of Audience . . ."

OUT INTO THE night again and along to another guarded doorway. That brought them directly into a vast hall, lit only at its further end, where perhaps two dozen men were sitting on a carpeted divan.

This place was well named, Marron thought; it wasn't only his unnaturally sharp ears that caught the murmur of those men's voices as they entered, to judge by the way Jemel stiffened suddenly, the way he stalked at Marron's side. Rudel was too well schooled to show any reaction, but

Marron thought that he too was listening intently to the muttered words that reached them. Something about the intricate way the chamber's roof was carved meant that the slightest whisper was channelled and amplified, to reach even the furthest corner of that tremendous space. He reminded himself to speak no secrets here, and only wished that he need not speak at all.

No chance of that: it was of him that the waiting men were speaking already, and in no terms of welcome.

"He is an abomination, we cannot permit . . ."

"He exists; we have to deal with what is."

"He could cease to exist. This should never have happened, but it is not too late to correct."

Small wonder that Jemel was so tense, walking with his hand on his sword-hilt now. Marron touched his elbow; when that had no effect, he took Jemel's wrist and drew it forcibly away, held it tightly. Let them see that, as he walked into the lamplight. Perhaps it would help; it could at least do little harm in such company, in such a mood.

They were lords of many different tribes, these men. He could read that much by their subtleties of dress, without knowing what each fold or adornment signified. Such a meeting would always be angry, he thought, each man would bring generations of wrongs and slights to it. Perhaps he should be glad to give a focus to that smouldering heat. Marron was incidental here, though they would not and could not see him that way. Rudel's mission was what mattered, the chance to talk peace instead of war; they might hear him the clearer, if they had burned out their resentments on another target first.

He set himself beside Rudel, on the floor before the divan, and drew Jemel up close. Hasan said simply, "Lords, here are the guests of my house, to hear your joint welcome to our place of council." Then he stepped to one side. There were messages here, more than the obvious. He was of course telling the council that these newcomers all stood under his protection, which was or should be potent; at the same time, he was telling the companions that although he might have summoned the council, he was not a part of it. He had said before that he was no prince among his people; he could be no more than a supplicant, as they were.

When the council spoke, whosoever voice it spoke through—and that would have been a debate worth hearing, Marron guessed, with no one tribe willing to accede priority to another—it should speak first to Rudel, as being so obviously the eldest and already known here. But the talk had all been of Marron, of the Ghost Walker; perhaps it would be he who attracted first attention . . .

He scanned the faces before him—old men and younger men, though none so young as Hasan; bearded and clean-shaven, scarred by war and blemished by old sickness—and saw no hint of welcome anywhere among them, only hard dark eyes and grim expressions.

Even so, he was startled when the first reaction to their arrival was no word at all, but a dagger thrown.

A dagger casually tossed, rather, to skitter towards them across the rock of the floor, spinning as it came.

It was a gesture of utmost contempt, as he read it; and he was doubly startled when it stopped not at Rudel's feet and not at his, but at Jemel's.

That was no accident, no miscast; so much was clear in his friend's reaction. The proud toss of his head, the glare, the instant tightening of every muscle and the leap of hand towards sword-hilt, that Marron fought to restrain: another message had been sent and received, though it bewildered him.

"We did not send for the renegade," a slow voice said. One man moved: a swarthy man in his middle years, burly in his body, one of the few who were beardless. He rose to his feet and went on, "He ventures where he was not invited; let him pay the price of it."

Hasan strode quickly back, to stand at Jemel's other side. "My lords, Jemel takes his rice with me tonight. I understood that you wished to meet all my new-come guests; if I have misunderstood, the fault is mine and not Jemel's. You will not dishonour me, I know, by offering offence to one of mine . . ."

"Is he yours, Hasan? Well, perhaps—though his robe does not say so. I say that he was ours, he was of the Saren, but he has turned from us. If the Beni Rus have taken to welcoming the tribeless, that of course is their affair; but in that case he should keep to your kitchens. He disgraces this assembly; he disgraces me. If he denies that, let him return my blade."

That was a challenge, plain and simple; Marron had to call on the strength of the Daughter to hold Jemel still, to save him answering it. Swiftly, before that silent struggle became too obvious, he said, "My lord, Jemel has turned from his tribe, so much is true; he has done so on my account," which was almost true, he hoped true enough to pass, "and stands here with me, as my man."

"Does he so? Hasan, show his left hand."

Before Hasan could move, Jemel jerked back his sleeve and held his hand up high, to show them all where his smallest finger was missing.

There was a hiss of talk on the divan, too many voices speaking at once to be clear even in this space; the words "Sand Dancer" came down, though, from several throats. More than one dagger was drawn.

Eventually, one strong voice cut across the whispers.

"The Sand Dancers are outcasts, of their own choice. They are forbidden Rhabat, with good reason; they bring nothing but strife, here where we strive for peace between our peoples. The penalty is death, for those who break this law."

"My lords," Rudel, speaking at last and too late, "this boy is not a Sand Dancer. He lost his finger in a fight we had with them; a coincidence, nothing more."

"Let him speak for himself." That was the Saren sheikh again. "He has a tongue, I presume—or did he lose that too? Or perhaps the courage to use it?"

"I have a tongue," Jemel said softly, against the sudden silence. "I have used it to forswear my tribe and my allegiance; I have used it again, to make new oaths. I have stood atop the Pillar of Lives and set a stone there, where I swore my life to the Ghost Walker. My finger was given in support of that oath; if Rudel says otherwise, he lies. Make of it what you will."

"Out of his own mouth," a grunt of satisfaction from the sheikh. "Shall it be my sword that takes him here, or shall we send him to die out of our sight and cognisance, as he deserves?"

"Neither one," Marron said hotly, choking almost on a flare of anger. "You know what I am; I have said he is mine, and he confirms it. I will not give him to you, for this nonsense nor for any true offence. If you try to take him from me, beware."

That brought all the council to its feet. Scimitars scraped from their sheaths; Rudel groaned audibly. Marron stooped, to scoop up the dagger from where it still lay at Jemel's feet. Another moment and he would have used it, he would have cut his arm and opened a portal, dragged Jemel through by force if need be to avoid his friend's death or his own, or anyone's.

But in that moment of delay, there was a ripple of new light at his back that threw his shadow forward; and a new voice yet, a clarion voice that stilled every other in the chamber, that needed none of the arts of that place to make itself heard.

"What is the trouble here, my lords? I came to seek my daughter; and I find you all in uproar, which is nothing unusual when Julianne is about, but I do not see her here . . ."

Marron dared not leave hold of Jemel, but he risked one quick glance over his shoulder. He saw a single man, a small man in a green robe with his white hair ruffled around his balding crown, as though he had been disturbed from sleep. He held an oil-lamp in his hand, and looked almost foolish as he blinked about the hall.

TWO

The Unexpectedness of Men

JULIANNE HAD BATHED slowly, had eaten quickly—with the promise that there would be more food later should she want it, that there was and always would be more food, more water or else fruit-juice or sherbet if she preferred it, more of anything and everything she wanted—and now she was exploring, while Elisande laughed at her heels.

"Oh, be quiet," she grumbled, "it's not funny. You've been here before; I haven't. I didn't dog you while you were crawling into every corner of the Roq, did I?"

"Only because you were too prim to leave your room without a man's permission."

"Nothing to do with being prim!" It was too true for comfort, all the same; and there was nothing conveniently to hand to throw at Elisande, in lieu of a rebuttal.

In fact it was still true, that she was always ready—perhaps too ready—to conform to local custom, however much it irked her; she was always reluctant—and her friend would certainly say too reluctant—to challenge convention without cause. Like everything that had gone to make her

what she was, it came down in the end to her father's training. *Work within the system, child, don't work against it;
you'll get a lot further, and achieve a lot more along the
way.* That had been after an argument over a new harness
for her pony, she remembered, when she was very small.
All the boys were using them, so she'd demanded one to
match; her father had flatly refused. And had gone on refusing, despite tears and tantrums and monumental sulks. In
the end she'd thought it through, washed her face and
changed her dress and gone in frills and flounces to sit on
the knee of her favourite adoptive uncle. She'd wheedled,
little-girl style, and the harness had been delivered the next
morning.

She'd thought her father would be angry; instead he had
applauded, added a new saddle that he'd had waiting, and
turned the whole affair into a lesson for life.

Her father's lessons clung. Even now: she was exploring,
yes, and unchaperoned, yes (except by Elisande, who most
emphatically did not count)—but only within the bounds of
the women's quarters, and she had been careful to ask licence even for so much unchecked wandering.

Whether she'd heard Hasan's crying her name, or
whether she took it on herself to welcome all the new ar-
rivals to her domain, Julianne hadn't asked and had no way
to guess; but they'd got no further than the hallway behind
the screen before another woman had come lightly down a
curving flight of stairs to greet them.

"Thank you, Tourenne," she'd said in brisk dismissal to
the girl who'd brought them this far, "I will see to our
guests' comfort now."

The girl had dipped her head submissively—in Marasson
she would have curtsied, Julianne had thought—and
whisked herself away without a word.

"I am called Sherett," which had been no surprise at all,
"and I am wife to Hasan of the Beni Rus."

She'd worn her hood thrown back with her black hair
loose and swinging heavily to her waist, no veil; her face
was strong and striking, as determined as her character. She

was in her middle twenties, Julianne had guessed, and she carried innate authority as easily as her husband. Likely she always had; it wasn't his rank that had invested her.

Elisande had pulled off hood and veil with a huff of relief, rumpled her flattened hair and said, "I am Elisande d'Albéry, granddaughter to the Princip of Surayon; this is Julianne de Rance, daughter to the King's Shadow." Then, abandoning formality, she'd gone on, "I think we met before, Sherett, when I was living here. You weren't married then. You rode a black mare and went hawking without permission, without an escort, which had you in trouble with your menfolk . . ."

A laugh had greeted that. "It did; but it achieved its purpose, it attracted the attention of Hasan. Unless it was the horse that caught his eye. But I remember you, of course, Lisan; and welcome back. Our house is yours, as it ever was. My lady . . . ?"

Slowly, Julianne had detached her veil and put back her hood. She'd felt herself surveyed, summed up, weighed and measured almost; and had returned that proud gaze proudly, although she'd been able to feel every one of the days and nights of hard travel and stress marked out on her sore and filthy skin. When she'd pulled her own hair out from under her robe, she'd heard the soft scatter of dry sand falling to the floor at her back.

Her wince had made Sherett laugh again. Not unkindly, but it had still left Julianne caught between a bristle and a blush. Which she'd resented, just enough to say, "We have a message for you, from your lord . . ."

"I heard it," which had answered the question only in part; Julianne still thought she would have been there and greeting them regardless. "Pay him no mind; he is a man, and therefore foolish. Very foolish, in his dealings with women. But he listens to me, which is rare."

"And you to him . . . ?"

"On occasion. When he speaks sense—which is rare. Now come, Lisan, my lady—"

"Julianne. No more than that, please, Sherett." Despite

herself, she had swiftly lost hold of her resentment; this
was a woman to deal with fairly. And to listen to, and learn
from . . .

"Julianne, then. Come, you have sand in your hair and
sand in all your joints, I know. We have oils to ease them
and water to bathe dry eyes, sticks to work the grit out of
your teeth. No doubt you can wash each other's backs, you
will not need my thorns . . ."

IN FACT SHERETT had joined them in the hammam, which
had proved to be a series of chambers that varied from
sticky-warm to roasting, with a shockingly cold plunge-
pool to follow; as promised, it put to shame the Sultan's
simple steam-room.

"The men hear rumours of this," Sherett had said, almost
chanting the words in rhythm with her strong fingers as
they'd worked aromatic oil deep into Julianne's back, "and
they mock us for it; but it is simple to achieve, where there
are braziers, rocks and water. Why make a virtue of denial,
why live as paupers amongst such riches?"

"They think you will grow too soft to face the Sands,"
Elisande had grunted, from where she'd lain stretched out
on a shelf, half asleep in the seductive heat. *Too dry to
sweat,* she'd called herself; too thin, Julianne thought
rather. All her friend's bones were showing; and she'd been
eating rapaciously since she came back from the djinn's
country. She and Marron both, which had only made it
more evident. They must have starved, living for a week on
what little food one girl could carry. Elisande denied it, but
Marron had infected her, Julianne thought, with more than
his lack of interest in food . . .

"They had better not say so to me."

"I don't suppose they'd dare," Julianne had smiled gently, "but they would think it in any case."

"Of course they would; they are men. Worse, they are
Sharai men; they think we were all born to suffer."

"Oh, and were we not?"

"Perhaps. Perhaps so. Lie still, this suffering skin I can at least attend to . . ."

AFTER THE BATH, the meal: fine cuts of tender meat, fresh fruit and bread and the miracle of clean, clear water. Julianne had eaten lightly, Elisande quickly; and then Sherett had given laughing permission for them to wander as they would. She laughed often, this confident woman; thinking of her man, Julianne was not surprised.

"Of course; this is your own home, for as long as you stay with us. Go where you will, we have no secrets here. You do not need me for guide, and there's more pleasure in exploring alone. Besides, Lisan will remember every corner of this house. Ask for me, if there is anything you want."

Only one thing Julianne wanted, that she did not have and hoped she might obtain; and that she had asked for already. "A message may come, from my father . . ."

"If it comes, I will find you, Julianne. If it comes not— well, he is a man. A fine man, who may deserve his daughter; but a man none the less, and they are playing men-games in the council . . ."

Games which could lead to war—but Sherett knew that, for all her seeming scorn. Julianne had nodded, had caught hold of her friend's hand and led her away without another word.

EVERY PASSAGEWAY WAS rugged with long runners of that same hardwearing midnight-blue stuff from which the Sharai made their robes. For these rugs it had been plaited into ropes, which were coiled and interknotted and sewn together into fantastic designs. Julianne's eyes saw them vaguely, in the shifting shadows of the lamp she carried; her bare feet felt their textures exactly, and she delighted in them.

All the walls in passageways or chambers were hung with colour, bright banners of gold and green and red, some embroidered with the unspoken name of God, Elisande said, or else with a tribal sigil.

"If the Sharai can make such as this," Julianne asked, fondling the silken swathes, "why do they dress so drably? Oh, I grant you, these are practical in the desert," and her hand plucked a little fitfully at the fresh robe she wore, that she'd been so grateful for an hour earlier, "and thrifty no doubt, for a poor people; but here, where they dress their walls so gaily . . ."

"The women do the work," Elisande said, touching her hand to the nearest embroidery with a gesture that was surprisingly reverent, that she must have learned by watching, "but they do not weave the silk; they trade for that, with caravans from the east. These robes are traditional, laid down by centuries of custom; they believe that this is God's own colour, the colour of the sky behind the stars. It marks them out for what they are, a chosen people, chosen to live in a harsh land where weaker blood would perish. They are not a poor people, Julianne, never make that mistake; they have great wealth in store, here and in their tribal lands. They live in poverty by their own choice, because they think that life enriches them."

"And yet they fight over goats and camels . . ."

"Oh, the Sharai will fight over anything. Including Outremer, unless my father and yours can dissuade them from it."

That was a cold reminder, that they were not here to play; a reminder too of her father's supposed danger, that she had fled her new-made husband and a promised life of comfort to forestall. *Fled from trouble into trouble,* she thought wryly, thinking of Hasan; and shook her head determinedly. Her father would come to her when he would, if he would. They could talk then, have a *long* talk, about a great many things in this changing world. *If* he came. That was as it always had been, a question without a dependable answer. She had lived all her life in doubt of him, and been constantly surprised; he came unexpectedly and left without warning, and that was her definition of a father.

Which was why, when they eventually did have that talk, she was not going to apologise for any choice she'd made since his last dramatic departure. If he left her alone, she must act alone; and tonight she was going to play explorer, whether or not she ought . . .

She plunged through a heavy tapestry that hung across a doorway, and found herself in a room of chests and bags. Opening one at random, she pulled out a rich velvet robe—storm-grey, like Imber's eyes sometimes, when he was unhappy; she stifled the thought, before it could stifle her.

"I told you," Elisande said from the doorway. "Great wealth, but they don't make a show of it."

"Then what is the point of it, what's it for? Why have such things"—and there were many of them, that her busy fingers found: dresses and chains and bangles, gold and silver plate in the chests where she flung them open in frustrated exposure—"if they only hide them away?" Dresses were made to be worn and plates to use, by her lights, or they lost all purpose.

"They are to have, to keep. To possess. This land allows them little permanence; they have to keep moving, and take with them only what they can carry or feed. They set great store by ownership. Of their herds, which is why they raid for them; to steal from an enemy is to wound him worse than a sword-blade can. And of their women, which is why they keep them in seclusion. Though they are hardly alone in that. Julianne, why did your father have you raised in Marasson, when he is King's Shadow in Outremer?"

"Oh, I was a bargaining counter," a possession, yes, a game-piece in a complex plan. "He always meant to marry me where I could be most use, within the Kingdom: to make peace with a restless lord, to shift the balance of power, to strengthen a bond that was weak. Whatever made most sense to him, when I came of age. He thought it would be better if I was kept apart till then; he said it would protect me from the intrigues of the court, no man could use me or threaten me if I was a thousand miles away. I think there was more to it, though. If I came to Outremer as

an innocent, I would be more pliable to his will; and also it
prevented me from forming any attachment of my own, of
course, which might have proved a terrible inconvenience."
Oh, Imber . . .

"Instead of which," a quiet dry voice spoke at their back,
"you have found your own way to inconvenience me."

Elisande gasped, and whirled around; Julianne was
deeply proud of herself, that she did neither. She turned
slowly, swept into the best courtly curtsey that she could
manage in a Sharai robe, and rose laughing to say, "You
cannot be here, it is most utterly forbidden . . . !"

Here he was, though, her father: as ever appearing unannounced, when and where he was least looked for.

He looked well, she thought, tanned and fit, dressed simply in her favourite green. As she always was recently, she
was momentarily surprised to find herself looking down at
him; she had spent too little time in his company to grow
accustomed to that, or else she always built him up bigger
in her memory than he was in body.

He examined her with no less candour, and nodded a
grudging satisfaction. All he said, though, was, "You've
grown thinner, Julianne—unless you've simply stretched a
little further. Either one was unnecessary. The dress suits
you."

"I think the life suits me, father," she said blithely. "May
I make you known to Elisande d'Albéry, granddaughter to
the Princip of Surayon?" She used the same form that her
friend did, always; she was never *daughter to Rudel.*

"I know who she is, girl," her father grunted. Of course
he knew, he knew everything; that was another definition
of fathers. "And her lineage. She's even thinner than you
are. If that's some new fashion among the young, you
should forswear it, both of you."

But then he bowed, and smiled; took Elisande's hand and
kissed it for all the world as though he could never behave
other than gentlemanly, and said, "I am a friend of your
grandfather's, and of your father's; I hope I can be a friend

to you too. Call on me, for any service you choose. I could never deny beauty."

Elisande blushed, to Julianne's high delight. She recovered quickly though, glancing over and saying acidly, "Now *that's* what I call a father. He should give lessons." Then, back to him again, "Tell us, though—how did you get in here? Past the guards, and past Sherett too, which I think would be harder? No man is allowed in the women's quarters, not anyone, not ever . . .

"It's no good, Elisande," Julianne interrupted her. "Never ask him a question beginning with 'how,' he'll give you no useful answer. Just an enigmatic smile and something that sounds like a quotation, only he turns out to be quoting himself. He'll tell you why, he'll talk to you for hours, why this and why that; but how is always his big secret. And this isn't worth wasting your breath on. He comes, he goes; that's all. He always has done. Nothing more to say."

He smiled, enigmatically enough for anyone, and bowed to her for the compliment of her understanding. This time she didn't curtsey in response, she only watched the mockery and thought how mock it was. He had always been a serious man, though often and often she had seen him cloak that with frivolous manners or a foolish smile; it seemed to her suddenly that the core of him lay closer to the surface these days, and so the cloak was correspondingly gaudy. Like his coming here to the women's house, however it was that he had managed that: there was no point to it, except to add a fragment to his legend. The man who went where he would, heedless of bar or custom—but he could as easily have had her fetched to his own quarters, where they could have been comfortable and cosed together half the night, sharing journeys and anxieties and memories and more . . .

Instead he was here, and she thought that this would have to be a hasty meeting conducted in whispers. She was a little surprised, that he would think the adventure worth the risk; but he was after all her father, and surprising her was his especial interest.

Then the tapestry over the door billowed and was swept aside, and her heart sank; Sherett stepped through with a tray, and her heart plummeted. They were discovered already, no chance even for that secret and rapid exchange of views. She wondered what the penalty was, for a man who broke so strict a sequestration . . .

Sherett smiled brightly at the girls, somehow contriving not to see the man who stood so close by her elbow. "I thought you two might enjoy a little *jereth,* to celebrate your safe arrival here."

Julianne's father took the tray from her, playing the invisible gentleman; she added, "No need to hurry. You will find us all in the kitchens, when you tire of your own company. Elisande knows the way."

And then she was gone. The tapestry fluttered and fell still, while Julianne was still gaping at the place where she had been.

"Now that is a sensible woman," her father said cheerfully, setting the tray down on a convenient chest. "A better choice for Hasan than his first two wives; I told him so, indeed, while he was still considering the matter. I have high hopes of Sherett."

Julianne said nothing, only watching as he poured out small measures of *jereth.* The jug was fine work, chased silver of a quality to outshine the plate inside the chests. The goblets matched the jug, and there were three of them on the tray.

He passed the first to Elisande; she took it gravely, with a little bob and, "Thank you, sir. Oh—what am I to call you, please? If I say 'sir' you have to call me 'my lady,' and I can't abide that. And 'Shadow' is ridiculous, but if you have another title I've never heard it . . ."

"I renounced my titles," he said, "when the King appointed me his Shadow. My name is Coren."

"Coren. Is it? I like that," she said artlessly, playing the giddy girl with all the art she could muster.

He smiled gently, entirely undeceived; gave a goblet to Julianne and took the other for himself, saluted them both

briefly, sipped and said, "So. Tell me, then, everything that
you have wrought or seen since I left you, Julianne, on the
road to the Roq."

SO THEY DID: they did it between them, telling their individual parts where their stories diverged and sharing the
tale where they had shared in its shaping. If Julianne kept
anything back, it was only trivial matter after all, what she
was sure her father would dismiss as trivial; if Elisande did,
there must still be secrets that girl had not yet told to her
friend.

They told of their meeting on the road, and of their meeting with the djinni; of Marron and Sieur Anton, of Marshal
Fulke and his call to arms, of Rudel's coming and the rescue of Redmond from the cells. They told how the Precep-
tor had sent them on towards Elessi, and how they had met
the Barons Imber along the way; how they had fled, had
encountered first the 'ifrit and then Jemel; how they had
been caught and brought back, how Julianne had been married that same day. Neither said anything of the night that
followed, how she had slept not with Imber but with
Elisande. They tried with inadequate words to describe
what had happened in the Tower of the King's Daughter,
how they had collected the Daughter and been balked when
they tried to go through to the land of the djinn; it was sim-
pler but no easier to say what had happened after, when
they had finally escaped the castle by means of Marron's
ignorance and fury.

Their journey since, their separate journeys were swiftly
covered. Much of what they'd said, perhaps most, Julianne
was sure her father had known already; he showed no sign
of that, though, listening in silence largely, his occasional
questions only for clarity's sake where their tales disagreed.

"Well," he said at last, "you have at least married the
man I chose for you, Julianne, though you seem to have
tried your utmost to avoid it."

"The djinni . . ." she said helplessly.

"Yes, the djinni. I have met your Djinni Khaldor, more than once; it takes more interest than the rest of its kind in the doings of mortal men. Even so, such an intervention is unusual. Unprecedented, I am inclined to say, though who knows the whole history of the djinn? It spoke to both of you, you say . . .

"And sent us both here," Elisande confirmed. "Ultimately."

"Ultimately, yes. Have the Sharai pestered you with questions, Elisande, as it predicted?"

"They have not. Although we've not been here half a day, yet; and it didn't say 'pester.' It said the questions would be a gift. I don't understand what it meant."

"The djinn are always elliptical, but very seldom wrong; I think you may depend on the questions. Whether you would be wise to answer them is another matter. Until I know what they are, I cannot say. Enough, for now. We will talk again. Julianne, I must find some way to return you to your husband; I am afraid it will not be a happy homecoming, there has been too much damage done already, but between us we may contrive to mend the worst of it. I still have some respect for your diplomacy."

If none for her wilfulness; so much passed unsaid, but not unnoted. "The djinni said that you would be in danger . . ."

"I am grateful for your concern, but I am always in danger. You know that. Less so here, frankly, among our enemies than I would be in Outremer, with friends. And Outremer's danger is great; I would risk much, more than my own life, to save the Kingdom. I wish Redmond were here, though. The Sharai respect old warriors; they respect my master, but not especially me. Nor Rudel—he has fought, but never under his own banner as a prince of his people. Spies and guisards command no respect at all. They will listen to him, but not be swayed. Without Redmond, the burden falls to me; so I cannot listen to your djinni's warning, even if I believed it to matter."

"The djinn are very seldom wrong." Elisande quoted his

own words back at him; he reacted only with a smile, and a nod of farewell.

The tapestry covered the doorway closely, but it seemed barely to twitch as he passed through. Sometimes Julianne thought that he had no physical body at all, that he was as much a creature of spirit as the djinn were, all purpose and intent and hidden thought.

"Well," Elisande said, "what now?"

Julianne shrugged. "There's no point asking the guards at the door, if they saw a man entering or leaving; they'd only laugh. Are there hidden gateways in the rock?"

"None that I know of, except that one we came down by, from the hills. Every child here knows of that. He came; he went. Does it matter how?"

She sounded like Julianne's father, dismissing the means and interested only in consequences. It was probably deliberate, a light teasing; Elisande was cat-curious, she must be aching to know the truth.

"I suppose not," Julianne said, refusing to play along. "We should go to find Sherett, and the other women. We're their guests; it's only polite to keep company with them."

But Sherett came to find them, apparently as well-informed now as she had been earlier. She retrieved the tray—though not before Elisande had topped up her goblet, and Julianne's—and led them briskly down through the house. Towards the kitchens, presumably, where she'd said the women had gathered. Why the kitchens, after the evening meal and when the house was full of greater comforts, Julianne couldn't imagine.

On the way, Elisande asked, "What would happen to a man who stole in here, and was caught?"

"He would not be a man for long," Sherett said, chuckling wickedly. "We would cut him and keep him, as a slave. It has happened, here and elsewhere, though not in my time. We are kind that way; the men would kill him, if we drove him out. The death of the scorpion, which is not kind at all."

Julianne didn't particularly want to hear about it, but

Sherett clearly wanted to tell; Elisande encouraged her. "Scorpion? Painful but quick, at least . . ."

"Not necessarily. After the sting, yes, they die quickly; before it, they can live for hours."

"Well, indeed. I myself have lived for years already, waiting for a scorpion to sting me . . ."

"You don't have one in your mouth."

"Ah. No. But again, I would have thought that quick."

"They use a small scorpion, which has been packed in ice and left for a day. It becomes slow, lethargic, even-tempered. Then it is placed in the offender's mouth, and his lips are sewn together. So it warms, it becomes active again. At first it is hungry; then it is enraged. I am told that men have survived half a day by keeping it placid, by holding their tongue quite still while the scorpion feeds on it."

"Ugh. I don't think I'd want to. If I'm going to die any-way, I'd rather have it over. I'd aggravate the thing, sooner than let it eat me."

"Suicide is an offence against God."

"*Suicide?*"

"Deliberately to anger a scorpion, knowing it will sting you—what else? It is the role of man to endure whatever God sends; when death must come, even in disgrace, it is still a man's duty to delay it as he can."

Was there a touch of cynicism to Sherett's smile, as though she thought a woman might be wiser? Julianne thought there was. Or hoped so, at least; she had small patience with religious orthodoxy, and none at all where it preached a hopeless fatalism.

DOWN THE STAIRS to the entrance-hall and down again, a narrow flight where the air was hot and heavy with smells of frying spices, clamorous with the clatter of pans and the high voices of women at work.

"The King's Shadow gives a feast tomorrow night," Sherett explained, "and so you find us busy. He gives the feast, but we must make it happen. Poor entertainment for you, to watch us cook; there are few of us, though, and I can spare none."

Julianne's polite demurral was overridden by Elisande's declaration, "You have two more sets of willing hands now. What can we do?"

"Nothing. You are our guests. Sit and talk with us if you will, but it would shame us to see you labour."

"It would shame you more if the feast were ill-prepared, for lack of a little help; and it would shame us to sit idle while you worked. I at least have peeled onions and scrubbed pots in this kitchen before now, Sherett. And Julianne is a married woman, she needs to learn all the arts of womanhood. It is a guest's privilege to breach a custom where they choose. Give us tasks, or we will take them on ourselves in any case—"

"—And likely spoil what you do not spill. I have worked with clumsy girls before," scowling momentously at them both. "Still, I don't deny that any help is welcome," and the scowl melted into a smile. "Come in, then, and we will see if you can scrub to Yaman's satisfaction . . ."

THE KITCHEN WAS small, airless and swelteringly hot, with open fires and ovens all stoked high and a dozen yammering women frenziedly chopping, kneading, basting. Julianne feared that she might soon regret Elisande's easy generosity; she was sure that she would soon want another bath. After so long in the desiccating Sands, she'd thought her body had forgotten how to sweat; two minutes in here showed her that she'd been wrong.

At least the scrubbing proved to have been an empty threat. Even Sherett deferred to another's authority in the kitchen, and was swiftly overruled. Yaman was the oldest woman there, wife to one of the tribal leaders and so doubly senior, and she was appalled by the very suggestion that guests in her house might wash dishes. It took another argument from Elisande to persuade her that they should work at all; eventually they were reluctantly permitted to occupy stools in the quietest corner and prepare a heap of garlic and ginger and turmeric root. Sherett was herself sent to the massive earthenware washpot—to Julianne's quiet pleasure, and Elisande's manifest glee—with a pile of roasting-trays to scour, though she quickly delegated that duty to a younger woman.

Julianne peeled and diced, while Elisande pounded in a giant stone mortar, with a pestle that reached to her waist when its bulbous end was resting on the ground. It must in the past have been the source of a thousand lewd suggestions; Julianne thought it might have provoked a few more tonight, except that good manners towards visitors forestalled them. The older women eyed the way it rose and fell in Elisande's hands, to a steady thudding rhythm, and snickered quietly between themselves.

"I don't understand," Julianne said quickly, before her friend could notice, "how my father can be giving a feast for his hosts?" Sharai laws of hospitality were stricter even than those in Marasson, or so she'd understood; and in Marasson a guest could neither refuse a gift nor return a kindness without causing deep offence.

"Oh, it's a gesture, an ancient custom, a form of words that doesn't actually mean what it says. The host provides the feast, of course, or rather his women do," with an expressive dash of her hand across her glistening brow. "The guest can contribute nothing to it, except a speech. It actually costs the host dear, when it's done properly; he must slaughter some of his precious herd, and spices are expensive. He takes honour from it, though, from his openhandedness; which is why it happens, because honour is all that a guest is allowed to give his host."

Put that way it made sense, she supposed, if you accepted the slightly peculiar notion that it honoured your host to drive him to great expense. She thought it rather dishonoured the guest to do so, but then she was not Sharai. Neither was her father, of course; but he would use that custom and any other, to bring about the ends he sought. She thought it unlikely that a grand feast that a Patric had required them to pay for would influence any of the tribal sheikhs against making war on Outremer; again, though, she was not Sharai. Nor would she have the opportunity to hear her father's speech. That was likely the greater purpose for it, from his point of view; that man had a gilded tongue, when he chose to use it. Give him a well-fed and mellow audience and he just might sway them, or some of them at least.

Some, she feared, would not be mellowed by any amount of feasting in his name. He was yet a Patric and an unbeliever, one of those who occupied not only fruitful land worth fighting for but also the holiest sites of the Catari faith. The Sharai were a religious people; even Jemel still said his prayers morning and evening, despite his loyalty to another unbeliever. It was a holy war to which Hasan was calling the tribes; however persuasive her father's voice and Rudel's, Redmond's too perhaps if he came in time, she thought that the tribes would come in answer.

She thought of Imber riding to that war as he must, her bright and beautiful boy, foolish with dreams of honour of his own, and she wanted to weep.

She thought of Hasan, equally brave and equally driven, and didn't know what she wanted.

Her first sight of Imber had seized her heart, perhaps even her soul; she'd thought that he possessed her, mind and body, that he inhabited her skin now as certainly as she did. She'd thought that he would stand in her eye for ever, blond and tall and reliable as rock—changeable as rock changes, that was, in sunlight or shadow, starlight or dark: mutable of mood but quite untouched beneath—and be a bar to any other man. What need another, she'd thought, when Imber was her own and she was his?

She'd been wrong.

Her first sight of Hasan had gripped her like a hand of fire, hard and hot. She thought him beautiful as his land was beautiful, as a hawk is: rapacious, unforgiving, deadly and yet breathtaking, limitless, free. As wide as the ocean, she'd thought him in that moment, as high as the moon; and so very different from Imber, who was beautiful as a rose is beautiful, young and thorny and close-furled petal on petal, showing only the outermost colour and shielding the heart . . .

So very different, it seemed that she could be owned and claimed by both; or at least that each could have his own, his separate Julianne. Imber had lost nothing of her, she was still entirely his own—and yet there was another Julianne who ached for Hasan's touch, whose body thrilled in his presence, whose heart had sung when he'd spoken so lightly of his marrying her. *Alas, my lord, I am married already*—but to her it had not been a joke, and still was not. She was eternally married to Imber; and yet, and yet . . .

And yet she had promised to ride with Hasan, she remembered, in the early morning. Or no, she had demanded that promise of him; and how loyal was that to her wedded lord, her love? Perhaps she would grow into one of those women whose affairs were the gossip of the court at Marasson, who had a new passion every summer, whose husbands were more pitied than mocked . . .

She didn't believe it, though. She would not. She had too much self-respect; she would return to Imber at Elessi as her father had said, and she would mend what damage had been done by her running away, and she would be a faithful, loyal wife to her tender and doubtful baron, and so they would both be happy.

Before that, she would go riding with Hasan. Before that, she would stone these apricots Sherett was bringing her, now that they had finally worked all that garlic and ginger and turmeric into a soft and pungent mound . . .

AT LAST THEY were chivvied out of the kitchen, and sent to bed like weary children. No second bath, she was too tired for that; only a quick, cool wash and she fell onto the pallet laid out for her, with Elisande beside.

"What happens in the morning?" she muttered, as the other girl put out the lamp.

"In the morning? I wake you, earlier than you want to be woken; I wash and groom you till you're beautiful, then waste it all behind a robe and veil that shows no more than your eyes. Then you wait like a tremulous maid, peering through the window-screens and refusing to eat, until Hasan brings your horse to the door. You mount, you murmur sharp-edged compliments at each other as you have these past days, and you ride away."

"Alone?"

"Sweet, where do you think you are? Of course, not alone. A Patric and a Sharai, a warlord and a married lady—oh, no. If you were his captive, then perhaps; as you are his guest, you will both need chaperones. I ride with you, and he will bring some company to protect him from two such fearsome creatures as we are. Why, did you want to have him alone?"

"No, indeed. Why would I?"

A snort was all the answer she received to that. For a moment she was tempted to be childish, cruel even, to ask *did you enjoy your time alone with Marron, all those days . . . ?* But she was too tired to fight, and too tired for the reconciliation after. She lay still and felt the numbness spread from feet and fingers, rising like an inexorable tide throughout her body; just before it reached her mind and took her off, she did wish fervently and truthfully to dream of Imber.

While the image behind her eyelids, the man who stood foursquare and certain of his place there was not so tall as Imber, darker, older . . .

MORNING CAME, WITH Elisande's predictions one by one: dragged up in the half-light with her rebellious body shrieking for more sleep and her recreant mind for the shadows of dream to hide in, that this had come too soon, she wasn't ready, she didn't want to go . . .

And her friend's bullying her into washing and dressing

and sitting still while she was petted and perfumed, while
her hair was combed into order and brushed to a high gloss;
and then her sitting on the window's ledge and peering out
through the lattice, watching the gloomy pavement so far
below and nibbling on a little fruit and refusing all break-
fast else, because how could she possibly eat when her
stomach was cramped with tension, when her thoughts
were so dizzy between duty and longing, between one man
and the other . . . ?

There was constant movement along the pool's side, men
and boys walking slowly this way and that; others were
busy in the fields on the further bank, carrying water to the
crops before the sun's first light could creep down the scarp
to burn them dry. She watched and waited, in a frenzy of
doubt and desire.

At last, at long last she saw the dim shapes of horses
coming down from the stable, a line of them, some ridden
and some led. Heard them too, the hard but quiet sounds
of hooves on stone, a single sudden whinny that sang in
the air, in her ears. That was what she wanted, she told
herself firmly, all that she was craving: not the man's
company at all but the height and liberty of a horseback
ride, a strong responsive body beneath her and the curious
communication she could achieve through reins and touch
and voice, till human mind and animal worked almost as
one, sharing the excitement of speed and discovery . . .

She tried to tell that to Elisande, and was laughed at; and
then was hurried downstairs, down many stairs to the entrance hall where Sherett was waiting for them, already
hooded and veiled, her black eyes mysterious and challenging today.

Her voice was sharp, as she told them to conceal their
faces; her fingers were quick but delicate, adjusting the
folds of their costumes with more grace than Elisande
could manage.

"Are you coming with us? For the ride?" Julianne couldn't
decide if she wanted that or not. Wisdom said yes, said *yes*

please, ride with your husband, so that I don't have to; but wisdom's was a cold voice, and she was too hot to heed it.

"Not I, girl. I have a feast to prepare, yes? I merely want a word with my lord, and then to see my guests on their way to their pleasure. Stand still and let me tighten this, shameless, or the wind will have your veil . . ."

When Sherett was finally satisfied, she led them out around the door-screen, into a cool breeze and the company of men.

MEN, AND HORSES. Five horses, and three men: and Hasan the first of those, sitting his mount a length or so ahead of the others and drawing her eyes inexorably to him.

He greeted her with a bow and a smile, and, "You see? I keep my oath . . ."

"Prince, I never doubted you," she said, and swept into a deep curtsey, deliberately Patric, alien to both the dress and the custom of these people.

"Lady, you relieve my mind. I chose this filly for you," a young chestnut mare, short and restive, her breeding showing in every fine-boned line of her and her reins tied to his saddle-bow. "Her name is Tezra, and she is eager for a run."

"And so am I," but first, even before making friends with her mount, she walked a little way further to bid good morning to his companions. He had chosen those, she guessed, with equal care: a quiet older man whose company promised much, and a blazingly handsome youth with dancing eyes whom she could appreciate as a work of art and beauty, who touched her heart not at all. She might wish him on Elisande, she thought, if that girl could possibly be persuaded to it; he might have been picked for exactly that purpose.

When she turned back, she saw Sherett at Hasan's stirrup. They were talking, too softly for her to overhear; they were not touching at all, but did not need to. Simply from the way he stooped in his saddle, the way she stretched up almost on tiptoe, she thought she could sense all that bound them together: the passion, the intelligence, the understanding and acceptance. *She is his wife, and I am someone else's* . . .

And yet he had two wives else, and Sherett accepted that. The others were not here and she was, which must count for something; but still, he was about to ride off for a morning's jaunt with another girl, and Sherett accepted that also.

A girl who is married to another man; in Sherett's eyes, that might make a difference. She doubted that it did in Hasan's.

Would a man with three wives already—and a relationship with one at least whose depth, whose true value was spelled out before her now, in every lineament of their two bodies—would such a man truly desire a fourth? Surely not; of a certainty he had been teasing only, praising her beauty in the most fulsome way he knew. *Tell me his name, that I may kill him*—that had undoubtedly been a joke. Though it might become a joke that acquired a grim reality, if Hasan were permitted the war that he craved so ardently . . .

She stroked Tezra's soft nose, and murmured endearments into the flickering ear. "You're so beautiful," which she was. "I have another horse I love, but I could love you too," which was true; and if only it were so easy to love two men, if only her culture or his would allow it . . .

One of Hasan's companions—the young one, of course, Boraj of the easy grace and astonishing beauty—slid off his horse to help her mount. She thanked him, and took the reins from Hasan with no more than a tremor when his fingers quite advertently touched hers. She wondered what it was about this man, or else about her, that he could affect her so profoundly when she'd thought herself utterly given and claimed already; and found no answer in his strong face or his strong gaze. She turned her head aside to watch Boraj lift Elisande into the saddle of the other spare horse, a mare of gentler temper by the look of her.

Tezra fidgeted, tossing her head and shifting her feet on the rock walkway. Julianne spoke to her sternly, preaching the necessity of patience; then laughed and glanced forward. Sherett had stepped away from Hasan's side, she saw. As though that were the permission he'd been waiting for, he saluted her gravely, then beckoned the whole party forward.

AS THEY PICKED their way slowly through the foot-traffic, Julianne watched the faces that they passed. Man and boy, occasional veiled woman or girl too young for such conformity, all gaped up at Hasan, pressing themselves back not to impede his progress.

She wasn't the only one, then. To be sure, he was the leader, he would attract first attention regardless of who came behind; but they kept their eyes on him long after he was past, swivelling their heads and sparing barely a glance for Julianne and the others.

Perhaps that was what she felt also, no more than the common admiration for a man whose charisma was undeniable, whose fascination was irresistible, whose power and potency were patent. Only that because she was a girl, a foolish girl, married but not yet made wife to any man, her romantic soul twisted her sense of him into something more . . .

Perhaps. She yearned to believe that, but could not. She knew herself better; despised herself almost, for being so weak and foolish.

And having nothing she could do about that, yearned instead to kick Tezra into a mind-numbing gallop, to blast all such idiocy out of her head; and couldn't do that either, here where there was so little space between rock wall and water, and that space too full of people.

SHE TRAILED ALONG behind Hasan, constantly tormented by the adulation that she saw and could not allow herself to replicate. Either as man or war-leader, he was not for her. Her frustration passed through inevitably to her mettlesome horse, so that she had to fight Tezra as she was fighting herself; to these skilled riders she must be looking incompetent or mismounted as she struggled to control the beast with reins and stirrups, to hold her to a steady walk. That only added to her frustration.

The long, long pool dwindled at last, as the valley's walls closed in on either side; she found herself riding a twisting path between them, a path that grew narrower at every turn until there was only a bare slit of sky far above, barely enough light to cast a shadow. This must be the siq Hasan had spoken of, the way Elisande would have preferred to bring her to Rhabat . . .

Here too there was traffic; they met a camel-train approaching, and hardly found room to squeeze their horses past the high swaying loads. Even the camels, Julianne thought balefully, turned their heads to watch Hasan as he passed.

At the far end of that winding defile—and it was far, perhaps half an hour's slow ride—the high walls that had towered above them broke down in masses of crumbling rock and shale. The horses picked their way delicately, where falling stones had invaded the path; as they came out into sunlight, viciously dazzling after so long in the dark, Julianne turned her head to look back. She saw a steep slope rising behind her, a chaos of tumbled slabs and shadow. If it weren't for that well-established path, she'd have no hope of finding the one sliver of darkness that masked the way through. Easy to understand how Rhabat had stayed hidden for so long, even from the Sharai.

"That is our shelter," Hasan said softly. "It cannot be climbed; every boy who comes here has tried it, but the rock shears away under your fingers, and leaves you clinging to dust. A dozen men with bows can defend the siq, and we can feed and water an army if we need to; but there is no water out here, if ever an army was led against us."

No water, but there was still an army here. She gazed

past him and saw a wide gravel plain dancing with light, where every separate stone seemed to glitter and burn under the sun. The plain was shrouded with shapeless black shadows, and she had to blink and rub her eyes to see them clearly. They were tents, vast tents, the homes of the nomadic tribes; each one could shelter dozens of men, and there were dozens of them, more, gathered in disorderly groups as far as she could squint against the glare.

"Every sheikh has come with his retinue," Hasan went on, "but only the sheikhs and their close supporters may come into Rhabat; the rest make camp here, and we supply them from our stores. Even so, there were not this many two days ago, and there will be more tomorrow. Word is spreading; the tribes are gathering, uninvited but welcome none the less. Welcome to me, at least. You may feel differently."

"I don't know what I feel," she confessed; which was true, except, "Hasan, I don't want war . . ."

"I know; but war must come. Tomorrow, perhaps—who knows? It is as God wills it. Not today, though. Today, we can ride in peace. Will you come?"

And he kicked his stallion forward, hard. Julianne had no chance to refuse the challenge; Tezra responded on her own account, almost unseating her dithering rider with an explosive surge of speed.

AWAY FROM THE stonefalls at the hill's margin, the pea gravel made good footing for the horses, hard and level. Julianne caught her balance, crouched low in the saddle and set herself and her mount to a grim chase. Hasan had the start on her—if a short one, thanks to Tezra—and he had a stronger horse beneath him; Tezra was lighter, though, all sinew, built for speed.

She was nimbler, too, quicker to weave her way between the clusters of tents; soon they were racing shoulder to shoulder with Hasan. He glanced across with a grin, and then expressively behind him; she risked a peek, and saw that they had far outpaced their companions.

Briefly she hesitated, thinking of what was proper, of his reputation and hers. In that moment he surged ahead again as Tezra slowed a little, sensing her doubts through the reins. Julianne gritted her teeth, drove in her heels and cried the horse on with a wild whoop. Devil take the proprieties; she might blush for it later, but she meant not to lose this race.

NEITHER DID SHE, though that was by his kindness. Slowly Tezra gained ground on the bigger stallion, slowly they drew level with his withers, with his shoulder; then they were running head to head again, and all the vast desert lay open and empty before them, no more tents now, only an infinity to run in . . .

Except that Tezra was blowing hard suddenly, not her will but her stamina failing her. Hasan knew as soon as Julianne did, or so it seemed; he reined back his mount, drawing him smoothly from that headlong gallop to a canter, to a trot, to a walk. Gratefully, she did the same. She would have hated to force Tezra on beyond her strength, but she might have done it regardless. She wasn't sure she'd have had the resolution to call a halt before he did.

That wild ride had left her breathless too, but joyfully so. Exhilarated, flushed behind her veil—she could feel the blood burning in her cheeks, and was grateful also for Sherett's care to fix her clothing firmly. There was no one but Hasan to see here, and he at least would not have been shocked by a glimpse of her face, she was sure of that; but she was equally sure that she did not want that exposure. Not now, not like this. Her eyes must be enough of a give-away . . .

His own eyes sparkled darkly, as he bowed extravagantly in the saddle. "The race is yours, my lady."

"No, not so! You checked your horse, but only out of courtesy . . ."

"Precisely so. He who will not press his advantage when he can is doomed to lose."

He said it lightly but meant more by it, she thought: that

this was a rare gallantry, that when it mattered more he
would not be so weak.

She nodded, to tell him that she understood; and thought
that he would turn his horse now, that they would go
meekly and quietly back to rejoin their chaperones.

He was standing in his stirrups, though, and shielding his
eyes as he gazed out across the limitless plain.

"Someone comes," he grunted. "One camel, riding fast. I
have outrunners on all the approaches; I think we'll wait."

Wait they did, sitting their stationary horses for so long
that Elisande and the men tired of waiting themselves and
came to join the raceaways. Boraj was dancing attendance
on her friend, Julianne was delighted to notice, sidling his
mount against hers and murmuring softly, offering her a
drink from his flask. The stubborn girl only shook her head,
though, and edged her horse away. Julianne sighed, and
willed him silently to keep trying. *He who will not press his
advantage* . . . And Boraj had one advantage at least, his
spectacular looks. Elisande was susceptible to beauty, after
all; and unclaimed, and likely to remain so, for all that she
might wish it otherwise . . .

Weeks in the desert had not given Julianne desert eyes;
Jemel would have seen it perhaps before Hasan did, Marron certainly. Slowly the little flicker of shadow that Hasan
had declared to be a man drew closer, though, and resolved
itself indeed to be a man, mounted on a running camel.

Closer still, and she revised that opinion. Not a man; a
boy. She didn't know when Sharai lads were recognised as
adult—when they killed their first enemy, most likely and
brought his head back in evidence—but surely it wasn't
this young. The Sharai were a small people, by and large,
and some of the men had shrill voices, good for carrying
far in desert air; even so, this one couldn't be more than
twelve. Emphatically a boy.

Good for carrying messages, she thought, a light-framed
boy; and on such a camel, made for speed as much as Tezra
was. She recognised the lines of the beast, much like those
the Sultan had displayed for them, Sildana's offspring and

their confrères. It made sense, that the Sultan's racing stock should have been bred from such as this.

The boy saw Hasan's wave and came straight to him.

"Halm—you are well?"

Of course, Julianne thought with a touch of spite, such a consummate leader of men would know all his message-boys by name. How not?

"I am, Hasan. And you?"

And, of course, he'd encourage them to use his name un-adorned: no title, no gesture of respect. That way the name acquires respect in itself, it accumulates weight that it still carries in night-time conversations around the fire, when the night's too cold for sleeping. This boy would half-worship the man, would certainly die for him, simply for being allowed to say his name like that, in this company . . .

They asked politely after each other's families—the boy's uncle had a poisoned foot, for which Hasan recom-mended a hot poultice of camel-dung and a certain kind of cactus—until Julianne began to wonder why the hurry, why the racing-camel and the bird-boned rider if they were going to delay the message another hour by talking? Might as well have sent it on foot, or by tortoise. She'd had a tor-toise once, a pet tortoise that she'd raced against her friend's along the palace corridors, a lettuce-leaf the prize . . .

Eventually, though, Hasan broke off the preliminaries. "You have an errand to me, Halm?"

"Yes, Hasan," and he sat straighter in his saddle to de-liver it, a soldier on duty reporting to his commandant. "There is a trader's caravan camped at the oasis of Tosin's Stone. They meant to leave at first light, and will be here by sunset; I left at midnight, to advise you."

"That was well done. I will give your family a pigeon, though, to spare you the ride next time. Which trader?"

"He is dead. The drovers are led by a Patric," and the boy's eyes found Julianne and Elisande, reading their breeding from their eyes alone, unless it was from the way they sat their horses. "An old man, a cripple; the drovers call him father, and are anxious for him . . ."

"Redmond," Elisande said. "He would be a father to the world, if it would let him; he was always my best substitute. I told him he was taking on too much. And he must have driven himself and them, to come this far so fast, only a day behind us . . ."

"We were delayed," Julianne reminded her. "The Dancers led us out of our way, and divided we were slower through the Sands, besides having to battle with ghûls en route." All that was really for the boy's sake, to put a bulge in his oh-so-experienced eyes and a gape in his dismissive, almost contemptuous mouth. Only women and only Patrics, but they'd had more adventures in a week than he'd seen in his short lifetime . . .

Hasan nodded. "Redmond indeed—and in time for your father's feast, Julianne, though he might be more weary than festive. He will be welcome, however he comes. We'd best take the news back now; a caravan of goods is no great matter, but the Red Earl deserves a better greeting. Besides, we should send a party to escort him in; he might be startled else, by the number of our gatewardens," with a gesture back towards the proliferating tents. "Halm, find your own people, and rest; the Kauram are camped to the south of the road. Tomorrow, come through the siq, say I sent for you; I will give you that bird."

No doubt he would, but the pigeon was not the prize. Halm bowed, hand to heart and lips and forehead; then he rode away, his head high and his eyes starry. He would see Rhabat, by Hasan's personal word; even now he would be thinking that this was a story to tell his children and his grandchildren, how the greatest general of the age—the man who would win back Ascariel, no less!—had touched his life with blessing, for the slightest favour done.

Oh, Hasan was good at this, Julianne thought, wheeling her horse in his tail, riding in his dust. He would leave them all behind: defeated, hungry, bereft . . .

THREE

What Comes from the Water

JEMEL WALKED SLOWLY along the gully that led down to the Dead Waters, knowing that he was taking a risk, or more risks than one; his life might be the least of what he risked.

But his life was of little value to him anyway, and less if he lost anything more of what he valued more. And so he was here, his scimitar loose in its sheath and his bare feet silent in the shadows, his nose scenting rank salt and his ears straining for any sound ahead.

He could hear nothing, neither what he sought nor what he dreaded. So he stepped forward more confidently, less guardedly, remembering that he was after all Sharai and so not born to skulk, especially here in Rhabat. He came out from the deep darkness of the gully into the lesser shade of the narrow waterfront; the sea lay dark and still within the bay, brighter beyond under the glare of the afternoon sun. So much water made him simply uncomfortable, regardless of its sinister reputation or its more recent annexation. He stood gazing at it, snared by the quiescent threat of this place, almost amazed by his own courage in venturing here; and was startled by a more immediate threat, the mundane sound of steel drawn at his back.

He spun around and found himself facing two men of the Ashti, who stepped forward from a cave-mouth, each with a blade aimed at his heart. A boy lurked behind them, a lad, a runner of the same tribe, watching open-eyed the best excitement of his day so far.

Well, this had been one of the risks, the smallest risk Jemel had faced. Hasan was bound to have set guards here, after the report of 'ifrit in the water and his own encounter with the ghûls. Jemel had been lucky; the tribes would be sharing the duty, and it might have been the turn of the Saren to stand watch.

He kept his hands carefully far from the hilt of his weapon, and said, "I am called Jemel."

"We know who you are. What you are, tribeless," replied one.

"Sand Dancer," added the other. "What do you want here?"

Perhaps he had not been so lucky after all; perhaps he should after all have stayed in the house of the Beni Rus, where he was safe. That had been the common advice, the instruction from Hasan. But a host could not give orders to his guest, and no one could command the obedience of a man without a tribe. Jemel would have obeyed Marron, reluctantly, if he'd added his voice to the clamour; but Marron had slipped away in other company, and without a word to his friend. And Jemel would not cower cravenly behind another man's guarded walls, he would not have that added to what was already being said about him . . .

"I came seeking the Ghost Walker," he said. "I was told that he had come this way." A child had told him, a barefaced girl, awe and terror mingling in her voice; it had only added to his humiliation, that a crop-tending brat had known Marron's movements when he did not. Asking the question had been bitter enough; getting a reply had been almost worse.

"He did. With his woman." The Ashti's voice betrayed the general confusion. The Ghost Walker was their prophecy made flesh, the talisman they'd waited centuries to see; and yet the boy who claimed that title was nothing of theirs, neither the company he chose to keep in defiance of all custom. There was no terror in this man, or none that he would show: again a mix of emotions, though, wonder and contempt uncomfortable partners.

"Him we passed through," the other said. *With his woman,* implicitly, adding further to Jemel's gall. "You, though—you are another matter. Why should we pass you?"

"Were you set here to watch the water, or to obstruct those with good reason to come this way?" That was temper only, and he regretted it immediately; if they challenged him, he could offer no good reason. His reasons didn't seem good even to him, only that the alternative was worse.

They gave him no answer at all; one said to the other, "A tribeless man has no honour; he might be a spy for the 'ifrit. Or he is a Dancer, and they are forbidden this valley. If we slay him, we would at least earn the thanks of the Saren, perhaps of the whole council."

"Does the gratitude of the Saren mean so much to the Ashti?" Jemel snapped back. Here he was on safer ground. "Does the anger of the Ghost Walker mean so little? Or the dishonour of Hasan, who has named me friend and guest?"

This was posturing only, on both sides; they wouldn't kill him now, he was sure. Not without greater authority. A Saren guard might have done it without a thought, to please his sheikh; these might have done it in the moment of recognition, but not once they'd let him argue for his life.

"You should have stayed in Hasan's house," one said sourly. "You offend us all. But go, then. That way," with a twitch of his scimitar's point. "Run and speak with your master, tribeless. If you are wise, you will keep in his shadow hereafter, or else in Hasan's."

If he'd been wise, he thought, he would not be here at all; or at least not tribeless, and not in Marron's retinue.

Grief had made him reckless first, but it was not grief that drove him now. Nothing was as simple as it should have been. God had made his a simple people, or God and the desert between them; complexity confounded them, and Jemel was not immune to that.

He did not run, but walked along the waterfront, foolishly close to the edge; posturing again, but he allowed himself the indulgence. The guards were holding back, hiding in their cave at the gully's mouth, where rock walls offered some illusion of shelter. Let them see him bolder . . .

Let them see him eaten by 'ifrit, to know him no spy—but he did not believe he would be eaten. He found it hard to believe in the 'ifrit at all, because he had not been there with Marron—

—Or because Elisande had. As she was here, though not with Marron now. He found her at the open gateway to the rising tunnel, Rhabat's secret exit; she stood just outside its black maw, fretfully staring within.

"You showed him this?"

"Of course. He asked me to."

Briefly, Jemel felt all of the Ashti's patent distrust of her. She was Patric, a friend maybe but still of the enemy and committed to its cause: its survival, its occupation of Catari land. She should never have been allowed here the once, let alone brought back; this gateway was a Sharai secret and precious to them, it should never have been taught to her . . .

It should never have been taught by her to Marron, but his reasons there were more obscure, and faltered before her gaze. Marron was also Patric, of course, also perhaps of the enemy; not committed to anything, though, so far as Jemel could tell, beyond the avoidance of war.

"And you let him go up alone?"

"He told me to. It's *dark* in there, Jemel. I didn't think to bring a torch, I didn't know what he wanted until he led me here. He said he could find his way without light, but I would slow him down . . ."

"Why has he gone up, what for?"

"I don't know, he didn't say."

Is he coming back? was the question neither one of them wanted asked, for fear of the other offering an answer.

Nothing to do then but wait, and find out. Wait together, as they must: caught in a reluctant companionship, bonded by a mutual love that only touched each other at its fringes.

The Sharai could wait in patience, in silence when they must. So could she. Talking was always better, though, talking killed relentless time; how many nights had he talked through with Jazra in their youth, huddled together over a low flame without a blanket between them to keep back the bitter cold of the stars? Uncountable nights, immeasurably precious to him still. Talking with her could never mean so much, but he would talk if she would; the alternative was all but unbearable, to watch the dark and listen to its silence, to wonder if trust and need were both to be betrayed again. Marron had said more than once that his only skill lay in betrayal . . .

Jemel's eyes shifted, away from the shadows of the gateway to the shadows shifting on the lapping water. Nothing was moving there, except patterns of dark on the surface and below; he set his back to the rock so that he absolutely couldn't stare any longer into that tunnel, slid down to a comfortable squat and asked, "What did you see, in the land of the djinn?"

What did you see, that I should have seen instead? was the real question, and she heard it clearly. "Little," she said, shrugging as she sat beside him, folding her legs neatly beneath the hem of her robe as his own people did. "You went through first, you know what was there, the Pillar's elder brother; other than that, gold dust and golden rock, gold sky by day and night. It's not a land for looking at. There's little there, and little of what there is is extreme, or even actually interesting. Except that simply being there is fascinating. Like standing at a spring when you know it's the wellhead of a massive trading river, when you've spent all your life on its banks: to be at the source at last is mindshaking, even when the source is a trickle of clean water through a simple pasture and no more."

Jemel had never seen a river such as she described, and hardly knew what she meant; but he knew how he'd felt when he stood in that other world, and so he nodded. He'd thought he stood in the heart of the sun, and was not burned.

"What of the mountain that was flat at the peak?" This was all a tale already told. She had narrated the whole journey to the entire party before they reached Rhabat; but stories were made to be told again and again. And he wanted to hear it alone, to have at least some sense of sharing.

"It was hardly a mountain, Jemel, no great climb." *You didn't miss that much.* "I don't know what to tell you about it, else. It wasn't just flat, it didn't happen that way by nature. It had been cut off somehow and polished after, unless what did the cutting left it polished as it went. The surface was smooth as glass—smooth as ice, if ice is ever warm. And it got hot towards the centre, hard to walk on. Perhaps we should have run and slid across, like children, but it felt like a cathedral. Like a temple, somewhere holy . . ."

"What did it mean?"

"I don't know, Jemel. Nor does Marron. What did the needle mean? It was something they could do, perhaps, no more than that . . ."

Jemel shook his head. Everything must have a meaning; he believed absolutely in signs and portents and significance, only not in the ability of women to read what was written in the world. Works so great had to have a potency beyond their sheer scale. If he had seen and could not understand the blade—*the needle* she had called it, but she was a woman—perhaps that was only because he had not seen the mountaintop. A man might need to walk far in that land to penetrate its secrets. The week they'd been gone, she in the Ghost Walker's shadow—and fasting by the gaunt look of them and the hunger now, though they denied it—that week should have proved plenty, in both time and distance. Would have done, he was sure, had he been there in her stead. As he should have been, but for the mischance that had set her in his place, at Marron's side . . .

It had been more than mischance today, it had been Marron's choice, or hers. Almost he twisted his head, to seek the Ghost Walker fruitlessly in the dark; instead, again, he looked to the water.

"What is it," he wondered aloud, "that lives in there?"

"The 'ifrit," she said, and shuddered.

"No, not those. Something more, something greater. This has been a place of evil for generations. Men used to sail these waters," though it was hard for him to imagine, who had never seen a boat; he knew the words from stories, but he had no pictures in his mind. He waved his hand towards the evidence, storerooms in the cliffs and steps from the quayside that broke the surface of the sea and went on down into mystery. "Now we watch them and whisper, and keep safe away."

"They stink," Elisande said, which was true but fell far short of the truth. "They are dead; nothing lives there, nothing could. That's reason enough. The rest is storytelling, nothing more."

"No," again. If he'd known no better, he still would not have believed her; she had the shifty look of someone driven to a lie. Against her desire, perhaps, but lying none the less. "Men have died, and been found dead on the shores. Dead in terror, or torn apart. Not many and not recently, but they are more than stories, they have graves." Or tombs or cairns, crumbling rock-piles in the Sands to cover crumbling bones. "You have lived in Rhabat, as I have not," and he hated this, that he must ask a Patric for knowledge that was Sharai. He hated also to press her past her defensive lying, it was ill-mannered and worse, humiliating for them both; but if he could not have her share of Marron, he'd have whatever less he could take from her, and give her as little as he could in return. "What do they say here? They must speak of the Dead Waters . . ." In the women's quarters, and elsewhere; she'd been a girl then, unveiled, licensed to roam. Girls were demons, he'd often thought:

they tormented the boys and plagued the men, and nothing could be kept secret from them.

"Surely," she said, her face tight against him. "They say that they are dead." And then, of a sudden, her expression changed: collapsed almost, like rock that had stood too long against the sand on the wind and was worn as thin as paper, too weak to hold its own light weight any longer. "Oh, Jemel, I'm sorry. But you know what the djinni called me . . . ?"

"Lisan of the Dead Waters." He had not forgotten. He called her Lisan himself, these days, when he called her anything at all. His tongue could find its way around her full name if he chose, but he preferred to emphasise the distance that lay between them, that he was Sharai and she was not.

"Yes. I didn't understand it then, and I still don't; but now we're here, and I don't want it, I don't want even to think about it. I'd forgotten, I think, how rank these waters are. More than smell, but you said that. I came down here seldom, except when the children challenged me. And that was rare, they were scared themselves; but it was forbidden, and so we had to come. Besides, there was this," a jerk of her head towards the open gateway, "though we never explored far up there, either. Too dark, and too dull. The water was dull too, to be honest. If we stayed long enough to be brave, it was long enough to be bored. Nothing ever happened; we were never even caught by the adults, there wasn't a guard then. Why risk men, against a devil? That's what they say, in Rhabat: that a devil lives in the water, and takes whoever dares to come within its reach. Takes and torments them, body and soul—that's what they say, that the water's fouled by the souls of all its victims, which it keeps so that they'll never find their way to paradise. It's worse than death, they say; it's death and hell together."

Jemel had—perhaps—stopped believing in paradise, and so in hell; he had stood however briefly in another world, and thought that two such might be enough for any man's faith to sustain. Belief was easy, for those who had not seen. Truth was heavier, and he could only carry so much in mind or heart. He said his prayers by rote now, and only when others were there to see it if he failed.

He could still believe in devils, though; that much was easy, where wickedness seemed to seep up through the damp stones, and hang in the very air he breathed. And if in devils, perhaps also in souls; he shuddered at the thought of it, being trapped past death in those murky waters.

Watching more alertly now, perhaps looking for souls among the shadows, he thought he saw solid shadows gather below the surface. It was hard to be sure, when the waters were more choppy suddenly—but they were choppy only in a small area above that cluster of black shadow, as though a wisp of wind stirred them only there. Or as if something were rising, disturbing them from below . . .

And moving too, moving swiftly now, sending little bubbles up to stir the surface as it, they headed cleanly for the steps.

Jemel leaped to his feet to cry a warning to the guards, drawing his scimitar and pointing it towards the broken arrowhead of ripples that was spreading slowly across the water.

Too slow, too late, and useless anyway; what could two men do, against a sudden eruption of ebony-shelled creatures from the deep? Too many to count, they scuttled up the steps like crabs, like giant crabs with claws like scything daggers; but they were growing, changing even as they climbed, swelling into something greater than those hard shells could contain. Their backs split open, and bony wings unfurled.

The guards shrieked like women, but neither of them ran. The boy ran, off into the gully as no doubt he'd been kept and told to do, but honour to the Ashti: the men stayed to face that dreadful onslaught with weapons drawn and ready, though they must have known their blades would be all but useless. One broke, indeed, on the back of a carapace; the other struck and skidded uselessly, was quickly seized and snapped between great claws.

Where two men could do nothing but die, three could do no more. Jemel made no move to join them in their deaths, felt only relief when Elisande grabbed his arm and hauled him back into the deep shadow of the gateway.

She at least had thought of something she could do; she cried out softly, up the curve of the tunnel.

"Marron! Come quickly, the 'ifrit are here . . ."

Whether the cry would reach him, who could tell? Marron had sharp ears, and the windings of the tunnel carried sound a long way before it died; but the tunnel climbed higher even than a voice could at full pitch, which hers was not. And he might have left it, Jemel thought; he might have opened the upper gateway—what other purpose could he have, after all?—and gone out onto the headland above. He might have gone altogether . . .

He had not. A scurry of light footfalls and he was there abruptly, not breathing hard, showing no sign of how far he'd come, whether he'd been one or a hundred turns above.

"'Ifrit?"

"See . . ."

Dozens of them, scores now, shapeshifting from crab to airy monster that Jemel could give no name to. If they were aware of being watched they paid no heed, but took wing one by one till the sky was full of them, a black flock rising high and swiftly.

Silently, also. No cries came back from that dread gathering. Jemel cried out, though, as he felt his wrist seized with a grip he couldn't resist; and Marron cried too, as he forced the edge of the drawn scimitar across his forearm.

Elisande's turn to add her own voice, "Marron, no . . . !"

A waste of breath: blood followed the blade, and the Daughter poured out of the wound.

Poured and rose, appearing as ever like drifting smoke but moving faster far than any smoke could in this heavy stillness, driving upward.

It chased after the 'ifrit like a dense, smudged arrow; but they flew faster, whipping at the air so savagely Jemel thought that he should feel the wind from their wings, even so far below.

Perhaps the Daughter did feel the turmoil of it, perhaps that was why it could make no headway, couldn't reach even the last straggler in the flock. Or perhaps it had simply gone too far; Marron seemed to be straining when Jemel glanced at him, his face tense and twisted with effort.

"Enough," Elisande whispered, laying a tentative hand on his shoulder. "You cannot reach them, call it back . . ."

He sighed, and nodded. Jemel looked up again and saw the Daughter pause, saw it hang for a moment, losing shape, as though it too felt the disappointment of defeat. Then it flowed down and back, insinuated itself into his bleeding arm and the wound sealed behind it, loose tails of leather drooping from the flesh like dark dead worms to show where Marron had slashed through the useless stitches in his haste.

"What were you trying to do?" Elisande demanded breathlessly. *Not to kill, surely?* There was shock in her voicelessness, as though that would be another betrayal, the worse for being so unlooked-for.

"I thought I might open a gateway that could catch a few of them, send some at least back where they came from. I brought them here," bitterly, accusing himself, "I might try to make amends. But I couldn't reach. I almost lost it, I thought, for a moment . . ."

That, they'd seen. It was a lesson learned, Jemel thought, and not to be lightly forgotten.

AS EVER MARRON was fully recovered in his body, if still shaky in his mind. If he couldn't open one gateway, at least he could close another; he turned round and gripped the wide slab of rock that stood ajar at his back. One heave of his shoulders and it swung into place, the ancient mechanism so well-crafted that even so strong an effort couldn't make it slam or spring open against its locking. Once it was closed, only the closest examination could find the hairline

cracks that distinguished door from rockface; not even the
sharpest minds could calculate where and how it could be
opened, if they weren't already privy to the secret.

Marron glanced at Jemel with seemingly both shame and
triumph in his face, *I know now, although you did not show
me.*

Despite his misgivings Jemel would have shown it, if
he'd been asked. How not? He remembered having felt
obscurely glad, though, that Marron couldn't slip that way
without his guidance. He'd forgotten Elisande's familiar-
ity with Rhabat. Now he would be anxious for as long as
they were here, and drawing small comfort from the fact
that she'd been left at the foot of the tunnel this first time,
at least . . .

No blame to her, though. She gave Marron what he
asked for, and Jemel would have done the same, as he always did. Not their fault, neither of their faults if Marron
turned from one to the other alternately, seeming not to
know which he wanted closest.

And this was distraction anyway, far from what mattered
now. Jemel's eyes met hers and seemed to share the same
recognition, as though her thoughts had marched in line
with his; even Marron's neatness of mind, closing the door
behind him, even that was only a delay, a way to fill a moment or two of time . . .

Enough. He gestured with his head, and led them forward; found Elisande unexpectedly at his elbow, where
he'd expected her to take Marron's at his back.

"We should say the *khalat* for them, Jemel. We two,
Marron doesn't know it . . ."

"I have heard it," his voice, strained and reluctant. "What
is in me has heard it many times; I don't believe it knows
how to forget. I will join you."

THERE WERE MANY forms of the *khalat*: from complex
sung choruses intended for a solemn funeral that could take
as long as an hour to complete, to a brief prayer-chant that

any lone warrior could remember, to sing his fallen comrade home in the midst of a battlefield if he must.

There were also inevitably variations between tribe and tribe, but with a strong voice to lead, any Sharai could follow and join in even the most elaborate rite. They all depended on the same few simple verses.

Elisande and Marron both looked to Jemel to lead them, she from where she was kneeling beside the bodies to do the woman's work, straightening the messy remnants and cloaking them as best she could with the ripped rags of their clothing. Marron stood back, coming no closer than he must for decency's sake; even that was too close, by the way his own blood—or that which was in his blood—responded to the stink of what was spilled, rushing vividly to his skin.

What *khalat* came most naturally to Jemel came from the Saren, inevitably, soft call-and-response they would sing over two avowed brothers fallen together, as such brothers should. He had begun before he knew what he was doing. He choked on the words then and fell silent, heard his friends' mingled voices take it up—and joined them determinedly, saying Saren words over Ashti bodies and thinking all the while of another who was not here, who had lived and died Saren yet had not heard this in his death. Elisande had sung Jazra to his rest, a Patric voice in a Patric country, using what bastard version of the rite Jemel did not know . . .

He thought again of trapped souls in the water at their backs, of Jazra's soul perhaps trapped in that alien castle if Elisande had faltered or failed; and clamped his mind against Jazra and Elisande and all, focused only on being sure this *khalat* was properly sung. If there were no paradise, even if there were no souls, he could still give that much respect to the fallen.

HE WAS SO concentrated, indeed, that when they got to the end of it, when they'd chanted the final words together, he didn't know what to do or say next. Nor were his companions any help. Marron lifted his head to the sky and seemed to lose himself in silence, though even his far-seeing eyes could surely find no hint of black wings now, no sign of where the 'ifrit had gone. Elisande had blood on her hands; she glanced once towards the corrupted waters of the bay and made a visible decision to live with it for now, but then apparently could think of nothing else.

The sound of rushing footsteps in the gully, many of them, was relief to all three, Jemel thought. They turned as one, to see Hasan lead a group of men out onto the waterfront. The boy had got his message through, then. Some carried bows strung and ready, the rest had blades drawn; when they saw no immediate work for their weapons, they milled together in murmuring confusion, Kauram speaking with Beni Rus and Ib' Dharan, no distinction. That was Hasan's special gift, Jemel thought, to bring the tribes together at need, in a crisis; if he could only hold them so for a period of weeks or months, he must surely win his war against Outremer.

It had been that same gift of leadership, though, that had led to Jazra's death and Jemel's survival, his outcast condition now. Jemel could see the value of it, and still feel a surge of furious resentment.

Hasan came walking towards them; with the *khalat* he'd never said for Jazra still echoing in his head, Jemel took a pace forward to meet him.

Hasan checked, gazed at him appraisingly and said, "There is blood on your blade, Jemel."

Jemel hadn't realised even that his scimitar was still in his hand, let alone that he'd half-raised it as he had, the point a short thrust from Hasan's chest. He shook his head in bewilderment at himself, and muttered, "The blood is Marron's. He unleashed the Daughter against the 'ifrit, but could not catch them . . ." *We did not face them at all,* but he felt no need to say that aloud; it was implicit, he thought, in his and his friends' survival.

"Where did they go?"

"Up. They flew, above the cliff . . ."

Hasan nodded and walked on, to stand above the bodies. Jemel hastened to wipe his scimitar—on his own robe, there was nothing else and he lacked Elisande's nice care for her clothes—and sheathe it before he followed.

Hasan noted how the bodies had been arranged, and thanked Elisande for it; then he asked, "You said the *khalat* for them?"

"Yes," Jemel confirmed—though no doubt the Ashti would say it again in their own preferred rite when they buried their men.

"Good. Thank you, Jemel. Thank you all . . ." His eyes seemed to count them off, though Jemel was sure that he had counted them already; there was no true surprise in his voice as he went on, "You seem to be one short in your number. The Lady Julianne is not with you?"

Elisande laughed shortly before catching herself, seeming to realise that her news might not be so funny now. She made an effort to keep her voice light, even so, as she said, "Julianne is becoming more adventurous, or less conventional. Her father has ridden with a small party, to meet Redmond on the road; they needed to speak, he said, before his feast tonight. Julianne went with him."

"Indeed?" Hasan's voice had no trace of humour in it, only a grave disquiet. "Are you sure? I saw them go; there were no women in the party."

Nor should there have been, at such a time, for such a purpose; though it was clearly not the lack of propriety that so disturbed him.

Elisande was still trying to smile, but finding it harder now. "No, she thought that would be inappropriate. She rode hooded and veiled against the sand, in the dress of a boy of the Beni Rus. I showed her how to wear it . . ."

If Hasan recognised the compliment inherent in the choice, he gave no sign of it. "She should not be so far from the safety of Rhabat, with 'ifrit in the air. I had best go after them, with men who know the danger."

"May I come?" The words were out of Jemel's mouth

before he knew his own intent to say them. It meant leaving
Marron, and the first time he had chosen to do so; it meant
choosing Hasan, which he had sworn never to do again; it
meant leaving Marron with Elisande, which was perhaps
greater yet.

"If you will not stay in my house, you had better ride at
my side. Swiftly, though, Jemel—fetch your bow, and meet
us at the stables. Tell my people, I would welcome more
company. You other two, these waters are not safe to linger
by. Elisande, I expect Sherett would be glad of your help in
the kitchen—"

JEMEL DIDN'T STAY to see her reaction to that barely
veiled order, nor allow himself so much as a breath of relief
that Marron could not join her there; he ran. Back through
the gully, which was peopled now with archers, better defence than swordsmen if the 'ifrit had come that way; past
the first small pool and so to the bank of the greater, and on
to the house of the Beni Rus. Hasan was seriously alarmed,
he thought, and with good reason.

He cried the warning to those he met in the hallway—
"The 'ifrit have come out of the water, and are flying above
Rhabat; Hasan rides, to protect the King's Shadow and his
party. Bring bows!"—and raced up to the chamber he
shared with Marron. It took only a moment to snatch up his
bow and arrows, another to be sure of the one specially
blessed by an imam, that had already proved itself sover-
eign and might again have to rescue Julianne from an 'ifrit.
Even so, by the time he regained the hallway, he found a
throng of men armed and ready.

He could not lead here; he named the stable as meeting-
place and followed the surge. Hasan was there already,
mounted and waiting, with a dozen men beside; the Beni
Rus made up a dozen more. Others would follow, Hasan
said, as the word spread; they dared not delay.

They kept to a fast trot as they rode the length of Rhabat,
and all through the siq; the way was too narrow for any

greater speed. Even so, it felt good to Jemel to have a horse beneath him again. The Sharai depended on their camels and treasured them accordingly, but it was on horseback that they felt truly alive. He understood Julianne's yearning; her disguise this afternoon needed no excuse. Hasan might blame her none the less, or Elisande for aiding her; Jemel didn't envy either girl his anger later. In truth, though, they couldn't have foreseen this danger. No one could . . .

ONCE BEYOND THE siq Hasan kicked his horse into an immediate gallop, racing away from his followers. Giving chase with the rest, Jemel thought that this too should bring more men on their tail; the tribes camped here would be growing restive, with nothing to occupy them and sworn enemies in tents on every side. The peace of such a gathering was vulnerable at best; give them a chance of action without violating their oaths, and they'd seize it with glee.

Which would teach them perhaps that they could ride together, tribe beside tribe, and fight as one if it came to fighting, so long as they had a leader all would respect. Oh, Jemel thought, that man was subtle. Genuinely anxious, he had no doubt of that; but using the opportunity regardless, always keeping his eye on his ultimate goal, one army under his command to lead against the unbelievers . . .

Or perhaps that was his immediate goal, and his dream looked further. One kingdom, under his command? It would not be impossible. Nothing would be impossible, if he led the tribes successfully against Outremer. If he won back Ascariel for the Catari, if he set imams once more in the Dir'al Shahan, the high temple, he could demand the moon; the sheikhs would ask no more than how he wanted it, new or gibbous or at the full.

His horse outpaced them all, as did his urgency. Soon they stopped trying to catch up, and only kept their horses at a steady gallop in an effort not to lose too much more ground. Hasan rode for Julianne, though that was a complication Jemel couldn't understand, let alone untangle. Ju-

lianne was married, albeit by infidel rites before an infidel
altar; the Sharai still respected such a marriage, and Hasan
would not take or claim her against all custom. Still, he
rode for Julianne; his men rode for him, and all these other
men besides. So long as they could watch him, see him
safe, they were content. Why kill their horses, for the sake
of a few Patrics? They would ride, and ride hard, but not at
his slaying speed.

So Jemel came through the troop, driven by his own concern for Julianne, and found that he led them after all, despite himself. Perhaps that would spur their pride, to be
outstripped by a tribeless man; perhaps he could hurry them
a little, just by riding a good horse well . . .

FOCUSING ON THAT—on style and speed, on laying
down a challenge to those behind—at first he misunderstood the sounds that overtook him. Confused cries and
wordless yells, they might have been anything. Simple
shouts of encouragement, furious protest when one eager
horseman rode his beast too close to a tent and tangled its
feet in the ropes—his was a rowdy people, and voices were
for raising.

Jemel didn't bother to look back until he heard the high
scream of a horse in agony. It might—almost—have been
the cry of a horse falling, its legs tangled in tent-ropes; he
didn't think it was.

Twisting in the saddle, he had time only to register terrible confusion, no time to understand it before dense
shadow blocked the light. Too fast, too dark for a cloud,
and there could be none in any case, not in this dry season;
startled, he glanced up to see a vast black shape swoop towards him, the sun making a dazzle around its silhouette.

His idiot horse flung its ears back, its head high and
reared in terror, lifting itself and him closer to the claws
that were outstretched already, iron-black talons curling out
of glossy black chitin.

No time to nock an arrow to the string; no time even to

draw his scimitar and try to beat those claws aside. All he could do was slip a stirrup and let himself slide sideways, almost out of the saddle altogether, to put the horse's body between him and the monster's strike.

For a moment he lost sight of it, as he clung to his frantic mount with both hands on the saddle horn and one leg hooked over; then that swift shadow was directly overhead and talons scythed the empty air, a hand's span above the horse's plunging back.

A blast of hot, dry air with a metallic taste to it, like the air a blacksmith breathed, and it was gone. Jemel hauled himself back into the saddle and quieted the horse with brutal heels and hands, while he scanned the sky.

There it was, rising to the peak of its arc now—and there were others behind it, hovering and striking where they pleased among the tents.

It turned in the air, graceless but swift; folded its wings like a falcon, and dived again.

There was nothing else about it that was bird-like. No feathers, no hint of feather. It had kept the breastplate of a crab, or something like it; in the brief time that it had hung exposed, Jemel had seen the sun glisten off rounded ridges that none the less made up a single piece of armour.

The claws he'd seen, close enough to test their razor edge if he'd had a mind to it; the legs were long, too thin for such an ending, and bent wrongly.

Two fatter limbs thrust forward and up, with pincers like lobsters'. Between them was a head like a disc on a short rod, two red eyes set in the foremost edge; behind were those wings, bent before the wind now but he'd seen them stiff to thresh it, and he'd seen them shaped earlier, down on the waterfront. Long and narrow, sharp like knives, with a structure of slender bone like fingers overlaid with a fine skein of sheeny skin: more bat's than bird's wings, they looked not strong enough to bear that weight of wickedness, but nothing in the creature's making was natural or right.

It plummeted towards him, those spider-legs stretching

far forward with their monstrous claws agape; again he had
no time except to duck down the other side of the saddle.

His horse bucked mindlessly, then seemed to stretch itself impossibly high; Jemel lost all grip with his legs and
felt himself dangling, swinging from his hands' locked grip
about the horn.

He threw his head back and stared upward, to see those
cruel talons sunk deep into the horse's skull. The 'ifrit's
wings were spread wide and beating now, raising horse and
man together; Jemel took a breath, and forced his desperate
hands apart.

He fell, twisting in the air, to land hard on his back. The
impact drove the breath from his body, so that he lay gasping, while the bizarre shape that was 'ifrit and hanging
horse together filled his sight.

An instinct of self-preservation had him rolling to one
side, before he knew that he could move. A second later the
body of the horse came crashing massively to ground, just
where he'd been sprawled a moment before.

He threw himself back against its shattered bulk, seeking
to hide in its shadow while he slipped the bow from his
shoulder and searched among the arrows in his belt. He had
only four, and one was broken; the one he sought had special fletching, though, and his frenzied fingers found it by
touch. It was blessedly sound, and whole. He fumbled it
free and lifted his head to spot the 'ifrit.

It was circling high above, out of bowshot and looking
for his movement, he thought, to stoop again. As he
watched, though, he saw it distracted; he saw it turn and set
its wings to dive, but not this time at him.

Scanning the near horizon to seek its new intent, he saw
Hasan.

Hasan, who must at last have realised that he rode alone;
who must have looked back, perhaps hearing some hint of
the mayhem in the camp or else simply wondering how far
behind his men were; who must have seen the lethal shadows diving and so had turned his horse—of course, what
else would such a man do, what else could he do?—and

come racing back to bring his sword and his authority to the battle.

To die with his men, Jemel thought grimly, and with all the men of all the tribes that were gathered here; because what good could one more sword do against creatures that were immune to mortal steel, and of what use was authority against chaos, against the turmoil of panic and terror . . . ?

Well, he had one chance to learn.

Jemel stood up and ran a few paces forward, then set his feet and set his arrow to the string. He sighted along its shaft, tracking the 'ifrit in its swoop; no wind that mattered, nothing to allow for except the speed of that dive, but that was almost too fast, he barely had a moment to adjust . . .

He held his breath, and loosed the arrow. He saw it fly, like a rip in the air, he saw the 'ifrit swoop; he saw Hasan realise his danger, and rein back his horse. He saw that maddened animal rear, as the 'ifrit closed from above.

And then, at last, he saw his arrow strike.

It might have been the finest shot he'd ever made, unless the arrow had some special virtue on it to meet his aim and his intent, to find its target as well as to destroy.

It caught the 'ifrit in the body, driving deep between belly-armour and wing. A little lower, and even that arrow might have glanced harmlessly away; a little higher, it might have torn somewhat at the fabric of one wing, done nothing to save Hasan or his people or the world.

But it struck true, and buried itself to the fletching. The 'ifrit tumbled suddenly in the air, losing all its impetus, changed in a moment from lethal raptor to broken drone. It crashed to ground, and Jemel's ears hurt with the high, edgy sound of its shrilling. He'd heard that before, and knew what it meant; even so he slung his bow, drew his scimitar and sprinted forward.

Hasan had his horse controlled, but could neither leave it nor force it close to the fallen 'ifrit. Jemel had trouble enough with his own legs, that were threatening to rebel; but he wouldn't show weakness before that man of all men.

It wasn't weakness in any case, only relief that he'd shot well, but Hasan might misunderstand . . .

So he ran all the way to the trembling, writhing monster, fighting against the awful hissing shriek of its distress. He'd done the same once before, but then he'd been sure of its death and his final stroke of the sword was for satisfaction and for show, no more. This time, the closer he got, the less certain he was. Its legs waved and tried to run against the ground, and could shift its body not a finger's length; its two massive claws threatened the wind; its head twisted and jerked on the short neck.

Perhaps he should wait, trust the arrow and the imam's words on head and shaft, hope that blessing would spread like poison through the 'ifrit's system and so kill it at last. Perhaps he should nock another arrow to his bow and try for its eyes, from a distance, from here where he was still safe. Certainly he should not overleap its kicking legs and come stupidly close. Within sword's reach meant within claw's reach also. Just because Hasan was watching, he didn't need to make public display of his own idiocy . . .

Just because Hasan was watching, of course, he did exactly that. One of those long wings lay stretched out on the tawny ground, fluttering the gravel; Jemel treated it as a ramp and a way of safety, and simply ran straight up it.

His bare feet found purchase on splayed ridges of bone or cartilage but only skidded on the slippery smoothness of the skin between, so that mounting to the creature's back was a harder scramble than he'd anticipated. The wing flexed beneath him, and nearly threw him off; it tried to beat upwards, but its own weight and his combined to keep it pinioned, though he had to stoop and use his hands for balance and grip, when he'd wanted to show his grace and courage by leaping lightfoot up it, like a tumbler leaping from horse to galloping horse.

As soon as he'd reached the wingroot and was standing astride the 'ifrit's spine—if it had one—one giant claw came groping blindly back to find him. He hewed at it with his sword; the blade rang falsely and juddered in his hand. So far as he could see, he hadn't marked the chitin.

That seemed to be the 'ifrit's final effort, though. The claw subsided and lay next its fellow on the gravel, too heavy to be held up any longer. The terrible screeing noise had faded to a whistle, sharp and harsh but barely whisper-loud; Jemel felt confident enough to walk forward along the broad back until he came to where the neck sprouted suddenly inflexible, overlapping rings of chitin, where the head still turned and jabbed the air. Head-high to him, and yet the neck seemed short, so big this creature really was. He'd been deceived, by flight and speed and distance; by memory too, perhaps, a little, because the crab-things that came out of the water had been no larger than a Patric knight's shield, and now they were the size of a Sharai tent, longer, wings the length of an evening shadow . . .

The head was straining to see him, he realised, and could not twist itself around so far. It was a flattish disc, like one rice-bowl or one round shield inverted upon another—and there was a budding, he saw, like a bubble under the chitin, just on the rim. It was swelling as he watched, and as he watched it opened like an iris, like an eye, and there was hot red underneath and it was indeed an eye, grown to find him.

That was as much shapeshifting as the 'ifrit could manage now, seemingly; and it was plenty enough for Jemel. He didn't need Hasan's shout to tell him that there was no time for foolishness here, nor for curiosity. The whistling had dwindled to little more than a sigh, a simple use of air with no sound added; he could hear again the screams and cries of the camp at his back, and knew that Hasan would be desperate to reach his men, for whatever little good he could do there. He knew too that Hasan would not leave him here. There was a task unfinished, and a debt to acknowledge . . .

So Jemel finished the task, with a single clean thrust of his blade through the 'ifrit's new-grown eye: deep and hard he thrust, near to the haft the blade sank and must have been close to scraping the further side of that strange skull. The head lolled as he withdrew, and then flopped down as the neck lost all its strength.

He saw a mist creep through the glossy black of the creature's armour, and it seemed to him as though it became thinner, lighter, more frail moment by moment. It didn't shatter under his weight, as he half thought it would; instead it dissipated, frayed into the wind and was gone, as immaterial as shadow.

So he fell again, through where the thing had been, and landed awkwardly from sheer surprise; and had barely got to his feet before Hasan was there, still ahorseback.

"I owe you my life, Jemel. That was a fine shot."

"It was necessary," he replied simply.

"Perhaps. I hope God agrees with you, or it may have been wasted; we may lie and rot together, if these things don't eat us instead. Come, seize hold . . ."

Jemel gripped his stirrup, and Hasan kicked the horse away.

The first tug all but wrenched arm from shoulder; but every boy ran like this at his father's stirrup, or his elder brother's. Any unhorsed warrior would expect to. It was close to flying, Jemel thought, or close to the mythical magic boots of story; every leap carried him further and faster than he could run, so that he seemed to soar over the ground, barely touching toe to earth between each tremendous step.

THAT SPEED BROUGHT them back too soon to the congregation of tents, before Jemel was ready to stop flying. He was flying in his head also, washed with victory, and far from ready for the turmoil of defeat.

That this was defeat, he had no doubt. Hasan reined in his horse; Jemel stumbled at the abrupt halt, his feet staggering on ground that was suddenly hard and ungiving beneath him. He let go the stirrup, his arms wheeling for balance, and reeled a few paces before he caught it. Then he straightened slowly, staring at the chaos before him.

There was nothing, of course, that could have prepared the tribes for an attack from the sky. Even knowing that, though, the devastation that he saw numbed his mind. Tents flapped, torn and empty, or else lay collapsed like vast black skins atop their broken poles. Men, camels, horses ran mindlessly to and fro, their feet catching in the sprawled bodies of the fallen; and all the time they were harried from above, as the 'ifrit picked their targets and swooped, to rise again with a struggling, screaming victim in their grip. Sometimes that victim—man or beast it might be, they seemed to draw no difference—would fall quiet quickly, as talons bit deep into chest or head or belly; sometimes death would be delayed a little, while the 'ifrit climbed high into the air before it opened its claws. Sometimes the victims were still screaming as they fell.

Jemel knew it was useless, even as he pulled his bow from his shoulder and reached for an arrow. Others were doing the same; he saw their shafts rise, he saw them fall. It didn't matter whether they hit or missed their target, whether they struck belly-plate or seemingly fragile wing. With no power but bow's strength and man's strength behind them, they had no effect.

Still he drew, aimed and shot, only to be doing something. Hasan's hurry and his own fall to ground had driven any thought of his more lethal arrow from his mind; it would still be lying on the gravel somewhere behind him, potent and wasted.

He loosed all the arrows that he had, and saw them all fail, all fall. Then he slung his bow across his shoulder again and drew his sword, looking round for Hasan. All his oaths were forgotten; if he must die, if they all must, at least he would die defending that man, for his people's sake.

THAT MAN, HE saw, was already the centre and focus of a small group, men of his own tribe and others. Hasan was

the only one horsed; animals were as maddened as their
riders by the stooping, swirling shadows that killed from
above, and it took a master to control both himself and his
mount.

As Jemel watched, Hasan stood in his stirrups and bellowed. It was the name of God he cried, that which all the
Sharai knew and were forbidden to utter; for as far as his
voice could reach, men turned to gape. That one word
could cut through even panic and despair, to draw their attention to him.

He whirled his sword above his head in a gesture all
could read, *come to me, gather about me . . .*

Whether it was Hasan's native authority, or simply the
sight of someone, anyone taking charge, men came running. Not all, not immediately: some turned and bellowed
in their turn, to spread the message further.

Jemel did the same, calling and beckoning, as loudly as
he could; then he followed the general rush, to cluster in a
dense pack around Hasan.

One man had made the difference; one man's clear sight
could yet turn a rout, a disaster into an orderly withdrawal.
At his urging they moved slowly, warily back from the
tents and towards the siq that would bring them into the
safety of Rhabat, their numbers growing every minute.

The soaring 'ifrit still fell on them, picking off those who
were slow or too far distant and assailing the main band;
but now they met a bristling hedge of blades lifted against
them. Even unblessed weapons could batter clutching
claws aside, if they could do no worse damage.

Men were still lost, plucked suddenly from the mass;
Hasan himself was in most danger, sitting so much higher
than those who surrounded him. Necessarily he made himself a target, even if he was not so already by virtue of who
he was. A hundred voices warned him, though, of every
diving 'ifrit. Most times he simply ducked, sliding down
and around his saddle as Jemel had done before him, and so
survived.

Once, though, Jemel saw him keep his seat, and swing

his scimitar against the talons that reached for him and for no man else. Jemel saw the blade connect, and slice through the creature's legs when its claws were only a moment from Hasan's body. That blade must have been blessed at some time, and held its virtue still . . .

The wounded 'ifrit rose high above them, seeming to lose the solidity of its body. It didn't fade as they did in death but rather contracted, from nightmare creature to spinning coil of smoke. Jemel soon lost sight of it in his steady march among the throng, with the need to keep alert against the danger of others coming.

Others came, inevitably; they hung in the air, wings flailing to keep them out of sword's reach, while their long legs thrust and grabbed towards the men below. No arrows met them now; no one had space to draw a bow, even if there'd been any purpose to it. They could choose their intended victim unmolested; they chose Hasan so often, Jemel was sure that it was more than his height above the pack that drew them to him. Men had to cling to his horse's bridle on both sides, to keep the crazed animal from bolting; Hasan himself had to keep his blade flicking this way and that as they snatched at him time and again. Still he refused to dismount, though. Jemel thought he was right; even those on the margins of the group needed to see him, to hold them together in that slow retreat. If once they lost that sight, that certainty, they would break and run; and then more would die, dozens more, and it would be panic and terror that the remainder carried with them into Rhabat.

Instead they brought a victory of sorts, a grim and unlikely survival. Gradually the high walls of the siq closed around them, until there was no space, no wing-room for the hovering 'ifrit.

Discipline broke briefly, as that dense pack of men tried to squeeze into too narrow a road; voices threatened, men surged and shoved, blades flashed between tribe and tribe. Hasan cried them to order, though, and drove his horse through the throng, the flat of his scimitar beating left and right.

And so he led them on, and so they followed, several hundred men with scarcely one wounded among their number; but they left many, many dead behind them, and the way out of Rhabat was closed at their backs. They heard its closing, the thunder of falling rocks; a cloud of dust overswept them as they walked.

They were halfway back through the siq before Jemel remembered why he'd followed Hasan in the other direction just that short time ago; and realised that if they were shut in, then Julianne, her father, Redmond were equally shut out. If they were still alive at all . . .

FOUR

Heights of Terror

JULIANNE HADN'T DARED ask for Tezra when she'd followed her father to the stables, with the half-dozen men who would accompany them. Her father had known about her disguise, of course—she would never have tried, never have dared to think of trying to hide the truth from him—and she'd thought that most likely the men knew too; but the stable-lads could not. She was tall enough to pass as a boy, but her voice might have made them wonder; her asking for a lady's mount would certainly have raised questions in their minds. Their gossip might have spread further than the stable yard, might have caused trouble for her father. She had perhaps been trespassing too much on his kindness already, with this escapade; the last thing she'd wanted was to have rumours reach the sheikhs, of how he'd blinked at such a breach of their customs.

Besides, there'd been the danger of Hasan's seeing them ride out. If he spotted Tezra in the party, he'd be sure to look closely at her rider. What he might do then she hadn't been able to guess, she'd only been sure that the consequences would have been public, and unpleasant. Hasan believed in the traditions of his people; he might, she thought, have other reasons too, for wanting to be assured of her safety.

So she'd kept quiet as the horses were saddled, and only sighed to herself when the lads had brought her a hard-mouthed, raw-boned little cob, fit mount for a boy permitted to ride with men. His name was Rubon, they'd told her; she'd nodded silently, and hauled herself swiftly onto his back before their dark, inquisitive eyes could see too far beneath her hood.

The party had ridden off, herself in a boy's proper station, last in line; and of course they had indeed met Hasan standing in the doorway of his tribal house to see them off. He had bowed to her father, had watched them all past; she'd kept her head down and her hands loose on the reins, trying to imitate the Sharai men's easy slouch in the saddle.

No summons at her back, no questions: she'd let out a breath she hadn't realised she'd been holding, and looked forward to the afternoon. An hour's riding, perhaps, before they met Redmond; another slow hour's return, telling her news and hearing his, sharing his thoughts and her father's. And of course escaping the call of duty, dull work in the hot kitchens. Yaman might make a show of reluctance at putting guests to work, but that was habit only; once past it she was a hard taskmistress, and seemed driven by demons today. Elisande had had her own plans of escape; Julianne might have gone with her, but her friend had made it rather obscurely transparent that those plans included Marron, had been formed indeed at his instigation. It had only been tactful to let her go alone, even if it was also courting trouble: young women were not ordinarily to be seen around Rhabat in male company. As an excuse, *he is the Ghost Walker* would be more likely to throw oil on the flames; particularly given this Ghost Walker, and this girl. *Particularly,* she'd thought, and giggled to herself . . .

*   *   *

ONCE BEYOND THE siq and the camping-grounds, they'd
broken the strict order of their riding, so that she'd found
herself at her father's side, while the other men followed at
a discreet distance—far enough to let the two talk in private, far enough to swear that they'd heard no squeak of a
female voice from their anonymous companion. She'd been
grateful but anxious still, now that she'd started worrying;
she'd asked, "Who are these men? I can't read their tribal
markings . . ."

"Can you not?" he'd replied dryly. "You should learn, if
you mean to spend time wandering their deserts. They are
of the Ib' Dharan, my honour guard for the time I spend at
Rhabat; which means of course that I am honoured to buy
their services. If you are worried where their allegiance lies,
don't be. I have it in my purse."

That might not have stopped a whisper reaching their
lord, that the Shadow's daughter had ridden out with the
Shadow this day, in the dress of a boy; but he would likely
say not a word, for fear of losing his own share of his men's
income. Julianne had been reassured, and had tried once
again simply to relax into the pleasures of riding slowly
under a hot sun. Pleasure was what she'd come seeking,
after all, pleasure in various guises; this was the simplest,
this steady progress through a barren landscape, and it
would have been such a shame to worry it to waste . . .

HER FATHER HAD said little, the rhythms of riding seeming to lull him into a contemplative mood. He'd be thinking
about his feast tonight, she'd guessed, and trying as ever to
anticipate, to be ready to meet whatever came. He hated
to be unprepared, always; which was why he could be so
swift to change a plan, because he was ever ready to be
redirected. Serving the King as he did, he had to be.

When he'd ridden half an hour without a word, she had
taken her horse on a short distance ahead. Let him ponder
in peace; she'd look for first signs of Redmond. His cara-

van should be coming into sight soon, surely, however unhurried its pace . . .

Either her father had been concerned to see her ride
alone, or else she hadn't been the only one grown a little
impatient; a couple of the Ib' Dharan had come cantering
up beside her. Rather than oblige them to slow down to
match her pace, she'd kicked Rubon into matching theirs.
And they'd been young, those two, if not so young as she
was, let alone as young as her dress implied; and they were
bored with her father's stately progress, so much had been
obvious. Nor would they ever have let themselves be out-
ridden or outraced by a child, boy or girl . . .

So they'd raced, or near enough to it, along the broad
and clear track. Nothing like that morning's head-to-head
with Hasan, neither their mounts nor their minds could
have managed the same focus of intent; this had been a
wild, dusty, laughing scramble and no more, play entirely
without purpose.

Remembering the morning's lesson, though, she'd given
way gracefully and hauled her horse effortlessly to a walk
before the heat could sap his eagerness. The other two had
swept past her, kicking up a storm of dust and sand which
their abrupt halting had only made worse; choking on it
even behind her veil, she'd turned her head and looked back
to see just how far behind they'd left her father.

"We'd better wait," she'd said as the young men came
back to join her. Her voice had sounded thick and hoarse,
almost boy-like to her own ears; they had nodded gravely,
still not challenging her disguise.

THEY'D WALKED THEIR hot mounts in slow circles, while
the breeze blew the hanging dust away; and now, still waiting for the rest of the party to catch up, she shielded her
eyes against the fierce light and squinted forward, thinking
that she could just make out something, perhaps someone
on the road ahead. Or just off the road, rather, a hint of
shadow against the gravel's glare that could possibly be a

caravan at rest. It was absolutely at the limit of her sight; it might only be a smudge of desiccated shrub, although she'd seen none so far and any growth on such a bare plain was likely to have been stripped long since, for forage or fuel.

It seemed a strange place for a caravan to pause, though, and a strange time for it, just a little distance short of better rest and water. She remembered that Redmond was still carrying old hurts, and without a companion from Surayon to ease them; the boy who'd brought the news of his coming had said the drovers were anxious about him. Perhaps he'd worsened, and was not fit to travel further today. Though if that were so, surely he'd have sent someone ahead to carry the news to Rhabat, perhaps to ask for a doctor; he wasn't too proud to know when he needed help.

Her father was laggardly, dawdling deliberately, she thought, to teach her not to be so impulsive. She turned to her companions and said, "Is that the people we've come to find, can you see?"

She didn't bother to keep her voice gruff; they disregarded it manfully. Both looked where she pointed, one standing in his stirrups to see better; he said, "There are camels there, and people moving."

That must be them; if there'd been any other party headed for Rhabat, the boy surely would have mentioned it. Julianne wanted to ride on, to reach Redmond first and so turn the lesson back on her father. But she was nervous suddenly, afraid of what she might find in that curiously still group. Pure cowardice, but if there were bad news she'd rather not be the first to learn it. Besides, she might need to discard her disguise, if Redmond needed nursing. Better to do that with her father there, to shield her against any reaction from the drovers. They'd be accustomed to meeting women on the road, but a girl in boy's dress might be another matter . . .

So she lingered, and the young men with her, until at last her father joined them with the other riders at his back. She suppressed her fretful impatience under his austere gaze, and simply pointed.

"Look, there are people and camels, up ahead there. We think it's Redmond and his caravan . . ."

He peered, grunted, and nudged his mount into a brisker pace. She fell into place behind him, keeping her anxieties to herself; he could make his own assessment, he didn't need her to list the possibilities. He'd keep his thoughts to himself, in any case. He always had. Only his sudden haste betrayed him.

He led them at a sharp canter, over the remaining distance; she rode in his dust for a while, until it became so dense that she was riding blind, her every breath a cough. Then she moved up to his side. Her watering eyes cleared slowly; now she could see, and what she saw worried her intensely.

There were all the camels of the caravan, couched together and hobbled, as they would have been for a noonday rest. She could see men slumped against them too, as it might be their drovers sleeping through the heat. But noon was long past, they really should have been on the move by now; and the only figures moving among them were women, gowned and veiled. As it might be, as it might well be if Redmond really were too sick to finish the journey, if the men had handed his care over to a group of local women and were dozing the time away until he was fit to go on. If he ever was, today or any day, if they didn't leave his body by the road . . .

No, she was being stupid. Redmond's injuries had been well on the way to healing, before they parted; he might be, he must be tired and weak after a difficult journey, and torture left damage in the mind that would take a long time to scar over, but there was no reason to imagine him dead or dying. Exhausted, perhaps, too weary to sit a camel for a full day; no more. For sure, no more than that.

Nor would the women scurry so, over a dead body. Julianne could see a couple clearly now, coming away from the caravan and trotting over to a string of scattered packs and bundles at the roadside. Their belongings, where they must have dropped them when the drovers called for help. They crouched over one of the packs, took out a flask—water, perhaps, or something stronger—and went hurrying back, their tattered robes kicking up flurries of dust. They spared barely a glance for the riders' rapid approach; Julianne had only a glimpse of shrouded eyes behind long veils. Peasant women, she thought, long familiar with the type: shy and silent in the presence of strangers, with a wisdom that belied their simplicity and a stubborn strength that far surpassed her own. These at least she swore to know better, if they had truly brought aid to Redmond. She had tricks learned from her father, to overcome that shyness. Offering them money would be an insult, but she could at least learn their tribe and the name of their sheikh, she could seek his favour for them . . .

She wheeled Rubon off the road and took him straight towards the line of couched camels and resting men. The beasts were restless, she saw, tossing their heads and straining at their hobbles; the drovers must be exhausted to sleep through that. Likely they'd been smoking *khola,* to ease the heat of the dreary day; she'd heard that that herb had a bitter flavour but brought sweet dreams to its users.

Closer now, she could see over the camels' backs; and yes, there was Redmond at last. He was sitting with his back to a rock, and seemed to be sleeping too, while the women fussed about him. Sleeping, or unconscious—perhaps he'd shared the drovers' pipes, to earn himself some brief cease of pain.

Rubon shied suddenly, his hooves skidding on the hard-packed gravel as he twisted violently away. Julianne cursed, and slipped perilously in the saddle before she caught her balance. Then she dragged at the reins, to haul the horse's head around. She'd seen nothing obvious to startle him, no bird flying up suddenly and no abrupt movement in the caravan; but an unknown animal could have unknown fears. Perhaps he simply didn't like camels . . .

She wasn't sure she liked the look of those camels herself, she thought, fighting to force Rubon closer. A foaming mouth and rolling eyes were common enough in an excited horse, but camels were more phlegmatic, or simply more difficult to overwork; she couldn't think what it would take to bring them to this condition. Poisoned water, perhaps? But then their drovers wouldn't be so relaxed. Abject terror might do it, but the same objection applied . . .

Abject terror was still her best guess, though. It was affecting Rubon too, by the way he planted all four feet firmly in the gravel and stood shaking beneath her, ears back and neck running with sweat. He would not go closer; and she didn't like to dismount and leave him in such a state, though she was desperate now to reach Redmond and find out how he was.

The men had got ahead of her, by dint of being patient; they had followed the road a little further and so approached from the other side of that line of camels, that wall she couldn't breach. She saw her father jump down from his horse and toss the reins to one of his companions; she saw the women make way for him, standing back to let him through to his old friend Redmond's side.

She wrenched furiously at Rubon's reins, meaning to take him back and around to follow the men's wiser tracks, if she could only get him moving again. What had she meant to do in any case, jump him over the hobbled camels? Couched nose to tail as they were, there was no path between . . .

Before she could persuade or bully Rubon into taking a single step, though, one of those frenzied camels suddenly managed to break its hobble. It surged to its feet and galloped off blindly across the plain—while its drover simply toppled and lay flat and unresponsive in the sun.

Even *khola* couldn't do that to a man. Julianne turned her head to find her father. No need to cry a warning; he knew. As she watched, he laid his hand on Redmond's shoulder and nudged it gently.

The old man slid slowly sideways, and settled to the ground with his face in the dust. His fall left a dark wet streak on the reddish stone of the boulder he'd been leaned against; between his shoulderblades, Julianne thought his robe was hanging open down the length of a savage tear.

Then she realised that it was his back that had been torn open, through the robe; those were flaps of skin and flesh that gaped.

Much of his spine was missing.

SHE THOUGHT THAT the world had slowed calamitously around her; she thought that she was the only one still thinking. It felt almost as though she'd been granted a gift of prophecy that ran just half a moment ahead of its realisation, or else that her thoughts governed the actions of those she watched, as though she were dreaming and yet ordering the progress of the dream.

She thought there must be hoofprints in the gravel all around her father, and saw his head dart bird-like left and right to spy them out.

She thought he should understand by now, he had to, he wasn't usually so slow; she thought he should straighten and defend himself, and so he did, or tried to. But he was slow again, too slow in drawing his sword. She thought those supposed women must show themselves now for what they truly were; and saw it happen, saw them grow tall and monstrous, their ragged robes shredding as their bodies swelled. All but one loped towards the men who were still on horseback, who were struggling to control their panicked mounts; that other swung a dreadful arm, and clubbed her father across the back of his balding head.

She saw him lifted off the ground by the force of that blow, saw him fly some distance before he fell. She wished, she prayed, she willed him to stand up; but the sense of foreknowledge, almost of power had abandoned her already. He only lay sprawled and still, as still as Redmond, as any of the drovers . . .

Thrown back into the physical world, where men and horses were screaming and dying, where her father was brutally hurt and perhaps dying also if he weren't dead already, she wanted only to go to him: to stand above his body with knives in hand and shriek defiance at the ghûls.

In the maze of confusion and fear that her mind had suddenly become, focused only on that one small thing, her father's empty form, she forgot that she wasn't sitting Merissa or Tezra or any of the pliant, courageous ponies she used to ride. A horsewoman to her bones, she dug in her heels and concentrated eyes and thoughts on that jump, clean over the struggling camels that lay between her and her goal.

Rubon tossed his head, to remind her of the truth; she saw how his nostrils flared to smell the blood and terror she was trying to force him towards, and she thought too late that she should have left him here after all, she should have slid off and run the distance, it wasn't so far . . .

Too late because he was on the move already, kicked into it by her own heedless feet. Not where she had set him, that living barrier; he'd turned almost on the spot and was charging blindly in the opposite direction, over the plain that was so smooth and flat it might have been made for such running.

She threw all her weight against the reins, trying to drag him physically to a halt, but he had the bit between his teeth and his jaw locked tight; there would be no stopping him now.

If she jumped she'd break a leg at best, going so fast over such a surface. Nothing to do but sit tight and wait for him to tire, or else for the panic to fade in his mind, for his grip on the bit to slacken . . .

She twisted round in the saddle, trying to see what was happening behind her, and almost lost her seat as Rubon shied again, turning abruptly to the west. Trusting his instincts now, when that trust was little or no use to her and none at all to her father, she tried to see what had startled him. There were birds flocking and wheeling in the sky to the south, but they were far away. Or no, they couldn't be that far, they'd have to be dragons else; but still, black birds were surely nothing much to a horse so far gone in fear . . .

To a horse so far gone, she supposed, anything that moved could be more cause for terror. Perhaps he was wise to turn to the sun, to run blind . . .

Perhaps not. He played literally into her hands by doing so; his pace slackened as the glare denied him even a clear sight of the ground he ran on, and she felt it through the reins as his teeth loosed the bit. One sharp tug, and she had control again. His mouth was hard, but not hard enough to resist her desperate strength. She hauled his head around by main force, and set him galloping back the way they had come.

This time, she was wiser. She murmured reassurance into his ears as soon as they started to flicker, hearing the sounds of battle ahead before she could; she let him slow to a uncertain walk, let him stop altogether before the scents of blood and death could overcome his courage, as they had before.

She had no thought of leaping off and sprinting forward now, to die beside her father. That had been a moment's yearning, a girl's stupid gesture, long since blown out of her head by the wind of that mad ride. She stretched high on Rubon's back for the best view she could achieve and watched numbly, wanting only to witness, to be a voice for others. If men had to die, they should not do so unregarded.

It would fall to her, she realised, to tell Elisande and Rudel of Redmond's death. That was a cruel twist after they had worked so hard to free him from the Roq, after he had come so far, so near to safety; briefly it felt almost worse than the loss of her own father.

But thoughts of her father brought back the memory of the djinni's voice. *You can save him, though it might be better if you did not.* Well, she had not; that might please the djinni, though she couldn't imagine how. Nor how she might have done it, unless she'd not paused to wait for him on the road, unless she'd ridden on and so found Redmond dead and died herself to warn him. That wasn't fair; how could she have known or guessed, how could she have seen ghûls in those women when more experienced heads than hers had not?

She caught a sob in her throat, swallowed hard against rising guilt and turned her mind deliberately back to follow her eyes, to witness.

The ghûls' sudden ambush had caught all the tribesmen unprepared, as it had her father; none had survived, that she could see. Bodies of men and horses lay scattered across the gravel, and the ghûls were shambling among the maddened camels now, slaying with claws and razor teeth. Some were pausing to feed, and not only on the bodies of the beasts.

If any tried to feed on her father, she thought she might yet do something stupid; but he lay yet where he had fallen, face down and seemingly untouched.

Close enough to see so much, she was also close enough to be seen; far enough away to have time to flee, though, she thought. She hoped, as more than one bloodied muzzle turned in her direction.

What would they see, though? A boy, on a pony. Offering no danger—and right enough there, alas—and offering no interest either; they had food in plenty, no reason to hunt for more. Besides, a fast pony could outrun a ghûl, at least a ghûl in that form, horse-headed but bandy-legged; Rubon she thought could outrun the wind, if it smelled of ghûl. They were dull creatures, or supposedly so, swift neither of thought nor limb. That was why they relied on guile to snare their victims, and fell back constantly on the appearance of a woman.

Well, it worked, so why not? Even on the intelligent, it worked. Even with one in the party who had met a ghûl all too recently, and shaped like a woman, too. Perhaps that was what the djinni had meant, that she should have been more alert, and so had failed it and her father both, and all her people too . . .

She could have mourned her father then, she could have broken down altogether; but at that moment she saw one of the ghûls leave its feeding, and go to stand above his body. She watched breathlessly, fearing to see it stoop, its jaws open; instead, though, she saw muscles ripple and surge along its back. She saw the sparse fur stretch, and split; she saw it raise its head and heard it keen as if in pain as dank wet matter slithered out of the opening wound. Slithered and spread, unfurled like distorted leaves—like a pair of leaves, rooted in its spine . . .

Wings, she realised at last, marvelling at the stupidity of her eyes; it had grown wings. And wafted them slowly now, as if in experiment or wonder. They dried rapidly in the hot sun; it beat them harder, and rose a hesitant length above the ground before dropping back.

As if satisfied with that, it reached its long arms down and hooked them into her father's clothing, perhaps through the clothing and into his flesh, she couldn't tell. Then it tossed its terrible head, flexed its wings, leaped into the air and flew.

SHE DIDN'T UNDERSTAND; did it mean to play with the body as she'd seen young tercels do, dropping prey from on high, only to catch it again mid-air? And why him, why did it have to be him when there were so many bodies it might have chosen . . . ?

Perhaps because he is not dead, she answered her own protesting question as Rubon flinched from the ghûl's shadow when it passed across them. Alone of all his company it might be that he was still breathing; it might be that the ghûl would take him up and drop him and not catch him again before he struck the ground, and so for a second time she could see her failure, see her father fall.

But *why?* was still a question, and not answered yet. If they wanted him dead they had teeth, they had talons, they had used them many times today; and this change at least had seemed to hurt the creature. Why put itself through that without need—and why single out her father, whether for play or for special execution? Her father was special, of course, this had been a careful ambush and he must have been the target, all those other deaths were incidental; but—

Because he is not dead, and they do not want him dead. Or not them, but their masters. The ghûls served the will of the 'ifrit, they had stones in their tongues to force them to it; perhaps that keening cry had been not pain but protest. Or pain as punishment, perhaps those stones burned hotter if they delayed or disobeyed . . .

But, *he is not dead, and they do not want him dead*—that was enough. There would be time later to work out why the 'ifrit should want her father alive, whether it was for some dread purpose or simply to kill him for themselves, to be absolutely certain he was dead. That would be like seeing Redmond's body, worse than cruel; but even the chance of it could be put aside, for now.

Redmond's body, this moment, she would always regret; he deserved better than abandonment, the chance perhaps of a later hunt for bones. The living outrank the dead, though; she would have left her father—she thought, she hoped—to chase Redmond, or any survivor. She wheeled her willing horse around, away from the scene of slaughter, and set him to pursue that shadow across the plain.

The ghûl was heading westerly, into the sun, all but impossible to spot a dark fleck against that dazzling light; but its speeding shadow ran before them and all they had to do was chase it, no need to catch up. Julianne was still no more than a witness. The 'ifrit were in the Dead Waters; if the ghûl meant to deliver her father to them, it must fly over that high scarp that hid Rhabat, that lay between plain and sea. Without growing wings of her own, Julianne could not follow it then.

There was still the chance, though, of something unforeseen: an archer chance-met, to wound the ghûl and bring it down; a sudden storm of sand, a wind it could not fly against; a djinni . . .

Actually, she thought bitterly, the djinni was all her hope, and so she had none. The rest was foolish dreaming. Djinni

Khaldor could save her father in a moment, but it would not. *It might be better if you did not,* it had said, which was a death sentence for him now, because without its help she could do nothing. A death sentence or worse, if the 'ifrit had other plans for him . . .

She reminded herself that the djinn did not interfere in the affairs of men, except when it suited their mysterious interests; and then only to send her into heartache and despair, it seemed, from love to desire and from doubt to hopelessness.

Well, she would ride as far as she could follow the ghûl, to the hills' rise. She would watch it out of sight, and try not to think of her father; then she would go to the tribesmen camped before the siq, and tell them of the ghûls at their feasting by the road. Then she would go to Rhabat, and through Rhabat, and ask if anyone had seen a man dropped into the sea, and if he fell with a splash or were swallowed silently by something other than the water . . .

AND SO SHE rode, and the scarp rose before her, more cliff than hills, steep and broken. And the rapid shadow that she'd hunted was gone suddenly, swallowed by the still shadow of the land; but once in that shadow herself she could look up and not be dazed by light, she could see the cruciform of the ghûl in black silhouette against the sky, not beating its wings now but gliding. Gliding and dropping, growing just a little bigger in her sight. And surely it must be lower than the cliff's height now, and was not trying to lift itself and its burden back up into free air . . .

Suddenly slightly hopeful after all, she stared upward with a grim determination to be certain. Shadow against shadow now, as the creature approached the cliff, but still there was no mistaking the abrupt backbeat of its winds as it lifted a little, slowed in the air and so settled. Settled onto a ledge a long, long way up the face, near to the top: just where an eagle might settle to tear its prey apart in peace, inaccessible and safe . . .

But the ghûl wouldn't have borne the weight of her father so far, only to eat him now. Of a certainty, it wouldn't. Perhaps it was tired, if such creatures did tire; after struggling such a way on new and unfamiliar wings, it might need rest before it tackled overtopping the scarp. Or else this might be the appointed place, where it was told or forced to bring him. Why this side of the ridge she couldn't imagine, when the 'ifrit were in the Dead Waters; but there were things, she knew, that were beyond her imagining, and they still existed in the world. Because an idea made no sense to her, didn't mean it didn't make sense . . .

Whatever the ghûl's reasoning—if such creatures did reason—the fact remained: there the ghûl was, for now at least, and there also was her father. And here was she, and there was a long climb, an impossible climb between them. Hasan had said it was impossible, and that even without knowing how impossible such a climb, any climb would be for her.

And yet, and yet. The djinni had said *you can save him,* and she had to try. If it had said *you cannot save him,* still she would have had to try . . .

She slipped off Rubon's back and hobbled him quickly Sharai-fashion with the girdle of her robe, thinking even as she did so that it was like a declaration, *I'm going to fail here, I'll be coming back soon . . .*

Her knives she stowed safely, pointlessly in her hood; little use they'd be against a ghûl, even if she did find a way up and contrive to climb it. It was a gesture, no more, to counteract the hobble. *Knives cut hobbles,* she thought, and almost managed a giggle.

She could find nothing more to giggle at as she approached the rubble at the foot of the cliff. At first she stumbled over loose shale, then larger chunks of rock that turned beneath her feet; then there were boulders the size of a chest that she must scramble up onto, and already she felt nervous, arms out for a balance that was never quite there so that she was teetering though both feet were firmly planted.

Then she was facing a wall of rocks the size of houses, and this was still detritus, pieces of the scarp that had fallen away. She lifted her head and looked up, and even in the dense shade she could see that the cliff didn't have one face, it had a thousand. Whatever god had built this ridge, the work had been done poorly; it must have begun to crumble almost before it had been finished. She could see deep cracks in it, and great overhangs where wind or rare rain had bitten a slab away; it defied her understanding of the world, that rock was a solid thing that could be trusted to endure, and only herself was weak and liable to falling.

Still, her father was up there, and in need of her; she had to try, before she could know that she'd failed. The rock might be as friable as stale bread, but at least there were plenty of holds on its rough surface; she stretched up, gripped with both hands and slotted one foot into a crack.

And stepped up, found another foothold by touch, put her weight on it—and felt it flake away beneath her, felt her hands slip at the sudden jerking shock and so slid down again, skinning her palms as she tried to cling to rock that grated before it fell to dust.

She stood where she had stood before, sniffing and swallowing hard against a threat of tears. This was only a boulder, albeit a massive one; she had to surmount it before she even reached the cliff-face proper. And there was so much of that, it stretched so high and the climb simply wasn't possible, even to one who was skilled at climbing; just the thought of it terrified her.

So brief an attempt didn't count as failure, though. She moved a step or two to the side, tried to read it with her eyes—*hold there and there, step there, stretch to that and hope, trust, pray that it would hold her*—and then reached out her stinging hands again.

Set her mind to climbing, tried to blank out all thought, all fear of a fall; took a tremulous breath, took a grip as firm as she could, as firm as she dared—and stayed, pressing her whole body against that insecure rock in a sudden shaking fit as she heard an unearthly voice speaking at her back.

"Daughter of the Shadow, you are no son of the rock, whatever your dress declares. You risk your life to no purpose; you need not hope to reach your father that way."

Djinni, rot you, I know that—but oh, where have you been? When I needed you more even than I do now . . . ? If it had come earlier, it could have saved Redmond's life, and the others'. To be fair, it would have needed to reach the caravan before she had, perhaps long before; but she felt no obligation to be fair.

She bit her tongue hard, till she tasted blood, to remind herself not to ask questions unless or until she simply had to; and pried her fingers slowly away from the rock, forced herself to turn around and stand straight, somehow managed a little bow before the slender twist of dust that was the djinni this time.

"Djinni Khaldor." She struggled to keep her voice from trembling as her legs were, without conspicuous success. "Your arrival is opportune. I know I cannot climb this cliff; and yet my father is in need of me," in need of help at least, though preferably something better than her own, "and you said yourself that I might save him, although I don't see how . . ."

"So you might, though perhaps you should not. Even a man such as he is expendable, at need. But you are human, and young, and will perhaps not see that as the djinn do. I may not raise you to the ledge where he lies, Julianne de Rance; if I touched your body, that touch would destroy you."

Indeed, she had seen that; but, "You could go there yourself, great one."

"I could, though again I might not touch him. I could destroy the ghûl, and the 'ifrit when they come; but he would still be on the ledge, where no man or girl could reach him. I will not do that. What I can also do, what I will do if you ask it, is to bring you to a cliff that you can climb, if you have the courage."

She doubted her courage for any climb, and she didn't understand; but she was used to bewilderment in this creature's conversation, and there had to be a point to it, surely.

"Very well," she said, "I do ask it." Was that, did that count as a question? She couldn't decide; and had to grit her teeth at the djinni's countering laugh, sure that it was reading her doubts, perhaps her very thoughts.

"Prepare yourself, then."

"Wait. One moment . . ." Wherever it took her, and for whatever purpose, she was fairly clear that she would not be coming back here; she couldn't leave Rubon hobbled in the desert.

She clambered down across the rocks and ran over to where the horse was standing; took a little longer than a moment to unknot her girdle and tie it round her waist again, and then to fix the reins about the saddle-horn, so that they shouldn't trail on the ground and trip him. She slapped his neck, told him lies about his beauty and courage and gave him a firm push away, back towards the road. If he were sensible or lucky, he might find his way to safety; any Sharai would gladly take possession of a stray horse. She could do no more.

As soon as she saw him start to move, she hurried back towards the djinni. It had moved a little distance towards her, so she didn't need to scramble over the rubble of rocks again; as she drew close, it said, "Stand still, do not fear—and do not reach for me, Julianne de Rance, if you value your own life and your father's."

She nodded her understanding, stood stiffly with her hands clenched on the seams of her robe, and waited.

For what she didn't know, and was too slow or too distracted to guess. It drifted closer to her, and began to spin faster and to stretch itself, to climb higher into the sky until it was only an insubstantial thread before her eyes. She felt the wind of its spinning, as a breeze first and then a gathering storm, battering at her. She closed her eyes for a moment but liked that less; it felt like the first time she'd been drunk, the world gone dizzy around her.

Opening her eyes again, she thought that perhaps she hadn't; at first she could see nothing but darkness. Then a golden thread in darkness, a twisting thread of light, and that must be the djinni; except that it couldn't be, because it opened like an eye itself or like a pair of curtains drawing back, and all a golden landscape was before her.

And beside her, as the dark swept further round; and so behind her, and there was no dark at all. She stood in golden light on golden dust, and the djinni was a shimmer of air, no more, that she could see only peripherally, in the corner of her eye when she turned her head away.

When she turned her head away, she saw a cliff.

This one cast no shadow, except across her thoughts. *I will bring you to a cliff that you can climb*—and the djinn might not lie but they could certainly, most emphatically be wrong. She couldn't climb that thing. She simply couldn't. It rose perhaps no higher than the broken ridge she'd been defeated by in the other world—and there at least was one small blessing, that she felt no need or urge to ask the djinni where they were; no question in her mind, she recognised Elisande's descriptions instantly—but this rose sheer, as though it had been punched up from bedrock by some almighty fist. The stone shimmered in the strange light, and looked completely smooth.

"Djinni, I can't . . ."

"If you do not," it said, quite matter-of-fact, "your father will die. Soon."

She wanted to ask how, and how her climbing this would help him in another world; and bit the questions back just in time, her numbed mind fumbling for some other way to phrase them. "I do not, I do not see that this will aid my father . . ." she said at last, only hoping that there was no suspicion of a query in her voice.

"When you reach the top, I can take you back. You will then be above him."

She didn't see how that would help either, but there had to be a way. That was implicit.

So she steeled herself, and walked forward to the base of

the cliff: No rubble here, to catch her feet and give her a premature taste of the fear to come. Only the level dust, running up to the great wall of rock.

When she reached to touch it, it was warm beneath her fingers although there was no sun to heat it. She snatched her hand back, startled; she'd forgotten what she'd been told, how the warmth of this world pervaded everything. How it rose from below, indeed, so that the underside of a turned rock would be hotter than the top. She wondered how hot this massive scarp must be inside, and decided she would be glad never to know.

This close, it didn't look so impossible, at least for any-one who could be confident high up, with nothing to catch her should she fall. Elisande might relish the challenge of it, she thought; as she would have done herself years ago, when she was young and carefree, when height delighted her past breathing.

Not now. Now she looked and saw ledges where strong fingers could grip, cracks where bare toes could find a pur-chase, her old skills of eye and judgement not deserting her; but already all she could think about was falling.

She tried to focus her mind on her father instead, on his imminent danger; but that was a distraction, it could be al-lowed no place in her head. She would need all her concen-tration to make this climb, higher and more dangerous than any she'd tackled in Marasson before she fell.

She bent and pulled her boots off, one by one; thought of stowing them in her hood along with her knives, but felt that that too would be a distracting weight. However light a burden, it would pull at her constantly, another reminder of the drop at her back . . .

So she tossed the boots aside, took one glance back but couldn't see the djinni, set fingers and toes to the rockface and began to climb.

AT FIRST, SHE thought that perhaps she could manage this after all. Her toes could find their holds by touch, she never

needed to look down; and so long as she could just keep
eyes and thoughts on her hands, her balance, her next move
along her chosen route, then she'd be fine. Falling was all
in the mind, she told herself quite firmly, and her mind was
far too busy to fall. Besides, it wasn't climbing that terrified
her, it was heights. She was a creature of such little faith,
she had to see a thing to believe in it; and she couldn't see
how high she'd come already, she couldn't see over her
shoulder. There was only the wall of golden stone, a
hand's-breadth from her nose. She'd been scared before
and she might well be scared after, standing on the top and
looking down; but for now there was nothing to be scared
of. So long as she was holding on and moving up, so long
as she could sight her grips and reach them, oh yes, she'd
be fine. Why not . . . ?

SHE THOUGHT IT was the warmth of the rock that made
her sweat so, fingers and face and feet and all her body
else; she thought it was some phantom breeze that made
her shiver when it played against her sweat-slick skin,
though Elisande had said there never was a breeze in this
bare land.

She thought it was the danger of a creeping darkness that
she felt behind her back, and building. She didn't look to
see—why waste the time, if time was precious?—but her
friends had said that night rose rather than fell here, and she
was sure that the light was dimming slowly, she was finding it harder and harder to see good holds above; and something certainly was reaching up for her, something insidious
and deadly was clutching at the hanging hem of her robe,
dragging at her shoulders, trying to pull her down.

She thought, she truly did think that it was only coming
night; until it tugged that little harder, and her foot slipped
off a ledge that was no more narrow nor any more slant
than a hundred others she'd already trusted her weight to.

She didn't dangle, neither did she scream. Her other foot
was firmly placed, both hands had solid grips, and this rock

wasn't friable; she thought it would endure the ages. Just the one foot slipped, and the shock robbed her of any breath at all. It chased like bitter silver through her bones, killing-cold and deadly heavy.

She clung. No more than that, she clung; while all her body shuddered convulsively, entirely out of any control of hers. She pressed her face against the rock for greater contact, and felt how cold she was against its warmth, how she repelled its heat. Chill throbbed through her, exuded from her; she thought she might cool the world if she were here long enough. She thought she would be; she thought she'd never move again.

Until she fell, of course. She thought she would fall now, she was certain of it. There was nothing else that she could do.

She understood what was behind her now. Not the night: she'd been deluded, lying to herself, persuaded by her own deceit. All this time, as she'd been climbing so the drop below had been growing, the awareness of it had been growing like a hidden tumour in her mind. Now it had declared itself. It had seized her and she had seen it at last, unable to prevent herself from casting one wild look down as her foot had scrabbled for purchase; she had screwed her eyes shut in a helpless response, too late. All light below, but the darkness inside her skull offered no escape. It was there, and she could hear it calling to her, singing almost, seductive and terrible. All she had to do was let go, release her grip on the rock and so fall. A few seconds in the air and then an end, it would all be so easy . . .

She couldn't do it. Almost she wanted to, only to spare herself what was worse, dragging that tremendous weight of horror higher, feeling it grow heavier with every inching step when there was so far still to go and so little chance of ever reaching safety. But she couldn't do it, she couldn't unclamp her rigid fingers any more than she could lift a foot, either foot, to feel for another ledge. She was caught, frozen into immobility. There was a slow and perilous way up, another down; or there was a fast way down, and she could take none of them. Only hold and cling, and wait for the inevitable moment when at last her hands would cramp and spasm and so she would fall regardless and die in defeat, against her choice . . .

Until she heard the djinni's voice again, speaking close and quiet beside her ear.

"You should not linger, daughter of the Shadow."

"It, it is too hard for me, spirit." *I'm only mortal and my flesh has failed me, and my courage too.* "I cannot move any further."

"That is not true," it said chidingly, "though it may become true if you wait too long."

"I dare not, then," she whispered. "I nearly fell . . ."

"Nearly to fall is not to fall. Your kind live always on the edge of death, a breath away from falling. You might have fallen; you did not fall. Nothing has changed."

Oh, it was so wrong. Everything had changed, in a moment's clear sight of the emptiness below her. And yet it was right also. The world, both worlds were still as they had been in the moment before she slipped; she was still here on the cliff-face, her father was still in deadly danger and his saving in her hands, perhaps, only that her hands were locked and useless . . .

No, that wasn't true either. It was her mind that was locked, trapped in a childhood memory that had become an adult nightmare. If she didn't move, then she would fall; that was inevitable as sunrise even here, where no sun rose. If she fell, her father would die. Again, inevitable. She had begun this climb with no sense of hope, only a grim determination to attempt it. The point and purpose hadn't changed. She was tired now, and her fear had broken out of its cage; but to balance that she was halfway up at least, and maybe more.

Fear lied, she thought; it said she had the choice, to give up now rather than fail later. That wasn't true. Giving up—no, be honest, call it jumping—was no option for her; her body wouldn't do it, even if her mind had genuinely wanted to. Climb or fall, live or die, her only route was on and up. She'd lied to herself also, she'd tried to pretend that she could leave memory and fear behind in her necessity, or bury them so deep within her that she couldn't hear their cries. Truth had caught her out, truth had snared her; but truth would lead her on. She would climb, and carry terror on her back for so long as she was able. She could do no more than that.

All she had to do was to begin, to move one foot—this foot, the right, the one that had slipped before. She lifted it slowly, tremblingly, and set it on the same little ledge it had slipped from, because there was none better that she could find by touch. Her toes tried to dig into the rock for a moment; she waited, focused, forced them to relax. Balance and judgement would take her to the top, not brute strength. She couldn't pit herself against the cliff and hope to win, any more than she could against the fall. They were both immeasurably older, immeasurably greater than she was; but they were neutral, for all that her fear said otherwise. If she could only trust her body as she used to, she might yet satisfy the djinni's faith in her. The djinn could see some aspect of the future; it would never have brought her to this, if failure were certain . . .

Her foot was in place, her hands were set; now she had to lift her left foot, and put her weight on the right. She had to do it now, or else she never would . . .

Because she had to, so she did. And found a crack she could wriggle her toes into, where the ball of her foot could rest upon the lip; and then she could slowly, slowly loose the fingers of her right hand, and stretch it up to find another hold.

SHE CLIMBED, AGAINST the endless rise of the cliff above her and the endless suck of the fall beneath. She climbed, and sweated from the sheer exhausting effort of that climb; she squinted and groped for holds, and did not, could not believe what her body and her failing eyes were telling her when at last she dragged herself over the cliff's sharp edge and onto its plateau top. She crawled a little way, until her numb mind recognised that there was level ground below her; but then she only lay on it to rest a little while, before hauling herself onward as she thought she must.

It was the djinni who called her back to herself, as it had before, though this time its voice seemed to come from a greater distance, she had wandered so far from the world.

"Julianne de Rance," it said, "rise up, and be ready. Time moves differently in this world, but it moves yet; I cannot hold it still. Your father's peril draws nearer; if you would save him, you must do it now."

Her father, yes. He had been the cause of all of this, hadn't he . . . ?

It took an effort, a tremendous effort to let go of the rock she clung to, to trust the air; but she forced herself to her feet and found that she could after all stand without holding on, with nothing to hold on to. That was good enough, for now. She nodded to that slender twist of air that was the djinni, hanging upright here, where it had always seemed a little aslant in her own world.

"I am ready, djinni," she said, though her voice was so faint and weary to her own ears that she thought it couldn't possibly believe her.

It did, or else its urgency was greater even than it had admitted. It spun itself into a tight cord; the wind of it whipped at her, battering her sweat-damp robe against her body, startlingly chill after the heat of exercise and the warmth of the rock she'd lain on, the warmth that was inherent in the very air.

This time she resolved not to close her eyes, but it made no difference. A sudden dark engulfed her, she felt dizzy and unrooted from the world, from either world; briefly she thought she was falling after all, and nearly betrayed herself by screaming.

Then the dark unfurled itself about her and she felt ground beneath her bare feet again, and the breath of a normal breeze. The first thing she saw was the sun, red and huge, close to setting in a glorious haze of purple and scarlet. As she turned, she realised that she was standing high on the scarp, that same scarp she'd been defeated by; the dangerous edge of it was only a few paces from her, and all the wide plain lay below. A pale line marked out the road; if she looked more carefully, if she peered and scanned, she thought she might spot Rubon's wandering, if he'd not found safety yet.

But if she looked that carefully she'd see the bodies of the afternoon, she'd see Redmond dead and unburied, or else what little that pack of hungry ghûls had left of him.

She looked for the djinni instead, and couldn't find it.

Her father, then: she must look for her father, and quickly. The djinni had been in haste; what irony if she wasted its efforts and her own, by dawdling now . . .

The lip of the scarp ran as far as she could see, to north and south. No telling from a glance in each direction, where below was the ridge where her father lay. Behind her there was a crumbling stump of rock that must once have been a pinnacle, that would have made a fine landmark even from the ground, from where she'd seen the ghûl set down; but it was too low now to be useful, she had no memory of it. She'd have to go right to the edge, and peer over; even then, the ledge she sought might be here or it might be a mile away or more.

Except that the djinni had been in haste. It could have put her anywhere; surely it must have put her close . . .

She walked slowly forward; nothing could have hurried her here, not the djinni, nor her own awareness of her father's peril. If she'd seen a squad of 'ifrit scurrying towards her across the bare plateau, she still would have measured her paces as though she were walking into a gale. Her conquering the climb hadn't conquered her nervousness of heights, only given her the courage to face it. With caution, with extreme caution . . .

The closer she drew to the edge, the slower her steps became. At least she kept moving, though, she didn't hesitate even when her legs began to tremble of their own accord, when she could see nothing ahead of her but the drop. She walked on, trying not to think how soft and uncertain this rock was, until her feet were absolutely on the lip; then she lowered her head by a tremendous effort of will and looked directly down.

And saw her father, saw the ghûl.

They were immediately below her, on a long and narrow ledge perhaps twenty, perhaps thirty feet down. She couldn't judge distance from above, when she daren't look too carefully. Her father lay stretched out, quite still; the ghûl had folded its wings and was hunkered down almost as far from him as it could get. Julianne thought that was deliberate. Even from this topmost and foreshortened view, even with the long, long fall below dizzying her eyes, she could see how it tossed its head as if in pain, she could hear how it sobbed to itself. It was in pain, or else cruelly, painfully frustrated. She thought it was likely slavering for meat, for the fresh meat it had won and carried to this height; but the control of the 'ifrit held fast, either on its body or its mind.

If it had been animal, she might have pitied it, almost. As it was not, as it was brute spirit and brutal with it, she need not.

She stepped back silently, hastily, before it could hear or smell or sense her presence. Then she sank down on her haunches, much as it had; and wanted to keen much as it was, and had to force herself to think.

The 'ifrit were coming, the djinni had said or at least implied as much; until then, clearly, the ghûl would stand guard. No hope, she thought, of tempting it away. Her only bait was herself, her only weapons two short knives that could do little damage, far too little from above against its massive skull or its hunched body and not much more face to face. It would have to be killed with one stroke; Elisande might chance a throw to its throat, but not Julianne. She might have earned the luck, but she doubted its delivery.

The rock was rough and gritty beneath her bare feet; there was a jagged stone under one heel, digging in. She shifted, and wondered briefly if she could drive the creature away by pelting it with pebbles. It wasn't a bird, though, to flee such a feeble attack. It had a mind, albeit a weak one; it had instructions, that were being viciously enforced . . .

She had to kill it, then. One swift and deadly blow, and she lacked the means. *You can save him,* but she couldn't see how; and that irritating stone was still there, sharp under her soft arch now, breaking her train of thought. She reached under her foot to force it out with her finger, and found it smaller than it had seemed, just a flake from that fallen pinnacle, most likely—

—and she rose suddenly, and turned to run to the heaped rubble of rock that crowded around the remaining stump. At first her ambition overreached her strength, she strained to lift a massive boulder and couldn't shift it; she tried something a little smaller and then smaller again, until she found the largest that she could carry. Whether it would be big enough she wasn't sure, but she could do no more.

She staggered back towards the edge, clutching the heavy rock against her chest. It was hard to be quiet, harder to be careful when it tugged so at her balance, trying to drag her forward; she leaned back against it, her feet groping blindly ahead of her.

Her toes found the lip before she'd expected it, reaching suddenly into emptiness. She snatched that foot back, and stood trembling for a moment under more than the weight of the rock. She peered over its rough mass, and found herself standing directly above her father; so she backed away, inched sideways as silently as she could, then tried the edge again.

Good: there was the ghûl. Another sideways shuffle, and it was beneath her. Her foot knocked down a little shower of dust, but it paid no attention, rapt as it was in its own misery.

Its head made a target that she hoped, she prayed she couldn't miss. She fought to hold the rock out with aching arms, so that it shouldn't catch the cliff-face and be deflected in its fall; nearly its weight pulled her down, but she let go just in time.

Suddenly free of it, her body and mind both tried to drag

her back; but she danced her feet against that urge to safety, intent on watching the rock's fall.

It fell straight and true, as it had to, and impacted on the ghûl's skull with a soft, devastating sound.

The creature collapsed, all in a moment. The rock rolled off and then went on falling, down and down into the deep shadow below. The ghûl's slumped body lost its grip on the ledge and slipped off, to follow the rock.

Julianne had just a glimpse of its crushed head, before it was gone. If that wasn't enough, if it wasn't quite dead, then its crash to land should revive it; she had no great concern about that, though, and no time in any case to worry. It was almost night; there was nothing to say that the 'ifrit would come with the darkness, but they had to come sometime, and likely it would be soon.

Which meant she had to climb again, down to her father. Quickly, down an unstable cliff towards a narrow ledge, and in shadow so heavy that it might as well be night already . . .

She knelt, turned her back to the drop, lay flat on her belly and swung her legs over the edge.

There were plenty of cracks and ridges that her groping toes could feel, but she was hanging with all her weight on her elbows before she found one that she trusted, a little hollow in the rock where her whole foot could fit.

She didn't want to trust it long; nor the next foothold that she found, a projecting knub of stone that surely must fall sometime, so why not now, when she put her weight on it, when better?

By then only her hands clutched the lip of the cliff above, and only briefly; she felt for holds and found them, and was committed.

And so quickly down, driven by anxiety that she tried to pretend was confidence restored. She could hear crackles and murmurs in the rock, she could feel it flake beneath her fingers, beneath her feet; soon she was scrambling in a constant fall of dust, grabbing at anything that seemed secure and finding nothing that was.

Her feet slipped and couldn't find a hold; she slid down the last ten feet or so, all her body stiffening in anticipation of a far, far greater fall; and landed with a jarring thud on the ledge, spread herself against the face and tried to embrace the entire cliff until the patter of falling stones had entirely ceased around her.

How she'd make the climb back up with her father a dead weight to carry, she couldn't imagine. First things first, though: and the first thing was to assure herself that he wasn't simply dead.

She inched along the ledge, face to the wall still, until she felt fabric against her foot. Then she worked her way down onto her knees, straddling his legs; and fumbled inside her robe to pull out the water-skin she carried, blessing Elisande's care in making certain it was there.

She moistened a corner of her veil, and wiped her father's face. There was at least a whisper of breath in him, she could feel it against her damp wrist; she poured water liberally over his head; and gasped her relief as his eyelids fluttered.

She put the mouth of the skin to his lips, dribbled a little water between them, and saw him swallow. His eyes opened, he shaped her name silently; she gave him another drink, then slipped her arm beneath his shoulders and helped him sit up.

"Careful," she whispered, "we're a long way up . . ."

"Too high for you, eh, Julianne?" No mockery in his dry voice, and no panic either, only a calm assessment as he gazed about him, blinking in the dim light.

"Much too high," she agreed. "And the 'ifrit are coming, soon, I think. It's not far to the top," though it might be too far for both of them, "but the rock crumbles under any weight . . ."

"Then we'd best not climb it. Give me your arm, and let me stand."

That confused her, and she was briefly afraid that he was too confused to make sense of where they were, despite his words; but she had a lifetime's practice at trusting her fa-

ther, and was only glad to cede authority to him, where it
had always belonged.

He was slow to rise and shaky on his feet, clutching her
arm with both hands. He took the outer side, though, leaving her the security of the wall, which reassured her further.

There was barely room on the ledge for the two of them
to stand side by side, and she didn't see the point of it; there
was nowhere to go, if they didn't attempt the climb.

But he said, "Walk a little, slowly. Don't look down, and
don't be afraid; you needn't look at all if you don't want to,
close your eyes if that's easier for you."

There was no question of her looking down, except at
her feet on this dark and untrustworthy ledge, certainly no
further down than that; nor was there any question of her
closing her eyes. Whatever he meant to do, she meant to
see it.

She matched her steps to his, slow and shuffling; and
they'd gone no distance at all before her feet were washed
with a softly golden light. She lifted her head in wonder,
entirely trusting now, and found herself walking into a
bright mist, as though an unnoticed door had opened to
pass them through.

She thought perhaps they'd find the land of the djinn on
the further side of that mist; and was wrong, knew herself
to be wrong even before the light was gone. Her feet stumbled over loose rock and she all but shrieked, terror suddenly resurgent and her turn to clutch at her father.

He gave way beneath her, no strength in his legs; but
they didn't fall, or only so far as the ground they stood on.
She lay clutching at it, panting for breath, surprised to find
the ledge so wide; and only slowly realised that this was
not the ledge, it couldn't be. Her dazzled eyes distinguished
shapes, shadows all around them, jumbled rocks and one
black edifice; it took a time for her to recognise that as the
stump, the broken pinnacle that had given her the weapon
she needed against the ghûl. They were atop the scarp
somehow, and her father was smiling at her, his teeth bright
against the night.

"I couldn't bring us far," he said, "not far at all; and that's my limit for a while. My thoughts are still jangled. We've a walk ahead of us, I'm afraid, and the 'ifrit may find us on the way."

Somehow, she couldn't care. If the 'ifrit found them, her miraculous father would undoubtedly whisk them both away on the wings of his will, no concern in the world . . .

Actually, she thought in all seriousness that he would, however tired or confused he claimed to be. He seemed as unconcerned as she felt, and that without any of the excuses that she had. She was elated, flying, the very opposite of falling; he was hurt and weakened and surely must be full of doubts and questions—if his last coherent memory were standing above the brutalised body of his old friend Redmond, how could he not be, finding himself high on a cliff and only his hypsophobic daughter for company?—but yet he was entirely sanguine about the prospect of 'ifrit, even a host of 'ifrit falling upon them. He wouldn't be so casual about his life or hers, unless he knew that he could walk her out of danger.

Walk her out of one place, and into another, apparently without breaking sweat. Even the djinni had to work, to carry her between the worlds . . .

"So that's how you do it," she murmured.

"Is it?"

"All that coming and going, and no one ever knowing where you are or where to look for you . . ."

"Oh, that. Sometimes, yes. Sometimes I'm just an old man in other clothes, and people don't quite see me. Coming or going."

"I don't suppose you're going to tell me how you do it?"

"Change my dress."

"You know what I mean." She'd earned something more than the distraction of jokes, she thought; but the shape of his mind was elliptical, and perhaps he was giving her what knowledge she could use. Though she knew that much already; wasn't she in boys' clothing now? And hadn't she

often and often slipped out of the palace in urchins' rags as
a little girl, to play with her urchin friends?

"The King finds it useful," he said, "for his servant to
move swiftly sometimes, between place and place. Sometimes to move secretly. And so he has gifted me this
power—if it is a gift. It can be a monstrous inconvenience,
to be convenient to the King. You saw that yourself, on the
road from Tallis."

"You were called away," she said slowly, remembering,
"and you rode into a furious light that terrified the horses;
but that was nothing like this just now, what you did on the
ledge . . ."

"I am nothing like the King. He can call me from Tallis
to Ascariel, and open a road that I ride in moments, a
month's journey in an eyeblink of time; I can carry you
from where we were to where we are, and it exhausts me to
do it."

He didn't seem exhausted, he seemed stronger by the
sentence, by the step. He walked beside her, one hand on
her arm still but hardly leaning now, as much for company
as strength; she thought how often she had walked so at his
side, her hand tucked through his elbow, and wondered if
he were also paying her a little tribute here, telling her that
she had grown in more than inches since last they were together.

As ever with her father, it was impossible to be certain
what he meant. He could be a snake that ate its own tail
sometimes, so subtle that his secret messages consumed
themselves in their own mystery.

The sun was gone, but the stars gave light enough for
walking on this high plateau. Light enough for the 'ifrit to
spot them, perhaps, that too, but she was still unworried.
They were headed south, towards Rhabat, which meant towards the Dead Waters too, towards where the 'ifrit lurked,
and she was still unworried.

"Julianne," her father said, "have you had much conversation with Hasan?"

"Not much, no." Too much, and not enough; but those

were both confessions, and she was a married woman. Her husband should hear it first if any man, but Imber never would, or not from her. She knew how deep a hurt could go with him, and wanted never to bruise those green eyes grey again.

If ever she saw those grey eyes green again, if ever he could find a way to take her back . . .

"Well. He is not a man to waste time with idle words. When he speaks, it is to the purpose; and he tells me he wants to marry you."

"He told me that, too." It was difficult to keep her voice as dry and airy as the breeze, as her father's was; but some things should be difficult. Concentration helped, it gave her a little distance from thoughts of Hasan, thoughts of Imber. "I told him I was married already." And he'd asked her husband's name, *that I may kill him*. She hadn't said it, she'd said something foolish instead. If he truly wanted to know, he could learn from someone else; she thought it likely that he did know by now, if he hadn't already known it then.

"Mmm. How did you get up onto that ledge?"

"Down, I came down, from up here. I climbed down . . ."

"Julianne, how did you get up here? You were on the plain with me, not so long ago."

"I climbed," another confession that she hadn't wanted to make, or not to him. No father should owe his daughter so much, and this one especially not. He ought to be untouchable, as he always had been; she hated to have seen him so defeated. "Not this. The djinni took me through to its own country, and I climbed there. It said it couldn't just lift me to the ledge, I had to climb . . ."

"It didn't say that, Julianne. The djinn do not lie. It could have done that much, or a great deal more. It could simply have brought me down to you; it could have taken us both to Rhabat, or anywhere else in the world. What did it actually say?"

She thought back, listening to its voice in her memory. "It said 'may,' it said *I may not raise you to the ledge*. It

said if it touched my body, it would destroy me. That's true,
I've seen it happen . . ."

"Indeed, that is true. It wouldn't have needed to touch
you, though. It didn't touch you when it took you between
the worlds, did it?"

"No . . ."

"No. Well, no doubt it had its reasons. Everything that
djinni does is curious to me. Let us get on; it's a long way
to Rhabat, when we have only feet to take us there."

THEY WALKED FOR an hour or more, talking lightly of
this and that, till the stars had drawn all heat out of the
world and it was only the chill that made her shiver now.
Gazing up at the great frosty blaze above her, she saw
shadows cross it suddenly, like vast and deadly birds that
couldn't be, like monstrous bats. She croaked, and
pointed; her father looked, and nodded calmly.

"'Ifrit," he said.

"With wings?"

"Why not?"

Why not, indeed? Their bodies were an artifice in any
case. And if a ghûl could grow wings, why not the 'ifrit?

"Perhaps they did not see us . . ."

"Perhaps not; but they will look. Time we were safe
home, child. Besides, I'm already late for my own feast,
which is unpardonable; and I find myself remarkably hungry."

And so it was a shimmering cloud of light that they
stepped into; and as they went, she wondered vexedly how
long it was since her father could have done the same as he
did now, just how far he'd made her walk to no apparent
purpose. And why, because he never, ever did anything that
had no purpose . . .

FIVE

Out of the Shadows, Into the Dark

ELISANDE COULDN'T QUITE believe that this was happening.

She'd been in the kitchens when the news broke: dutifully where Hasan had sent her, pounding almonds grimly into paste and watching her own sweat drip into the mortar for added flavour. She had hoped vaguely that telling Sherett about what had happened at the water's edge might have won her some more interesting task; she'd been disappointed but not surprised when the only response was, "Hasan will see your friends safe. Now come, if you will; we have only a few hours left to us, and we have missed your help already. And Julianne's . . ."

You have been playing like silly children, her harassed frown had said, *meddling with men's business when there was work to be done.* It had been true, too, at least by her lights; Elisande didn't want to see the world that way, but it was hard to resist. What she'd stolen for Julianne—a boy's clothes, and so an afternoon on horseback—had been precious to her friend; what she'd stolen for herself, time again and Marron's company to spend it with, had been perhaps more precious to her. No one could have predicted that the 'ifrit would choose that time to rise, and so make both their adventures seem foolhardy. Even so, though, a glimpse of Sherett's strained and weary face had made them both seem selfish at the least. Another woman would have been shocked, and angry too: two girls her guests, and one chooses to dress and ride with men while the other slips away to be private with a boy . . . Elisande had followed Sherett meekly to her labour, feeling glad to be taxed only with self-indulgence, and that obliquely.

An hour later, she'd not been meek; she'd been hot and tired, bored and resentful. Resenting Jemel, who was at least allowed to do something, to ride to Julianne's rescue if she should need it; resenting Marron, who could do exactly as he pleased and was no doubt doing exactly that, though she didn't know what it was; resenting Julianne for her borrowing of Elisande's tricks, for her meeting with Redmond, even for the risks that she was running.

Above all, Elisande had been busily and deeply resenting each and every one of the women who surged and jostled at her back, adding more at every moment to the steam, the heat and the cacophony of the kitchen. Real and deadly things were happening in the world just beyond their door, and they paid it no attention; that wide world belonged to men, and so they were cramped in this little space and frantically cooking for the later pleasure of those same men, and not one of them had seemed to feel any resentment of her own.

Even Sherett had been trained to accept this role and wouldn't challenge it, content to waste her strength and intelligence on the paltry matters with which she was permitted to concern herself. Even when the news had come, leaking back through the guards at the door: even when word had cut across the women's gabble, a single voice raised loud enough to silence all the others, still Sherett had only paused for a moment in her frenetic chopping, had only bowed her head to Yaman's sharp observation that more men in the valley meant more call on their stores and more work for them all.

'Ifrit had attacked the tribes, where they were camped before the siq. Hasan had rallied the survivors and brought them into Rhabat, but many had been killed and there was now no safe passage in or out. The party Hasan had been riding to protect—Redmond's caravan, Julianne, her father—had not been sighted, and was either stranded or lost . . .

Elisande had abandoned pestle and mortar, and headed for the door; Sherett had stopped her, with a hand tight on her elbow.

"Where are you going?"

"To the stables. You heard . . ."

"And so did you. You cannot pass the siq; what, will you fry 'ifrit with your glare, Elisande? Your friends are in God's hands now, or else in the hands of the Shadow, which are nearly as strong. Trust and pray, and return to your work; or if you cannot pray, trust Julianne's father and work anyway. Work will keep you from pacing and bothering people, when there is nothing you or anyone can do now. It will also keep you within my doors, where you belong. This is not the time to go blustering among the men."

That she hadn't been able to argue with although she'd wanted to, or she'd wanted to go bluster regardless. She'd wanted to plague Hasan for details, how far had he got, had he really not seen any sign of those he pursued or those they'd gone in search of; she'd wanted urgently to check on Jemel, was he living or dead, was he hurt? Most urgently of all, she'd wanted to find Marron. There was one who could leave Rhabat, if he chose to. He could open a doorway, make the journey in another world and so come back beyond the danger. Surely, he would go. And if he went, when he went, she'd wanted to go with him. He might need her help, if any were hurt; he might need her courage in a fight. He should not go alone . . .

He should not, but it had seemed that he might have to. Sherett had refused to let her go.

"What, will you scour all of Rhabat in search of that one? He may be of your people, but he is half ours now, he is the Ghost Walker; where he goes, you may not follow. That is written."

"I have been there already, Sherett."

"Even so. What if he is gone already? He is no fool, he will take men if he needs them, better help than you could be."

"He can be a fool," she'd said, thinking of the shy boy she'd first known, who sometimes resurfaced even now. "He might not ask, he might not think to ask . . ."

"Let his wisdom make the choice, Elisande. Every girl thinks her boy a fool. You would not find him in any case. There are thirty houses here, with thirty or forty rooms in each; will you invade them all? When there are men in each now, hundreds of unsettled men, and more in the huts across the valley? They would not welcome a wild girl. No, stay where you are truly needed."

"To make a feast? How can you think of feasting? When the man who gives it is one of the missing . . ."

"I have not heard that the feast is cancelled; only that we must make more food for the hungry. The men abandoned their camps, they have nothing. And the man who gives the feast is the Shadow; he will not be missing long."

"I thought I was your guest," she'd grumbled, "not your prisoner. Nor servant to your men . . ."

"Because you are my guest, I will care for you. Child. Here, under my eye. The care of children does not include letting them run headlong into stupidity or danger."

"Don't call me that, I'm not a child . . ."

"No? Very well, then. Still less does proper care of a woman allow her to disgrace herself before men of my tribe or any other. You wear the dress of a Beni Rus, Elisande, and you will behave accordingly. I am sorry, girl," she'd gone on more kindly, "I do understand your distress, and your impatience; but there is no help for it, or none that you can give. We women learn to wait; sometimes what comes back to us is not what we have waited

for. We learn to accept that, also. It is the most useful lesson the desert has to teach us. It would be easier to show
you in the Sands, but I will do my best within these walls.
Take this mortar, here, and these nuts . . ."

AND SO SHE had stayed, because she'd had to. She had
mixed her paste with honey and whole nuts and saffron
steeped in rose-water, to make sweets for the men to amuse
their tongues and their bellies with after they had feasted,
while they talked and drank coffee—which thought had
struck her with another, suddenly. She hadn't considered it
before, but of course someone must serve this feast to the
men, all those grand sheikhs and warlords, and their coffee
afterwards. The young men of their tribes might do it, but
she'd fancied not. The young men might have helped with
the preparation, and had not. In the desert, yes, at a meeting
of men where the women were left with the herds; but here
there were women enough if they worked, and what more
were they for . . . ?

She had checked with Sherett, standing on tiptoe to peer
over that woman's shoulder as she spun sugar-syrup into a
fantastic confection of towers above a cake of camels'-milk
boiled stiff with honey.

"Of course, we will serve the food. Not you, though. I
would not see my guests demeaned so far as that."

"Sherett, I'm not so proud. And if you don't let me fetch
and carry at the feast, Yaman will have me back here scrubbing dishes all evening, you know she will . . ."

Sherett had slapped stingingly at Elisande's hand, where
she was dipping a finger into the hot sugar-syrup; then,
laughing, "Scrubbing or boiling rice for the new-come
men. There will be work enough, that is certain. Can you
behave, though, can you curb your tongue? We must be
swift, and silent. A girl's voice has no place at such a feast;
I will not have you disgrace us all."

"Silent as the Sands, I swear it. It won't be the first time
I've played servant. Truly, I'll be good."

"Your father will be among the men. Would he not be shamed, to see his daughter at such a task?"

"Not he. He'll deem it fitting, and thank you for the lesson. He thinks me too forthright, too independent; he says I get above myself, and need knocking down . . ."

"A wise man, your father. Does he hope to see you married soon? He should do, you're ripe for it, girl. And there's one at least here who would offer for you, I hear."

"Boraj? That pretty, laughing boy? Oh, please . . ." The only boy she wanted was as pretty, or nearly so, and solemn as rock; she couldn't remember having made him laugh, but a moment's smile from him was worth a day, no, a lifetime of the giggling, flattering Boraj.

"His father too would welcome it; and I think so would the Shadow. An alliance between Patric and Sharai, at this time—that would be no bad thing. Boraj's father has a strong voice among the sheikhs . . ."

Elisande had gazed at her doubtfully, an appeal already shaping itself on her tongue, *don't lend your voice to such a notion*—but she'd swallowed it in fury at herself, seeing how Sherett's eyes danced in the hot light.

"You're teasing me," she'd scowled. "And even if you weren't, my father will let me make my own choice."

Would he? It was the custom in Surayon, she couldn't remember a girl ever being married against her will. If her father knew where her choice lay, though . . .

Well, it didn't matter. Her choice was hopeless; she was resigned to that. Nearly resigned, only tormenting herself by snatching stray threads of hope.

"I may join you tonight, then? You owe me, now . . ."

"Don't growl at me, girl—and don't sulk, those brows will show it above your veil. But yes, you may join us, if only to save your fingers from the scrubbing-sand. Don't thank me, you're sure to regret it later; for one thing, you may expect to see Boraj at the feast. I'll dress you up prettily, for his sake if no other's," and her eyes had been sharp then, seeing too much. "It would be a shame to let ourselves be outshone by the food we serve . . ."

*   ·   *   *

SMALL CHANCE OF that: when they were finally finished
in the kitchen, she'd been towed away to the baths by a
crowd of women, and then up to a room that was gaudy
with hanging dresses of silk and satin. Some had been so
gossamer-thin, even she had thought them indecent; Sherett
had made her blush, simply by fingering one of those with
her eyes on Elisande and her lips seeming to shape the
name of Boraj.

But the older woman had laughed then, claiming her victory, and turned aside to find another, a gown of heavy gold
brocade.

"We will wear blue," she'd said, "as we always do; but
you need not. This will suit your colouring admirably."

"That will make me stand out like a lamp in the shadows. I'd rather not . . ."

"I insist. You may play the servant, Elisande, but you
must dress as a guest. I won't have you hide among us. Let
the men see you, and understand the courtesy you do them.
It will reflect to your honour, and your father's also."

She cared not a whit for her father's honour, nor her
own; but the dress was lovely, falling over her skin like
spun sunshine, warm and enfolding as woven flame. One
touch, and it had stolen from her the capacity to argue.

IN ROQ DE Rançon, she had played lady's-maid to
Elisande; in Rhabat, where once she had played rapscal-
lion, now she played serving-wench to a hall full of men.

She had only ever glimpsed the Chamber of Audience
when she'd been here before, peering through the doorway
to decide that it was vast but dull, it had nothing to offer a
youngster. Now she wanted to stand amazed by its height,
its width, its decoration, its massive pillars hewn whole
from the same rock that made the ceiling that they sup-
ported and the floor beneath her bare feet. Her soul cried
out for time to stand and stare, but she had none; she could

only snatch moments of wonder, an occasional pause in the shadows to gape upward or around.

It was the light that made the difference, she thought, more than any added years affecting her reactions. A child then, she felt a child still; she didn't understand how anyone could feel otherwise, enclosed within such an ageless weight of rock.

The hall was ablaze with light, torches in sconces on every wall and pillar and a leaping fire in a pit in the centre of the floor. There were veins in the rock of the walls which caught that light and ran with it, as though it were their lifeblood; they glittered and pulsed in rhythm with the hurrying women, whose deep blue robes shimmered as though there were starlight trapped in the silk. Even the men's drab desert dress seemed to quicken, while the skin glowed on their hands and faces; the dishes gleamed on the floor before them, and the food was jewelled.

And yet Elisande knew that she was the brightest thing in the hall that night; she shone as she scurried to and fro. Single or married or many times married, every man followed her with his eyes; she felt the weight of their gaze on her shoulders, heavier even than the weight of that roof so high above that even this much light couldn't reach it, and left it swathed with shadow.

Those young men privileged to be there, sons and nephews of the powerful, they called her to come to them, to fetch them bread and rice, meat and drink when there was plenty still before them. She chose not to acknowledge their brashness even by ignoring them; she served them as she served their elders, quickly and efficiently and with what they needed, nothing more.

Boraj was the loudest and the most obvious among them. Trading on earlier acquaintance he made great play of his soft eyes and lustrous hair, flirting with her so outrageously that in the end his father called him to order, loudly across the hall. He flushed at the raucous laughter that followed, as it had to; the looks he gave her after were quieter, but spoke of some more serious desire.

She treated those with the same disdain she had awarded
his coarser efforts, and searched in vain to find Marron anywhere among the several score of men around the hall.

Her father she had no trouble finding; he sat among the
sheikhs, higher even than Hasan, and spoke with them as
an equal. He spoke to her not at all; she had better from his
neighbours, soft words of thanks and occasional polite re-
quests that she hurried to fulfil.

His silence towards her was nothing unusual, she had
lived with it before and paid it back a hundred times, in
contempt or vitriol. What was rare was to sense the disquiet
that underlay the grave courtesy that he gave to his companions, if not to her: to sense it, and to share it. She was
not accustomed to finding herself at one with her father. It
had happened too much for her liking already on this journey, since its beginning indeed; she almost yearned for the
old antagonism to run as it used to, far below the scornful
surface.

Much like hers, his eyes shifted around the hall, following the shifting shadows as if seeking constantly for the arrival of those who were missing and much missed, much
needed. Seeing that, she felt suddenly overwhelmed by the
futility of this great feast. Its author was among the missing, as were two good friends of hers, the father of her soul
and the friend of her heart; guests of these people who
claimed to prize hospitality higher than their own lives,
they were cut off at best, surely in danger. And yet their
hosts feasted in their absence, and talked of nothing that
mattered because that was the custom, not to speak of the
day's business until the meal was done; and she couldn't
believe that it was happening like this, it didn't seem real
after all the desperate business of the day.

She wanted to break out, to protest, to fetch a horsewhip
from the stables and drive them off to search, to rescue or
revenge. She wanted to hurl a plate of glazed and roasted
mutton across the floor, right in front of the sheikhs there,
to splash them with its seething juices while she harangued
them for their cowardice, their idleness, their discourtesy to

guests. She wanted to forswear herself and all her promises, to humiliate Sherett and her father and anyone else there who thought she could or would behave herself under such provocation.

She could name three, perhaps four people whose good opinion she valued enough to hold herself in check for their sakes—and they were none of them there, and that was the point. Someone had to do something, and she was forbidden to, and none of these men apparently would, or not without urging. She was forbidden to do that too, but oh, they needed it . . .

She might have done it; she felt as close to it as she had to all the mad things she'd ever done in her life, that brief moment before she did them.

What held her back was Hasan, a sudden glimpse through custom and manners and normally iron control to the heart of him, the real man. His voice rose abruptly above the general babble; nothing unusual in that, the Sharai didn't feel they'd eaten well unless they'd had an argument for seasoning, and they didn't feel they'd argued well unless they'd shouted. But she heard him say, yell rather, "—And if she die, how then? She died in our care, and we left her blood unmarked in the Sands, shall we say so . . . ?"

A hush followed, sign of deep shock. Like everyone, she stared at Hasan; like everyone she saw him colour, saw him turn to the sheikhs and bow, seated as he was, hand on heart, profound apology.

He'd broken age-old tradition, and had made what amends were possible for such a breach; talk started up again all around the hall. No one laughed at Hasan, no one referred at all to that moment; they all politely turned their heads away, not to add to his embarrassment.

All but Elisande. She watched him, and saw that there was a third to be added to the list, that short list of her father and herself. Hasan was more than anxious; he was racked tight with tension, eating little and speaking less, speaking hardly at all since that outburst.

The time would come, when he could have his say and men would listen. If he could wait for that, then so could she; these lean men couldn't eat for ever, surely, though they showed no signs of slacking yet. She'd follow Hasan's lead, and only if he failed her would she bring shame on herself and all who loved her, by telling this whole gathering what she thought of them and their feast, their craven greed, their passivity. Their god too. He would not be immune to her tongue if they dared suggest that the fate of her friends lay in his hands now . . .

Determined on that, she threw herself back into the role of willing servant-girl until the time came. She gave special attention to Hasan, though she had almost to fight for that privilege, pushing ahead of other women equally keen; even here and even after he'd disgraced himself, it seemed that tribal prejudice wilted in the face of his fierce charisma. She could fear for her land and her people, she could fear deeply if she weren't so eager to see him use that power to claim and lead his own tonight.

With all her attention, all her hopes focused on him, she forgot to keep checking the entrance to the hall, against the fading chance of longed-for latecomers. It was the sudden stillness of the men she served that alerted her, the way their heads all turned toward the doorway, while the constant flow of voices all around her dwindled slowly into silence.

She straightened, backed away, finally allowed herself to look. Even as she did so, she was struggling to expect nothing that she wanted—and lost that struggle gladly, gave it up in a moment as she saw Marron striding down the centre of the hall. Jemel was with him, which answered one lingering question; but that was the least of what had troubled her all evening, or she hoped it was. She hoped she was not so petty.

The two boys came marching past the firepit, towards where the sheikhs sat assembled with her father among them. She thought she was not the only one there whose breath was stilled in their bodies, as they waited for what might follow.

Properly it should be Coren de Rance who challenged the boys; this was his feast, after all. But of course he was not here. The sheikhs looked at each other, as though waiting for any one of them to claim precedence, so that the others could instantly deny it; it was not Julianne's father but her own who stood eventually, who spoke to them in his clear jongleur's voice, not loud but carrying, as all clear voices carried within this hall.

"You will have some good reason, Ghost Walker, I am sure, for disturbing the gathered tribes at their meal; I would be glad to hear it. You were not invited here, neither you, Jemel . . ."

Jemel scowled, as though it had been an insult to be omitted and another to be reminded of it; Marron only smiled.

"You need not talk to me as though I were a djinni, Rudel. It's safe to ask me questions. I know we were not invited, and I apologise for intruding; some number of your company would rather see me dead than living, let alone here among you."

"That is a matter to be resolved another time," Rudel said quietly, without disputing the fact or declaring his own position. Elisande thought she knew where he'd stand; another reason why she would always, always stand with Marron. "Tell me now, why have you broken in on our feasting? What is so urgent that it could not wait an hour?"

It might be news of Julianne; it couldn't be good news, though, or he'd have brought her with him. Wouldn't he? He was breaking custom simply by being here, he challenged the Sharai simply by existing; he'd have no hesitation in fetching a girl to stand before them, if that girl were their friend and freshly brought safe back.

Elisande listened, almost dreading to hear Julianne's name; and almost felt relief when Marron said, "The imam in the high temple, who watches your hidden gateway for you—that man is dead, and an 'ifrit guards the gate now.

We have been up, we have seen. If they attack the valley, there will be no escape that way. Or that may be the way they choose to come . . ."

"Perhaps; though sea or air might serve them better. Well, thank you, Marron, Jemel. You came to no harm?"

"None. The 'ifrit did not attack." And neither of course did he.

"Curious, if it knew who you were; curious if it did not. They must be content to keep us penned, for now—though we are not, of course, with you here. We could all of us leave, at any time . . ."

"If the Ghost Walker opened a way to the land of the djinn," one of the sheikhs said abruptly, "the 'ifrit could slaughter us there. I will not lead my men into that."

"There is more," Marron added heavily. "We have been there, Jemel and I; we met no 'ifrit, but we came back onto the road, and found Redmond's party. I am sorry, but they are dead, all of them. They met ghûls, by the look of it."

It was cold news, coldly spoken; Elisande fought down a wave of sorrow. Later, she would mourn that old man as he deserved. For now, she had to hear what more had not been said yet.

"What of the King's Shadow, and his daughter?"

"There was no sign of them. There were many dead, including some Sharai of the Ib' Dharan, who may have been the men they rode with. The bodies had been desecrated, but we checked them all, and those two were not among them. Casting about, Jemel found the tracks of one horse that went away westward, that we thought it better not to follow."

"Very well. Stay, both of you, eat if you are hungry. We must discuss this. Marron, would you go back, and take me and a number of men with you? It is a risk, perhaps, but I would like to bring their bodies here. We can at least give them an honourable burial, they have deserved that much of us."

Marron nodded; Jemel took his arm and led him away, to the opposite side of the hall. Elisande watched, ready to go to them, to bully them both into eating, but she wasn't needed. One of the other women was ahead of her, with a plate of bread and meat; the two boys sat close together in a space apart from the men, and Jemel pressed food into Marron's hands before he took any for himself.

She sighed quietly, and tried not to keep looking over: not to see how their shoulders pressed one against the other, how neither of them shifted to give the other more room, how it was Marron who reached first to touch Jemel more deliberately, and not the other way around.

WHEN THE MEN were finally done with eating, there was coffee to be served. Elisande steeled herself, determined not to be a coward in this; she carried her tray towards her friends, greeted them with a determined smile that they should at least be able to read in her eyes—that might disguise what else they might have read there—and knelt carefully on the floor before them.

Jemel first: Marron could watch, and be reminded. She filled one tiny cup brimful of thick sweet coffee, and passed it to the Sharai. He took it with a nod, drained it and held it out. She refilled it, he drank again; and so a third time. He set the cup back on the tray, inverted, to show that he had had enough.

She poured another cup for Marron; when he took it from her, her fingers tingled at the touch of his. She had to fight not to snatch them back, nor to let them linger. She could feel Jemel's eyes on her, and struggled to play the perfect Sharai woman before him, veiled and submissive. It was all play, but not in any sense a game; they both knew that.

She wondered if Marron knew anything at all; he was so hard to read, since the Daughter had begun to change him. He smiled at her, though, as he imitated the way Jemel had drunk, the way men were drinking all around the hall as women carried coffee to them one by one. There was even perhaps a hint of mischief in his face as he took his third cup, as though he were thinking of a scandalous fourth.

She shook her head fractionally, *don't do it, Marron.* He was being watched, to see if he could follow custom at least this far; he faced trouble enough, he didn't need to add a trivial irritant to the offence of his presence, his very existence.

She moved on, from her friends to the nearest group of men; but couldn't resist one glance back as she went. His eyes were following her, but she saw Jemel reach for his hand and hold it loosely, and she saw how his head turned back immediately toward the Sharai.

Oh, Marron, she thought, heartbroken, *I'm sorry, I'm so sorry I couldn't be a boy for you . . .*

WHEN THEY CAME, she was watching Marron again: one last look to last her through the night, because she'd not see him again before the morning. Some women would stay to serve tea or sherbet for as long as the men should call for it, but not her. Sherett was sending her away with most of the others.

"You need not scrub dishes," she'd said, "though they must. It's time to shed the servant, and be a guest again. Go to bed, Elisande—and thank you."

And so she would go to bed, she thought; her bones ached with weariness. She wouldn't sleep, though. How could she sleep, when men were talking of taking war to her people, and there was only her father to stand against Hasan; when Marron was so very much in her head, so very much with Jemel; when Julianne and her father were still missing; when Redmond was dead and unburied, his body lying open to any desert scavenger and perhaps abused already?

She trailed miserably to the doorway, last in a line of women, and paused for one last lingering look back. The firelight had died to a low glow and some of the torches had burned out, but she could still see Marron in the shadows, Jemel's arm flung around his shoulders. As she watched, he lifted his head and gazed into the furthest corner of the hall. After a second, Jemel looked the same way.

And stiffened, half lifted his other arm to point. She couldn't hear what he said above the constant babble of other voices, but she saw his mouth working. Other men turned, as she did; she saw a misty gleam and two slow figures walking forward, arm in arm. One was taller than the other; something in the way they moved said that the taller was a woman, the shorter a man.

Something in the way they moved held her rigidly in place, before she started jerkily back towards them.

The strange light faded, but she could see them more clearly with it gone, as torchlight touched their faces; and she was running now, dodging between the men as they rose and stared.

She was swifter even than her father, though she'd had so much more distance to cover; she was first to reach Julianne, though her legs failed her at the last, stuttering to an awkward halt a couple of paces short of her friend.

Not tiredness had slowed her so, or dragged her to a stop. She wanted to hug, but was suddenly afraid to touch. Julianne looked exhausted, all too solidly there and feeling every ounce of her own weight; and yet the light shifted and she seemed to shift with it, she seemed ethereal almost, uncertain of her own skin's containment.

And a quick unnecessary glance confirmed what Elisande knew already, that there was no doorway in that corner they had come from . . .

"Are you real?" she whispered stupidly.

"I don't know. Am I? You tell me. Elisande, I climbed a mountain . . ."

And it was, it had to be the true Julianne who stepped away from her father and came unsteadily to Elisande, who clutched at her with hard hands. She felt the bite of nails through her silks, inarguably real; her voice choking on a protest that came out as half laugh, half sob, as she reached to peel the fingers gently away and found those nails chipped and broken, the skin of the palms roughly torn.

"Have you been breaking rocks with your bare hands, sweet?"

"No, I told you, I climbed a mountain—"

"Indeed? And where did you do that, lady, when all the mountains hereabouts have defeated me, and all men else?" It was Hasan, of course: appearing at Elisande's elbow and taking Julianne's hands from her. Dark thumbs worked gently over pale knuckles, as though they had a claim there that none could dispute. "And why did you do it, why go climbing mountains when there were those here who were anxious about you?"

"It was in the other world, prince, the djinni took me. And I had to do it, I had to save my father . . ."

She looked back then to find him, but Elisande's own father had claimed the King's Shadow, taking his arm and steering him towards the sheikhs. Late for his own feast, but he had come at last; his slender back and Rudel's broad one said that there would be no place for the girls in their coming conversation.

By the same signs, though, Hasan's place was manifestly there and not here, with the man and not the daughter. His reluctance to leave her was more than seeming, Elisande thought, this was no lordling showing off his pretty manners in the court.

Go he must, though, and go he did, if not before touching Julianne's fingers to his lips. Patric-fashion, that was, and nothing Sharai about it; Elisande wondered if Julianne had any idea of its significance, with all these tribal leaders watching. Its significance to her, at least, seemed clear. Her hand lifted as if to hold him back, her throat worked as if to call him; how he managed to keep walking, not even to turn his head with such a summoning so close, Elisande could barely imagine. The determined strength in him was something terrible. When he set his mind to a task, it seemed that no one alive could deflect him from it. And yet he was not single-minded, he was able to set himself more tasks than one, when the need arose.

She thought it was a need, in him at least, if not in Julianne. For her it might only be a yearning; but Hasan was the perfectibility of a Sharai, he sought only what was necessary and would chase only where he was driven. She thought he'd never hunt for pleasure, only to eat.

Well, but he has a full larder already, one wife here and two more with his tents, wherever his tents are pitched. What need he another?

The answer was easy, of course, that it wasn't another wife he needed, it was Julianne. Why was another question, and she could put it off one more time, she thought; shrug it off for the moment, at least, to attend to her friend's more immediate comfort.

"That's a story I want to hear, sweet—but you can tell me later. You're here, you're safe, that's what counts. Are you hungry?"

"Elisande, I'm starving."

Sherett was there suddenly, at her other side. Sent by a gesture from Hasan, perhaps—or perhaps not even needing to look for it, knowing his will or her own, or simply her duty. "That we can take care of, if you're content with what small pickings the men have left. You too, Elisande, you need to eat now. Come with me, the pair of you . . ."

BETWEEN THEM THEY half led, half carried the stumbling Julianne out of the hall and into the clear night, along by the water to the women's quarters. The way was crowded with men, hurrying between the bright-lit houses or else gathered in small groups to talk; they made room for the women to pass, but jostled each other in a way that might lead to fights before the night was over, despite the tribal truce that supposedly governed Rhabat. They were nervous, watching the sky continually for shadows against the stars; many held bows ready-strung. Elisande at least was glad to pass the guards at the women's door, and come through to the comparative peace beyond.

She was desperate to hear Julianne's story, but food came first, food was urgent. Elisande recognised that same hunger in her friend that she'd brought back herself from the land of the djinn. Her own was with her yet, though its edge was duller now; and besides, it was late and she'd been serving delights all evening and never had the chance to snatch a mouthful . . .

"Small pickings" Sherett had said, but the woman lied. Nor had the leavings from the feast been distributed among the men outside, despite their need; the tireless Yaman and her cohorts must have given them plainer fare. Sherett brought the girls to the same long chamber where they'd eaten the previous night; they found it already full of women sitting quietly around a steaming array of dishes heaped high. Too weary to eat with any fervour, they were nibbling while they murmured softly between themselves.

Neither of the girls would let that restraint inhibit them; nor did they need Sherett's injunction to sit and eat, and save the talking till later. They headed for the nearest clear space they could see, and were reaching for food almost before they'd settled onto the carpet.

Flavour didn't matter, it was bulk alone that counted. They chewed and swallowed with frantic haste, and couldn't have spoken if they'd wanted to, so busy their mouths were. Not till she'd worked off that first demanding appetite did Elisande begin to taste what she was eating. Sherett passed her a bowl of rice bright with saffron, fragrant with spices, studded with chicken and almonds; she worked it into little balls with her fingers, popped one into Julianne's mouth and another into her own, and decided that this feast was none the worse for having been served and picked over once already. Time to slow down, time to enjoy both the food and her friend's simple company, uncomplicated by where she'd been or what she'd done; it was a time to feel truly appreciative of that custom that forbade earnest talk during a meal. Simply to have Julianne safe back was enough for now. Even Elisande's ever-burning curiosity faded to a glimmer under the combined effects of exhaustion, relief and a comfortably full stomach, especially when she had the chance to fill it fuller yet. Desert wisdom, that was, to eat whenever and as much as she could; it was some consolation to find that she could still be wise, in this at least . . .

JULIANNE OUTLASTED HER, even so. Sherett laughed at them both, even as she pressed them to another sweet, another little cake of pressed fruits and nuts. When at last Julianne cried for mercy, with a plea of imminent bursting, the older woman said, "Come, then. I know you are tired, but it is not good to sleep too soon after a gorging, and you two have gorged like the children you are. Besides, Julianne is as filthy as a goat; and she has a story to tell, which Hasan has charged me to hear . . ."

She led them to the hammam. Elisande stripped off her gorgeous silk dress with only a brief pang of regret, then helped Julianne, who was fumbling with sore fingers at the ties of her robe. Baking-hot rocks cracked and split as Sherett transferred them with tongs from a glowing brazier to a tub of water; steam billowed about the girls, making their bodies gleam with sweat.

"Lie down, Julianne, here on this bench. I have oils which will soothe you, where you ache."

Julianne stretched out obediently, her head cradled on her folded arms; she groaned softly under Sherett's hands, yelping occasionally as hard fingers dug deep into stiff muscle. Elisande grinned, and searched a crowded shelf until she found sharp files to attend to her friend's broken nails, balm for her skinned palms.

She knelt at the bench's end, took one of Julianne's abused hands and began her work.

"Tell us, then," she said softly "You can talk and suffer, it'll take your mind off the pain. And you'll go to sleep else, however much she hurts you. Trust me, you will . . ."

*   *   *

JULIANNE TOLD THEM a story about a ghûl with wings, a djinni and a mountain; but her mind was drifting between worlds, she told it briefly and badly. Eventually Sherett hauled her upright, and threw a bundle of dried herbs onto the brazier. Smoke mingled with the steam, adding a sharp, bitter perfume that had both girls coughing in chorus.

"Breathe deeply. It will clear your heads."

"What, will it bring our brains out through our noses?" Elisande grumbled, rubbing at stinging eyes.

Sherett only laughed, and said again, "Breathe deeply."

After a minute, it was true, the weariness had lifted from Elisande's thoughts, if not her body. Julianne's voice had been slurring on the very edge of sleep, but it was brisker now as she said, "I'm sorry. The Sharai value tales, I know, and I was spoiling mine. Redmond deserves a better eulogy than I can give him, and I did not see his death; but let me try again."

This time they questioned her as she spoke, to draw out more detail; anything she'd seen or heard might prove to be important. When she talked of seeing Redmond dead, she wept a little, which brought tears to Elisande's eyes as well. At her first mention of the djinni, though, Elisande straightened her back, pushed away her sorrow to wait for a better time, and said, "You didn't ask it any questions, did you?"

"No, love, I didn't."

"Are you sure?"

"Positive, yes. It helped me, I think, not to do that."

"It is not always a mistake," Sherett said slowly, "to put yourself in debt to a djinni. Sometimes the answer to the question is worth any price."

"I got no answer worth the having, when I questioned this djinni," Julianne replied.

Elisande snorted. "You didn't put any question worth the asking; but what it told us was still important. It sent us here."

"Which cannot have been incidental," Sherett said. "And remember, the djinn do not lie. If you ask, they will tell you true. It's worth bearing in mind, children. Your paths cross this djinni's more often than is comfortable, but it clearly means you no harm."

"No—but it can cause harm regardless," Elisande retorted. "Redmond is dead, who only came this way because of us."

"Because of me," Julianne corrected her. "He said so. He would have gone to Surayon with me."

"True, he would—and then come to Rhabat after you were safe. The ghûls wouldn't have killed him, no, or not today; but the desert might have done, or else his injuries. He knew the dangers, sweet, but he couldn't have kept away, where his voice might have helped our people live."

Julianne gazed at her doubtfully. "In which case his death was not the djinni's doing. Was it?" When Elisande gave her no answer, she shook her head and went on, "In any case, I asked no question of the djinni this time. Even when I was terrified, I remembered that. And it gave me courage to finish the climb, although it was—equivocal, about what I did. It said again, it might be better to let my father die; and the djinn do not lie, so it meant that truly. But it helped me anyway. I don't understand it . . ."

"Why should you? You're human, and it is not. Just don't forget that it used you, it uses us both; and its uses are not for our good."

"Julianne's father is alive," Sherett said dryly, "and I say that is good for both our peoples, whether my husband has his war or not. True, I have not the djinni's sight; but what the djinn see, of whatever future, they see dimly. That's why they are equivocal sometimes, Julianne. If you must ask a djinni questions, never ask it what's to come; it may deceive you without meaning to."

"Be safe," Elisande grunted, "and never ask it anything at all. It might send you to the uttermost east next time, with me dragging along like an unwilling dog in your wake."

Sherett smiled, and rose to her feet. "Those who talk

often with the djinn are not doomed to live safely. Go where it sends you, Julianne—"

"—And marry where I must. I know." Her gaze met the older woman's, challengingly; Sherett's smile didn't falter, though it perhaps acquired a quizzical edge.

"Take your time here, children," was all she said, "linger as long as you please. There is cool juice to drink, in the pot on the shelf there. Lisan, your friend still has claws that need your attention."

Then she was gone, a figure quickly lost in the steam. Julianne stared after her; Elisande reached for her friend's hand, where she hadn't finished working on her nails.

"Julianne," she said quietly, with no tease at all in her voice, "are you going to marry Hasan?"

"Oh, I expect so, yes. The day you marry Marron . . ."

Elisande's file twisted in her hand, came close to stabbing deep into Julianne's thumb; she barely caught it or herself in time. "Claws indeed," she murmured, working busily away. "But I thought Marron was going to marry Jemel?"

"Not he, he's married already. To Sieur Anton d'Escrivey. Oh, Elisande, why's it all such a mess?"

"Ask the djinn, sweet, don't ask me. If it's that important to you, ask the djinn . . ."

"Perhaps I would, if I knew where to find one. Elisande, I'm sorry . . ."

"It doesn't matter."

Of course it didn't matter, that was why she wasn't crying. Her face was only wet with sweat and Julianne couldn't see it anyway, she'd turned away deliberately to make sure. When she felt fingers stroking gently through her damp hair, it was just a sign of friendship, nothing more.

AFTER SUCH A day, such an evening, such a meal and such a bath, she should have slept as Julianne did beside her, like the dead. But Redmond was truly dead, and she

couldn't forget that, she couldn't stop thinking about him as
he had been, wise and kind, the father of her heart; she
couldn't stop wondering how he had died, how terrible it
had been, whether he'd felt much pain before the end. That
old man had known too much pain in his life; he hadn't deserved such an ending, ripped away too soon for all of
them, far too soon for the world which needed him maybe
even more than she did.

And when she turned her thoughts away from him, there
was always Marron waiting, and that was a different kind
of need altogether and a different kind of loss. She was sure
now that he was lost; Julianne's barbed reaction confirmed
it to her. Which likely meant that he had never been there to
be won, that she'd been a fool from the start; but he might,
he just might have been foolish too. She thought he almost
had been, those days they'd spent together in the land of the
djinn. Another country, truly—here he was all Jemel's,
when he was not all his own. Nothing of hers, whichever.
He might not have realised that yet, but Jemel had, she
thought.

So she turned between Redmond and Marron, and could
face neither one of them, and couldn't shut them out; and
so at last she rose up off her pallet and slipped quietly out
of the chamber, anxious neither to wake Julianne nor to dis-
turb anyone else in the house. She couldn't face questions,
and she couldn't face company just now.

Occasional lights had been left burning through the corridors; by their kindness, memories of her time here before
and an odd fumbling moment where the dark was too much
for her eyes and her hands had to do their work for them,
she came down to the hammam by ways that didn't take
her through the central hall. She didn't at all trust Sherett
not to be still watchful. She thought that woman could read
minds, perhaps. For sure she read Julianne's; Elisande preferred to keep her thoughts private, and especially a night-
time jaunt such as this.

The two girls had been last to bed, or last of those who
would see a bed tonight. The hammam was still as they'd

left it—promising each other that they'd tidy in the morning, knowing full well that come morning others would be up and tidying before them—with even their discarded clothes lying where they'd laid or dropped them. Her bright silk Elisande had folded and left neatly on a bench; Julianne's torn and dust-drenched desert robe, a boy's robe at that, had been simply abandoned on the floor, only kicked a little out of sight.

There was still a flicker of light in the lamps here, enough for Elisande to find it without groping. She stooped to retrieve it, felt it damp under her grip—even here in the antechamber to the baths proper, the walls glistened with water, and there were pools in the uneven floor—but shrugged and pulled it on regardless, tying it swiftly with long-practised fingers. How often had she dressed as a boy? Times without number; and not only for reasons of disguise. It was quicker, easier, more practical by a distance . . .

Tonight, she had another reason yet. She pulled the hood up to cover her growing hair—then checked, scowled, and pulled it down again. Went to search that useful shelf in the hammam, and found a fine pair of scissors. No mirror, the Catari god had forbidden the making of images and the imams had ruled against reflections too; but she didn't need a mirror, she'd done this often enough by touch alone. And with a knife, too. These scissors were a luxury . . .

As she chopped, she thought of knives and wondered whether to go back for hers. Decided not, the added risk wasn't worth it. She felt half naked without them; but she'd have felt simply stupid padding entirely naked through the house with a blade in each hand like some God-sworn fanatic assassin. Perhaps, if she didn't have her knives, she'd be more likely to avoid any situation that might come down to knifework. That would be no bad thing. Tempers would be short and hot out there in the cold night; she'd be wise to tread carefully, if she trod as a boy.

Besides, she could always keep these fine sharp scissors

in her sleeve, just in case of any trouble she couldn't duck away from . . .

At last she was done cutting, and there was more mess for someone to find in the morning; something more for Julianne to be distressed by, she thought without a pang of guilt, and for Sherett to disapprove of. Let her, let them all. She very much wanted to be a boy again tonight, as best she could contrive it. For herself, though, this time, not for Marron. Which was all the pride she could find, and barely, perhaps barely enough.

She left all her hair where it lay in a circle on the floor, and walked out running her fingers through the rough crop on her scalp, as crude as any desert lad might wear it. Now there was only the guard at the door to be evaded, and that she could manage without fuss.

There were few children here at the moment, just as there had been few men beyond the sheikhs and their retinues, few women too; but all the children in Rhabat slept in the women's quarters. They had their own part of it, that they called the Children's House. The boys still resented it, though, from about the age of six until they were allowed to eat and sleep with their fathers, after their tenth birthday. Penned up by women, of course they sought to escape, to have wild adventures, particularly at night; of course the guards knew, and of course said nothing if they saw a figure slip out through an opened screen. They remembered their own boyhoods, and stood silent and blind.

Not only boys could be wild. Elisande had exploited their licence time and again during her time here, frustrated beyond endurance by the restrictions placed on her after the freedom she'd known in Surayon. Even though she'd been allowed to dress and run as a child here rather than a woman, still she'd needed to break out, to be unwatched and unprotected under the stars.

Alone or with like-minded friends, she'd followed this path so often: along the passage which was always well-lit for the sake of wakeful children, and into the boys' dormitory; on tiptoe between their pallets—wondering as she al-

ways had whether they truly were all asleep, or whether
some were kindly snoring for the sake of their wandering
sister, not to spoil her adventure—until she came to the
window, the one particular window where somehow no
adult ever seemed to notice that the barring screen was
loose, and could be swung quite easily open, so . . .

THEY MIGHT HAVE been more watchful of the children
tonight, with the valley under siege and the skies so dangerous; but that very danger meant that the guards were watching the skies tonight, as were all the men who lingered
along the poolside. No one seemed to mark her, as she
slipped from the window and jumped to ground.

Hood up and head low for added security, she mingled
quickly with the restive tribesmen as they surged aimlessly
this way and that. She kept her elbows tight to her sides and
dodged through the crowd, trying to avoid any contact for
fear that it might be interpreted as a jostle; that kind of adventure she could well live without.

In truth, she wasn't really seeking any adventure at all.
She'd only hoped to leave grief and misery behind her, in
her vacated bed, as escape into sleep had proved impossible. Now that she was out and on the move, though, she
found that she'd brought both with her. It was no great surprise. What she had tried to run from was inside her head,
riding her thoughts with spurs and whip; even as she
ducked and weaved, she felt the twin pains of her twin
losses goading her.

If she couldn't sleep and she couldn't run, she might as
well sit down. Her body felt as leaden as her spirits. She
found a clear space by the water's edge and sank onto her
haunches, hugging her knees against her chest like any
Sharai lad out too late and trying to keep inconspicuous.

She didn't know why the men around her were twisting
their necks to stare upward all the time. Even the imams
hadn't been able to forbid the world from making its own
reflections; she could see all the sky laid out before her,

across the still surface of the pool. The stars glimmered like silver chasing on a blue-black blade; she looked for Redmond's face among their patterns, but couldn't find it.

Behind her, she heard voices:

"What of the Ghost Walker, then, what does he do to help us?"

"Nothing. What can he do?"

"He could see us all safe, he could take us out of this trap . . ."

"It is forbidden. Only the Sand Dancers may go with him, to the other world. You know that."

"I know that they say that, not he. They speak against the imams—but there are none here, imams or Dancers. And I know that he has taken the tribeless one before this, and a girl."

"The girl is of his own people, and does not respect our laws any more than he does. And I have heard that the tribeless one is a Dancer, or claims to be."

"No matter what he claims, or what he is. The Ghost Walker does not follow the imams' teachings; so I say he could save us, if he chose."

"But he chooses to dally with his tribeless boy instead, that's the only one that he'll save. They're off together now, in this world or the other, it makes no difference to them. Nor to us. They play at lovers under the stars, while we wait for the 'ifrit."

"Do they so?"

"Aye, I saw them. Heads together and holding hands, walking through our people as though they did not see us, eyes only for each other . . ."

You would have let them go as if you did not see them, Elisande thought furiously, *if you did not need him so . . .*

But she couldn't sit and listen to such talk, repeated again and again, as it must be in this forum of fear and despair. Nor could she challenge what they said, nor what they assumed: not without revealing herself, laying herself open to their scorn. A Patric girl caught playing at Sharai boy, trying to be what she was not, what he wanted—no.

She had too much pride for that. And she had no defence to offer, for Marron. For all she knew, it might all be true; most of it certainly was.

She stayed silent, then, until they'd moved on; then she stood and moved on in her turn. *Running again,* she thought, withering herself under the lash of her own hot contempt; but she moved regardless. Restlessly, pointlessly, she wandered along past the stables, where she could hear horses whickering, infected with her own insomnia or their masters' anxiety; and so to the pool's end and further still, looking only to be private, to find some place where she could hear nothing but her own bitter thoughts.

She came through to the smaller pool, but there were men there too, sitting around fireglows in the trees' shadows: guards, she thought, against an attack from the gully that led to the Dead Waters. She stole past, hugging the rock wall to avoid their eyes and their suspicious questions, and went on.

There were guards in the gully too, but they had climbed high onto ledges from where they could shoot either up or down, whether the 'ifrit came from the air or the water. One spotted her and called out, "You, boy—go back! This is no place to be foolish, and no time to be alone. Go back, and ask your father for a beating . . ."

She ignored him, trusting that he'd not come down after her. Nor did he; one moronic boy wasn't worth the risk of an adult warrior.

At the gully's end, where it opened onto the waterfront, she was afraid of meeting more guards on the ground, as she had before when she came here with Marron. That post had been abandoned, though; not even Hasan could order or persuade men, even his own men to stay so close to the Dead Waters after dark. Nor would it have been the fear of 'ifrit that backed their refusal, if he'd been so heedless as to give such orders.

She wondered if it was strange in her, to fear guards but not the legends of the Waters. The first would only send her back, the second might destroy her. But discovery meant humiliation, now and later; she thought she might almost prefer destruction. At least that would bring some sense of drama with it, a potent ending, even if it were terrible: something for the Sharai to weave a tale around. And perhaps she was after all looking for adventure, a match for Julianne's, to give a purpose to her being in Rhabat. *Lisan of the Dead Waters,* the djinni had called her; and here were the Waters, and here was she, and surely there should be some acknowledgement of that, surely something should *happen* . . . ?

Oh, she was thinking wildly and acting worse, acting stupid. She could almost laugh at herself, for being so childish. Except that she'd forgotten how bad the air smelled out here, sick and sour; she'd choke, if she tried to laugh.

Breathing shallowly, she stooped to pick up a stone and skimmed it out across the water, watching how it bounced and skittered before it sank, how the ripples spread.

Well, she'd announced her presence now, she'd made her gesture. She could turn and go back at any moment she chose; she had no need to stand and watch those ripples die in the heavy water, nothing compelled her to wait breathlessly at the edge of the pavement there, scanning the dull, dark surface for any response. The djinn might not lie, but even they could be simply wrong, they didn't always see the future truly . . .

Wait she did, though, long after there seemed no point in waiting longer. Even the stars' reflection was blurred into drab pewter, on this poisoned water; she thought that was a symbol of her disappointment, now that she felt brave enough to be disappointed by the lack of any answer to her stone. Only a hint of breeze made any stir in that reflection; she was about ready to leave, when the thought suddenly struck her that there was no breeze here in this deep bay, the rank air moved not at all against her skin . . .

Startled, she stared and saw it again more clearly, a definite break in the ghost-band of the stars, a ruffle on the water. A zephyr, perhaps, visible only by its effect—but a zephyr did not have to be a wind . . .

She felt abruptly clammy-cold, deeply regretting her bravado. She remembered the djinni, though, she remembered more than one djinn and the conversation earlier; she stood still, waiting, watching.

As it came closer, she saw that the disturbance was within the water, not above it. The surface rippled across a broad span, as far perhaps as both her arms could reach; the ripples seemed to grow more solid, as though the water were woven into coherent strands and those strands plaited together into an endless rope, the coils of it twisting down deep into the dark.

Then it rose like a pillar, like a shaft thrust up from below; the rope climbed the air and bound itself into a body three times her height and width, a body that shimmered darkly and stank worse than the air or the water had before.

This was death, the most intimately she'd ever faced it. Her mouth worked, she felt lips and jaw and tongue all move, but no sound came; she swallowed dryly and tried again, hurling words out as she had hurled that stone, hard and flat and low and with a tremendous effort of will, acting against everything that she knew was wise.

"Are you a djinni?"

Just that, four simple words; but they changed her world as they were designed to do, as they had to.

The creature stopped, in its relentless progress over or through that foul water. It was silent for a moment, she might almost have thought that it hesitated; then it said, "Yes."

Just as simple, just as direct. One word. Elisande felt it close about her like the jaws of a beetle, or the jaws of a trap.

She was no prey, though, it would not kill her now; if she were a victim, at least that was deliberately so. She was almost not pretending as she sat on the chill, slimy stone of the waterfront, folded her legs like a man and said, "Well, then. Tell me your name and how you came to this, then say how I may serve you. I am called Elisande, though one of your kind has named me otherwise."

A hiss, like an overboiling pot damping a fire; the water grew choppy for a moment all around where the djinni stood or balanced or was rooted, where its spinning darkness met the darkness of the sea.

"Perhaps I am not djinni now," it said, and its voice was as murky as its substance, far from the high clarity of its kind. "Once I was, and I was called Esren Filash Tachur; but the djinn are free, they wander where they will and are enslaved by no lesser creatures."

"The djinn are changeless too, or so I've heard it. Gold does not lose its lustre, for being buried in the earth. You must have been in these waters for many years, Djinni Tachur; there are stories of you that have been told through generations." *And each of them a cruel one,* but she had no need to say that; it would know.

"I have been centuries in these waters. I came for pleasure, because they were beautiful; now I am trapped here, and they are foul to me."

"To us also." She tried to think of the Dead Waters as a place of beauty, and could not do it. Perhaps they had been, though; perhaps the death had followed the djinni, and not the other way about.

"I have made them so," it said, confirming. "Nothing lives here, but I have killed it. Your kind, too, I have killed many of them. Some I asked for aid, I *asked* and still they would not give it, and so died. Now I do not ask, I simply kill. People come to me in my anger; they are stupid. You have said it, tales are told."

"Indeed. I have heard them; and yet I came. We are a stupid people, perhaps. But I am in your debt, djinni, I acknowledge it, and I will pay your price. Tell me first, though, how it is that you are trapped. I had not known that anything could trap a djinni against its will or against its power . . ."

"Our will is our power, and so was I trapped. This lake, this puddle enchanted me; so small a thing, but I found it worth my time. I had enough of that, I thought, to choose to waste it here. And so I did, and welcomed all as though it were my home, as though I dwelt here like some mean spirit in a bond of flesh. Even the 'ifrit, when they came, I made them free of this water as though it were my own.

"I showed them my vanity, and so they snared me. They had intended it; the 'ifrit have some sense of what will come, as we do, though mine was darkened then. They penned me in a trap of my own making. I spread myself through all the water that this sea contains, and so they caught me, as a rock will catch a net and hold it."

"I don't understand. What rock?" she asked, deliberately deepening her debt.

"A rock they had, that I had not seen: a stone, a pebble they had brought from my own world. A piece of the living land, that has great power here. They use the same to control their ghûls; I had never thought they might use that trick against a djinni. They dropped it into the water, into me; it lies at my heart, and I cannot touch it. It burns, it holds me here and binds me to their will. They have stolen that which makes me djinn, my freedom."

"Tell me what it is that they would have you do." Good: that was a command, and not a question. It was a hard game, this, a balance of power: to put herself in its debt but not too far too soon, to keep it well aware how much it needed her good will.

"Nothing, yet. They have only kept me here these many years, far from my land and my kind. Caged as I am, I cannot see beyond the moment; they have blinded me to what will come." There was a hissing hatred in its voice; time itself could mean little to ageless spirit, but imprisonment within it must be bitter, worse surely than the physical containment. "They are here now, though, in numbers, as they have not been before; I think they will use me soon."

So did Elisande. She had a brief and terrible vision of the djinni's rising higher and broader than it was, as it surely could do: of its drawing up vast quantities of water and then hurtling like a dust-storm through the gully, dragging

ever more water in its wake. It could fill the valley, she
thought, flood Rhabat, drown every man penned in there.
Why the 'ifrit would want that she couldn't imagine, how
slaying a human army would satisfy any need of theirs; but
they had made the pen and they held here a tool, a mighty
weapon. It couldn't be coincidence.

"Djinni," she said slowly, carefully, "you have answered
me two questions," *and given me much information besides, but never mind that,* "and I stand in your debt. I will
help you, I will free you if I am able—but there is a further
price. You must answer me one more question."

Its body surged and shivered; she fought not to flinch
from a hail of stinging water. "Debtors do not bargain," it
said.

"I do. Come, you have faced this with others. Whether
you begged or threatened, they refused you what you
need." She was guessing, but not wildly.

"They did. They died."

"Even so. One more question, djinni; it is not so much to
demand, in exchange for your freedom."

"Very well, then. Ask."

She took a breath, nerved herself to it, and spoke. "If I
free you from this bond, will you serve me instead? To do
my bidding for a time, for a short time, here or elsewhere?"

All the waters of the bay were churning suddenly; the
pillar of darkly solid sea loomed above her, spinning frenziedly. She had been spattered before; now she was soaked
in a moment, gasping under a weight of falling water. She
thought more might follow, she thought that in its rage it
might engulf her altogether and so lose its hope and her
own.

"Come," she shouted, "you have been enslaved for centuries; slay me now, and you may be a slave for ever. Or do
as I ask for a little while, and then be free." For how long?
A day, a week, a year? No—it wasn't the length of service
that enraged it, the djinn were all but immortal. Let it be for
the period that she might be mourning Marron, then: a poor
substitute, but something at least that she could call her

own. "For the length of my brief lifetime, djinni, come when I call for you and act at my command. Will you do that? I swear I'll not abuse the privilege, I'll take no more than I need from you. Now answer the question, and answer truly."

It might, of course, answer her no; that would still be an answer. But then she might fail in the task that it set her, she might not try too hard. They were both gambling here, girl and djinni; she might fail anyway . . .

Eventually it spoke again, it gave the answer she sought. "I will," it said, no more than that.

"Very well, then. I stand in your debt," and she did stand then, dragging herself up against the trembling in her legs and the drag of her saturated robe, the stinking chill of it setting all her skin to shiver. "Tell me how to free you."

"The stone lies deep in the water. Swim down, and bring it out."

She opened her mouth—and closed it sharply on a question, took a moment to rephrase before she said, "I do not know if I can dive that deeply; and I will never find one stone, in all this sea."

"You will know it, when you see. I cannot touch the stone, but I can bring you to it."

That at least she didn't doubt; whether she'd survive the swim was another matter. If she refused, though, it would kill her anyway; better to die trying.

Wondering just a little quite why she wanted a reluctant djinni for servant, she stripped off her sodden robe and let it fall. The djinni drew away, sinking its bulk down into the water again till there was only a slender column of dancing dark to mark its watchfulness.

The sea's surface fell still, lying dead and drear before her. She took slow, deep breaths, barely tasting the reek of the air against the sour tang of fear in her mouth; then she lifted her arms and dived cleanly, neatly into the Dead Waters.

And felt the djinni receive her, sucking her brutally down and down, into the uttermost dark.

SIX

Breaking Through

MARRON HAD WATCHED it all, from where he stood
with Jemel at the foot of the hidden stair.

Neither one of them had moved or spoken. Too far away
to help Elisande if the djinni attacked her, there was nothing they could do but witness, and be prepared to take the
news to her father—and to Julianne, which would be
worse, he thought—if it should come to that.

They saw her dive, and they saw also how the waters did
not close above her head: how they opened, rather, so that it
was as though she dived into a twisting funnel, a wormhole
whose mouth writhed away across the bay and out into the
open sea, further than even Marron's eyes could follow in
the dark.

"Will she live?" Jemel asked, in a whisper.

"You know the djinn better than I."

"I know not to trust them, although they do not lie; and I
know not to ask them questions. She did it deliberately.
Why did she do that?"

"Because she needed to," Marron said briefly. For her

people's sake, or for Jemel's? Perhaps; but he had seen her eyes on him at the feast, as he thought Jernel had not, and he understood a little of her turmoil. For her own sake, then, because she could: because she was distraught and desolate, because she would risk more than her life to win something, anything from this night of loss. *A gift of questions, yes . . .*

He could understand that. Who better? His eyes turned against his will towards the north, towards a man he could not see and should not ever see again; he dragged them back to find Jemel, there as he was sworn to be, anxious now about Elisande but still instantly aware of Marron's gaze and responding to it. Dark eyes huge and liquid in the dark, black hair and skin of bronze that would gleam gold under the sun, that was stretched over whipcord muscle and prominent bone, no spare flesh on him anywhere and yet he was constantly urging Marron to eat more, as bad as Elisande like that . . .

Her name brought a memory with it, that glimpse they'd had of her body as she dived, lean as any boy and as graceful. Thinking of bodies, thinking of boys, he thought of Aldo; and then, inevitably, of Sieur Anton, his only full-grown man, a body so different, scarred and strong and demanding . . .

He twisted around to stare into the dark of the open tunnel, to escape them all, even Jemel; and was not allowed to. Long fingers gripped his waist, a stubbled chin touched his cheek, a soft voice whispered, "I am not so easily left behind, Ghost Walker. Not in this world."

"You none of you are," Marron muttered, grumbled almost; but he was learning to accept his memories, as he was learning to be what he was. He leaned back into Jemel's resilience, accepted a kiss, barely hesitated before turning his head for another.

It was an effort then to tug himself free, to say, "This is not what we came here for."

"No—though everyone will think it was."

"Will they? To the edge of the Dead Waters, to play boys' games with each other?"

"This is no game, Marron. The Sharai know that, if your people do not. And there is no privacy in all of Rhabat tonight."

"And none for the Ghost Walker anywhere, where there are Sharai. My people call it no game but a sin, Jemel, a crime against the God. Men have died for it, and boys also. But we came to watch . . ."

To guard, because he did not believe that the 'ifrit had had no purpose in slaying the imam above. A guard was needful, but even Hasan would not listen; the men in the gully were enough, he'd said. And so Marron had come himself, and so Jemel, as ever at his side to watch with him—and to watch over him, of course, and perhaps simply to watch him also. Jemel could read his mind sometimes, he knew that Marron had looked at that climbing tunnel and thought of running.

Marron wouldn't do it now, when danger threatened his friends and all the people in Rhabat; but still he'd come back to the tunnel. It preyed on his mind. A way out of the valley, but 'ifrit had not blocked this as they had the siq, they had only seized and guarded it; a way into the valley, but 'ifrit did not need it, they could fly at will . . .

He wondered very much what else might be coming down that tunnel, and had stationed himself here against the chance of learning. Elisande had been a complete surprise; he thought perhaps she had surprised herself.

"We have two ways to watch now," Jemel said.

"True. There's nothing else that we can do for Elisande; you look for her, I'll guard the gateway."

He meant to move a few paces into the dark, perhaps up and around the first winding corner of the passage, to give him rest from more than Jemel's questing hands; he needed to feel those eyes not on him, he couldn't think under the weight of that implacable possession.

It was hard to move even such a little distance, though, and leave Jemel behind him. All the more reason to do it—

*a delightful cage is still a cage, and soon turns dank and
deadly: ask the djinni in the water there*—and swiftly: if he
lingered over the walk, he thought Jemel might follow him.
What use is a guard who will not kill an enemy? They'd
had that argument already, more than once. He needed to be
gone, suddenly and ruthlessly, if he wanted to be free of the
other's company. Jemel couldn't follow him where no light
burned.

But still, it was hard to do; and he'd taken no more than
a step before he paused, and was briefly too glad of the
chance. He'd heard something from the tunnel, a distant
whisper, the rhythm of light feet; it took him a moment to
remember what this meant, that it wasn't simply a gift for
his sake, an excuse to stay out in the open with his friend.

This was what he'd been waiting for, what he'd been
afraid of; what he'd been certain of, that something was
coming and that it was not 'ifrit.

Some*one* was coming. Those were human steps. He concentrated, and was almost sure they were Sharai: bare feet
for certain, backed by a man's breathing and the faint rustle
of a rough woollen robe.

Jemel had heard nothing yet; his eyes were fixed on the
water, looking for any sign of Elisande's returning. Marron
reached out to touch his shoulder, and gestured him back
with a jerk of the head. No words: the rising shaft before
him carried sounds a great distance. No man's natural ears
were as sharp as his, but even so he was cautious. He eased
Dard from its sheath, glad to have that sword at his waist.
With the speed and strength he borrowed from the Daughter, he could fight with a Sharai scimitar or any weapon
else; but nothing felt so native to his hand, so well balanced, so much an extension of his arm. Besides, this blade
had been given him by Sieur Anton. This blade had cut
Sieur Anton, indeed, as the knight's blade Josette had cut
him. There was a connection there that he treasured, dark
though it was. And Dard's whole history was shadowed by
betrayal. That was another connection; Marron felt bonded
to the blade, body and soul.

That he had sworn never to kill again, with Dard or the
Daughter or any weapon else, was a complication he would
have to face time and again. The better he fought, he
thought, the easier it should be; and so he was glad to have
Dard in his hand, as he faced the tunnel's black mouth.

Glad to have Jemel at his back, too, a fine swordsman
himself with no inhibitions about killing. Though it would
be as much a betrayal of his oath to let his friend kill for
him. Marron glanced over his shoulder and waved Jemel
further off; the Sharai lad hesitated, before taking a few
grudging steps backward. Oaths in conflict, Marron's and
Jemel's; he wondered if all his life would be a series of be-
trayals, if he could ever find a hope of peace and trust.

There was the faintest glimmer of light in the tunnel
now, fading the black to grey: the man coming carried a
torch, or a lamp. Marron stepped to the side, not to stand
too obviously in the gateway.

The glow grew, but then died abruptly before its source
or its bearer were visible. No fool, this man, to bring a light
out into the open, where there might be guards. No friend
either, Sharai though he might be. But that had never been
likely, with 'ifrit at the upper entrance to the passage.

Marron held Dard close to his side, to kill any glimmer
of starlight on the steel. Not so the man in the tunnel: his
blade was what Marron saw first, the curve of a drawn
scimitar reflecting the glow of the sky. And then the figure
that held it, edging out onto the pavement, cautious and
alert. A hiss of breath, as the man must have seen Jemel
outlined against the water; Marron moved immediately, to
step between them.

Another hiss, this time of recognition. Marron had
guessed already, who the man must be; now he knew.

The scimitar's point rose against him, just beyond Dard's
reach; Morakh's voice rose behind it.

"Have you been waiting for me, Ghost Walker?"

"Why not? You are my servant, sworn and promised . . ."

"I give no more service to an unbeliever. You are a freak,

a thief; what you have is not yours, and will be taken back. By your death, Patric."

"Is that why you give your service to the 'ifrit instead?"

"The 'ifrit do not deny our God; and they will do what has been promised us, they will drive your people from our land. With me and mine among them, the Sand Dancers following a true Ghost Walker."

"Come, then. Slay me, and take what you seek . . ."

Morakh laughed harshly, contemptuously. "You are like their ghûls, an animal hard to kill. One cut, and I face not you but what you have stolen. I will kill you, thief, with the single blow that is needful; but not here, not yet. Not while you are on guard and ready to use my own against me. Instead . . ."

Instead he was gone, suddenly vanished, and Marron faced only the emptiness of air. He whirled around to cry a warning to Jemel, too late; he saw Morakh behind his friend, saw the scimitar flash across his throat, saw Jemel flail and stagger, and fall.

He plunged towards the Dancer, roaring, and could have killed then despite all his oaths. But Morakh disappeared again, and this time even Marron's eyes could not find him.

One raging stare around was all that he could spare. Seeing nothing that moved anywhere this side of the gully, he let the man go—*for now, for the moment, not for long*—and the sword too, and fell down beside Jemel.

IT HAD BEEN a hasty, almost a clumsy blow, and Jemel had been twisting away from the blade as it hacked; what might have half-severed his head—and had been meant to, surely—had in fact not cut near so deep.

Deep enough, though, Marron thought grimly, seeing how blood gushed from Jemel's torn throat, how he gasped desperately for air he could not draw.

The Daughter surged in Marron's veins, in response to so much blood. He fought it down with a desperate effort and ripped the sleeve from his robe with one hard tug, thinking as he did so that it was futile, that no bandage could hold such a wound together. Jemel was doomed, was all but dead already; anything he did would be only a gesture.

Still, he had to make the gesture. He reached to lift his friend's head, to slip the sleeve beneath his neck, and was startled to find how cold Jemel's skin felt against his fingers. Only the pulsing blood was warm. Swiftly he wrapped the sleeve around the dreadful gape of the wound, and knotted it as tight as he dared.

Jemel's lips moved, shaping a word he couldn't speak; Marron read not his own name, but Elisande's. *Lisan,* Jemel was saying.

Marron wouldn't spare even a moment of his friend's dying, to look round for any sign of the girl.

"Don't worry about Elisande," he murmured, stroking Jemel's chill, sticky forehead while the Daughter raged in his body. "The djinni will keep her alive, it needs her."

Jemel was trembling now, shaking with cold or fear; Marron wrapped his arms around his friend, but they were as useless as his improvised bandage, which was already dark and sodden.

He couldn't stem the flow of blood, he couldn't help the hoarse, rattling breathing; all he wanted was to force some heat into Jemel's body, to give him some comfort as he died, and it seemed that he couldn't do that either. He saw the world through a cast of crimson, his ears roared with the Daughter's hectic thunder; suddenly he laid Jemel down again and snatched Dard up from where he'd dropped it.

He thrust the point into the wound on his arm, and gasped as the Daughter poured out. Pain followed, but he could manage that. He let the sword fall again, lifted Jemel again, opened a doorway and stepped through into the world of the djinn.

HE DIDN'T EXPECT a miracle, he knew there was no healing to be found here. But there was warmth, at least, and light; Jemel needn't die in the bitter dark of the waterfront. Let him die in wonder, in a mystical and alien place. Perhaps Marron would bury him here too, say the *khalat* and only hope that Jemel's soul could find its own way home, while his body stayed for the djinn to ponder over. He had cut himself off from his tribe, from all his people, by his choice; let him be truly outcast, then, let him lie where none but the Ghost Walker could find him . . .

Marron stood in brightness, by the shore of a steaming golden sea. That was something for a man to look on, as he died. Perhaps that dying would be slower, here where time moved so strangely; or perhaps not. Marron bled more quickly in this world, so Jemel might also. That might be a blessing.

What was surely a blessing was the heat, striking into Marron's bones already. He found a great slab of rock, and laid Jemel atop it; and couldn't think what to do then, except to stand witness to his friend's death. But the Daughter still pulsed in the corner of his eye, in time with the blood that pulsed from his arm, the pain that wracked him now; he lifted his hand to call it back—

—and checked himself, remembering.

Lisan . . .

He'd been sorely wounded when he'd come through with Elisande, and she had healed him. She'd healed her father too, when he was struck by a killing arrow . . .

Had it been hard to leave Jemel before? It was cruelly hard now, knowing he might come back to emptiness, to absence. He resented every blink of his eyes, for fear that his friend might choose that moment to leave him.

He went, though, because he had to. Walking with his head twisted around, finding the Daughter with senses other than his eyes because he couldn't bear to take his eyes from Jemel a moment sooner than he must, he stepped backward through the doorway and was in darkness again, the land of the djinn only a dim, misty glow framed by the smoky red of the Daughter.

He turned to face the sea, seeing nothing but darkness;

and cupped his hands about his mouth and bellowed her name, "Elisande!" although he was sure that she would never hear him, wherever she was beneath that implacable surface.

He'd lied to Jemel, he wasn't at all confident of her safety, her survival even; all he had was hope. The djinni would try to keep her alive, for its own sake; but its body was close to immortal, hers was frail human flesh which it might not understand. Or she might simply fail to find or raise the stone that imprisoned it, and it was not likely to be patient with failure . . .

Marron saw nothing, heard nothing in response to his call. He glanced behind him, towards the gully, thinking of Morakh slipping unseen by the guards, a lethal servant to the 'ifrit; his greater duty might lie that way. If Jemel died without or despite Elisande, and some other died too because he'd lingered here, he'd have another burden of guilt to carry and perhaps a great one.

But he couldn't abandon his friend so long as any whisper of chance remained to save him. It was the Sharai way to be loyal even in despair, and Jemel was his sworn companion; others must face their own risk. That was Sharai also: matters came out as they were written, or as their god decreed.

He lifted hands and voice again, "Elisande! Come swiftly!"

Whether in answer or not, he didn't know and couldn't guess; but there was a surge beneath the water, and her body burst suddenly to the surface, shattering the murky image of the stars.

He thought she might be dead, she might have paid the djinni in full for failure; he could see no movement in her bobbing body. She floated face down, only her bare shoulders showing pale amid the rippling dark. Something buoyed her up, though, something propelled her toward the stone embankment where he stood; and as he watched, her head thrust upward and she gasped for air.

There were steps that led down into the water; they were

bitter cold and slimy beneath his feet, but he plunged down till he stood waist-deep and ready to receive her.

She was pushed, almost, into his arms. The steps were cold, but she was colder: as cold as Jemel, he thought, and caught like his friend in that unworld between life and death. Her body was stiff, clenched around something that she clutched against her belly; her breathing came hard and irregular, as though she had forgotten the natural way of it and had to wait, to fight against the urge until she was desperate.

He carried her up, staggering a little under the weight, and laid her out on the pavement. Her robe was close, fallen in a pool of water; he wrung it out and rubbed feverishly at her back until at last she moved, stretching out and groaning, rolling over to lie belly-up. The thing she'd held fell from her grasp then; it was a stone the size of her head, and it glowed warmly golden in the night.

Marron reached to touch her stomach, and found it hot against his fingers. She opened her eyes, staring blindly up at him and gasping like a landed fish.

There was a sudden eruption from the sea; the djinni hung above them, a pillar of swirling water.

"Break it. Break the stone . . ."

It was half command, half plea. Marron had no thought to disobey; he glanced around, saw Dard and snatched it up. Held it reversed in his hand, and brought the hilt smashing down onto the stone with all the native strength he had. Not much, with the Daughter outside his body and his arm hurting terribly; but it was enough. The stone splintered into shards that skittered wildly across the pavement.

For a moment, Marron thought that the air, perhaps the world itself had split also, unless it was simply his head. There was a high and terrible scream, and he was knocked flat by a deluge of stinking water that washed all those shards back into the sea.

He pushed himself up one-handed, and gaped around. There were the cliffs; the gully, the sky, all as they had been; but there too was the djinni, bound no longer, a spinning rod that hovered in the air close by Elisande's head.

"I am free," it said simply. Its voice was high and pure and clean; Marron wouldn't have recognised it. Pity its release hadn't cleansed the water, too . . .

"No," he returned breathlessly. "You are not free, you are sworn to Elisande. Wait, and serve."

It said nothing, but it stayed; that was, that must be enough.

He turned to her, dragging her up from the stone. "Can you stand?"

"No," she whispered, clinging to him, making him hiss with pain as her fingers dug into his bleeding arm. "Marron, I'm so cold . . ."

"I can take you where you will be warm. But you must come, Elisande. Jemel is wounded, dying; he may be dead already. If not, you might heal him, though he is dreadfully hurt."

She whimpered, struggling for balance on unsteady legs. "I feel so weak, I want healing myself—but I will try. Where is he?"

"In the land of the djinn. I took him. You will be stronger there, as you were before, for me. Come, we must hurry; Morakh is in Rhabat. I need to give warning, but I cannot leave you there. Nor can I leave the way open for you to return; I can't go far from the Daughter."

"Wait." She stood, frowning with the effort of thought; then said, "Djinni, can you—"

"Lisan, do not ask me questions again. Even now. I said that I would serve you, for the debt I owe to you; you should not put yourself in my debt also."

That startled them both; she took a precious moment to recover, before trying again. "Djinni, you can travel at will between the worlds; I think you can take me too."

"That is true."

"Good. You take me, then, to where my friend is. Marron, take back the Daughter, and go. I will do what I can."

He could ask no more. He touched his lips to hers in

gratitude, tasting bitter water and her surprise in equal measure; then he left her, pausing only to press her robe into her hands with an incoherent mutter.

HE WAS TRULY and unequivocally glad for once to have the Daughter back in his body, and not only or even largely for the relief from pain. He felt his senses reach out, as though he stood at the heart of an expanding bubble of understanding. He didn't need to look behind him to see Elisande taken over to the other world. He could hear how fast the djinni spun, so fast it unpicked the threads that divided this from that, and forced a gap between; he felt it when that rupture came, like a hole torn in everything that was solid. He heard Elisande's squawk that wasn't truly driven by her voice, only by all the air being squeezed out of her as she was plucked up and flung through. He was smiling as he felt the rupture healed from the further side; that djinni would be obedient to its oath, but it was never going to make an amenable servant. Elisande had interesting times ahead, he thought . . .

And turned his thoughts deliberately away from Elisande, and so away from Jemel also. There was no more that he could do; life or death, it lay in her hands now, and no blame to her if she failed. The wound might have been too deep, or the delay too great in fetching her. She would do all that lay in her power, and she had no responsibility else.

That same delay was much on his mind now, and all blame to him if it caused more deaths than one. For all that stretch of his senses, he couldn't find Morakh: couldn't see him ahead in the gully, couldn't hear his footsteps padding in the dark, couldn't scent him on the still, dank air. He knew the desert smell of the man, but it was too dry, too dusty a scent to survive the teeming assault of this damp, enclosed space which funnelled the reek of the Dead Waters through to meet the rich perfumes of trees and pool beyond.

Besides, none of the guards admitted to having seen a man pass this way. Morakh must have done so, but Marron thought it likely that he'd shifted from one hidden crevice to the next, blinking in and out of presence; moving like that he wouldn't have left a clean trail of scent or print to follow.

He was going to be very, very hard to find in the teeming disorder that was Rhabat. Unless his actions marked him out, unless he made himself very, very easy to find; and more even than for their centuries of patience, the Sand Dancers were famous for their stealth.

MARRON RAN THROUGH the gully and out to the lesser pool with its attendant trees. There were men on guard here too, or there were meant to be; he found them all on their feet and massing together beyond the pool, where the high walls drew close again in a narrow defile that led through to Rhabat proper. Duty was warring against some greater distraction. Marron heard it more clearly than they possibly could, but even to him it was only noise, the sound of many men shouting, each individual voice losing its purpose under the sheer volume of the others.

He elbowed his way through the crowd, moving faster even than the rumour of his coming, so that it was only as he squeezed past that he was recognised. He left a clear path uselessly in his wake, where men pressed back from his star-shadow and whispered their name for him, *Ghost Walker,* half in awe and half revulsion.

Breaking through at last, he could run again, and did; through to the bank of the greater pool, that wide and shallow stretch of water that fronted all the houses of Rhabat.

Here again there was a crush of men, along that narrow front: too many and too tightly thronged for Marron to force even his slender body between, too hot to make way for him even if he'd shouted his arrival. There were blades drawn here, the traditional truce trembled on a knife's edge, and that knife was working.

The cause lay clear to be seen, a body floating in the pool. As Elisande's had, face down and shoulders showing; but this was a man in his tribal robes, not stripped for swimming, and the clear water was clouded all around him.

Marron looked in vain for any figure of authority, who might contrive to quell the building riot. It needed Hasan, and likely several sheikhs beside; he could see none. They'd be in the hall still, in council, or else dispersed by now to their several houses. Either way they'd be trapped, held withindoors by the same press of bodies that was frustrating him. Their names and ranks would pass them through at last, but that would be too late. Those blades were sparring now, but they'd be used in earnest soon, and even one more death would splinter this small army into a dozen battling factions, tribe against tribe.

Marron did the only thing that he could think of to do; he plunged feet-first into the pool.

The bed was slippery, and loose stones shifted under his weight, but his bare feet found purchase enough to keep him upright. The water rose to his chest, and had long since given up the heat it had stolen from a day's sun; he hardly felt its chill, though, with the Daughter warm in his blood. Warm and growing warmer, growing hot as he waded slowly towards the body.

The surging crowd fell slowly still, as he'd hoped it would, as his progress was marked and followed. Even those with weapons drawn drew back from instant fighting, though they didn't sheathe their blades; even the loudest voices dropped to a low murmur. Again he heard his title, *Ghost Walker* passed from mouth to mouth.

When he reached the body, he gripped its shoulders and rolled it over in the water. A man in his middle years, a hint of white in his dark beard; his head lolled back, to show the terrible gash in his throat. Marron struggled against thoughts of Jemel—was he living yet or dead already, had Elisande come too late?—and against the Daughter also, as it reacted fiercely to the blood that swirled around him. All the blood this body had contained, he thought, was in the water now.

He turned to face the staring line of men, hundreds there were, there must be, massed along that bank.

"You all know me," he cried, "you know what I am, and you know that I owe allegiance to none of your tribes. Tell me, who is he?"

A dozen voices answered him, in chorus: "Bensallah, of the Kauram."

"Very well. How did this happen?"

This time the answers were more various. He had been slain, cowardly murdered, by the hand of the Ib' Dharan, or of the Saren, or of the Beni Rus. Knives and scimitars were raised again, as other voices heatedly denied the accusations.

"Enough!" Marron bellowed. "Who saw him die?"

A babble that dwindled as Marron emphasised, "I do mean saw him die, saw the blow, saw who made the blow. Who among you saw that?"

Silence followed; at last a single voice said, "He was walking alone, towards his fellows. I saw, I saw a shadow rise behind him, and then he fell . . ."

"You saw a shadow. A shadow from what tribe, could you see that?"

"It is dark, Ghost Walker, and I was not close."

"The eyes of the Sharai are sharp—or said to be."

"None the less. I cannot say, I could not see."

"Could you see the tribal ties of the victim, could you see his face?"

"Of course. I saw he was Kauram. And the attacker drew his head back, to use a knife; I saw then that it was Bensallah, I knew him."

"You saw that clearly, but not even the dress of the attacker?"

"I—no, I did not."

"Could it be that the attacker wore a black robe, with no tribal ties?"

A murmur ran through the crowd, at that; Marron lifted his voice above it.

"There is a Sand Dancer at large in Rhabat. He fights for the 'ifrit, and is here plainly to sow dissension among the tribes; you have seen how easy that is. Let all beware; there may be other killings. Do not blame your neighbour, blame your enemy."

The murmur grew, while Marron waited; at last someone shouted, "The tribeless one is a Sand Dancer, or claims to be."

"He does not wear black," another voice objected.

"Black, blue—what difference, in the dark? He is tribeless, his dress proclaims it. Where is he?"

Marron answered, with a roar. "Jemel,"—and he used the name deliberately, to silence them—"Jemel is in the land of the djinn where I left him, or else he is in paradise by now; I do not know. His throat was cut by the same hand that did this," and he lifted the body out of the water to show how the head hung loose. "We met the Sand Dancer by the Dead Waters; he would not fight with me, but he near slew Jemel. If you want his name, I can give it you. He is called Morakh; some of you may know that name."

Many of them did, clearly, and knew enough to fear it. Marron saw a lot of sidelong glances as people checked the faces of those around them, some shuffling at the fringes of the pack; no one felt comfortable with their backs exposed.

And now, at last, here came Hasan, shouldering through to the water's edge. He leaped onto a rock that raised him above the mass, and lifted his arms to draw all eyes to him.

"You have heard," he said, his voice booming back from the high carved cliff. "Those of you who have the watch, double your guard and watch each other's safety too; danger may not only come from above. Let some of the Kauram take their dead brother, and say the *khalat* over his bones. The rest, get you to where you are safe, within walls, with those who are known to you. The man who is alone in darkness will be most at risk; where there are eyes and lights, the Dancer will not dare to venture. Go!"

Swiftly—and amazingly, to Marron—they went. That was this man's power, to cut through allegiance and ancient grievance, to speak directly to all. Marron's voice they resented, even where it spoke patent truth; Hasan's they loved, because he was of their people and yet could transcend his tribal loyalties and their own.

Some few men lingered, close beside Hasan; those he spoke to quietly, while he beckoned Marron to bring Bensallah's body to the bank. He startled them all, Marron not excepted, by jumping into the water himself to help lift it out.

The tribesmen raised the dripping body between them, and bowed their heads to Hasan; one or two even managed a brief nod to Marron, before they hurried away with their burden.

Hasan laughed shortly, before he levered himself up onto the bank. He turned then and extended an arm down to Marron, who didn't need it but took it anyway, feeling the man's strength as he was hauled bodily out of the water.

"That was well done, Ghost Walker. You have my thanks." His eyes said more: that he was surprised to find a Patric quelling a near-fatal riot in the Sharai army. Truly, now that he had time, Marron was surprised at himself. If he'd stopped to think—or if he'd still been certain where his fealty lay—he might have stood back and let them slaughter each other. He thought Rudel would have done that, at least, for the greater good of Outremer . . .

"It was you they listened to," he muttered awkwardly, against Hasan's waiting.

"No. It was you they listened to; it was me they obeyed. They know that Morakh was of my tribe, before he took the Dancers' oaths. But you had convinced them already. Come, let's find dry clothes and get warm; we have much to talk about."

More even than Hasan knew; Marron remembered

Elisande, and the djinni in the water. But then, inevitably, he remembered Jemel.

"I have to see my friend . . ."

"Marron, you have said it; living or dead, Jemel is beyond any man's harm at the moment. Nor should you go anywhere alone, at the moment. You of all men are in the greatest danger."

"And you," Marron returned briefly, though he wanted to say more; he wanted to bless Hasan for using Jemel's name so easily. That too was the man's power, he thought, to find anyone's weakness and play upon it with quiet skill.

"I, too," with another laugh. "We should stay together, then; and I am going to my house, to change my dress and sit before my fire. With my friend, I hope," and he laid an arm around Marron's shoulders and steered him off along the path, still talking. "That water is cold, and the air is colder; I am chilled to the marrow. Do you feel it? At all? Or does what you carry shield you from such crude contact with the world? You are not shivering, as I am."

Marron had to think about it, before he could frame a sensible answer. "I am aware of it," he said eventually, carefully. "I know that I am wet, and cold—but I don't feel it as I used to, before. In the same way that I don't feel hungry, or thirsty, or tired. I don't feel anything truly . . ."

"That is not true," Hasan observed. "You feel anger and confusion, those I have seen in you. And you feel love, that is evident in your concern for Jemel. And for others, the remainder of your party. Do you know where Elisande is, by the way? Sherett tells me she is not in her bed. That disturbs me now; I had thought that she might be with you. Should I have her searched for?"

Marron shook his head slowly. "She is with Jemel; I, uh, I sent her there. But you need not fear for Elisande; even here she'd be safer than any of us." Unless the djinni sought a quick end to its service, by slaying her itself or letting another do it. She should give it explicit orders, to guard her life; he must remember to tell her, if she hadn't thought of that herself . . .

Hasan eyed him oddly. "Would you care to explain that? A girl alone, secretly out of her quarters, how could she be safe?"

"She's not exactly alone any more, Hasan. I'll explain, yes—but let's get dry first. I may not feel the cold, but I can feel your shuddering."

HASAN TOOK MARRON to his own quarters, a modest room with an immodest view: set high in the house of the Beni Rus, the long, narrow chamber looked out over the breadth of Rhabat and all its length, from gully to siq.

"The sheikh has fewer stairs to climb, and far more space to play in," Hasan said as Marron looked and looked, "but from up here I command all the valley."

How he meant that, Marron wasn't subtle enough to determine; but what he meant didn't matter, the reality was plain to see. Hasan commanded all the Sharai, except perhaps the council. He might yet be denied his war; Marron thought he might wage it anyway. The tribes might follow Hasan even without their leaders' blessing.

Hasan flung open a chest and plucked out a pair of robes. One he threw to Marron. "Too broad for you, but belt it tightly, it'll do. I'm not much taller. I'll do the ties for you; my people will be upset if you wear it wrongly. Stupid to make a blood insult out of a matter of knots, but it's been so for a long time. They think they need these little things, to remain who they are. Times are changing; it frightens them, I think."

A minute later, after he had rubbed himself vigorously dry with a linen towel and then belted and knotted his own fresh robe with swift, accomplished fingers, Hasan turned to help Marron—and checked his hands, cocked his head on one side, whistled softly through bright teeth.

"You learn quickly, Marron. That is exact."

"I've been dressing Sharai for weeks now . . ."

"Not in the manner of a young man of the Beni Rus."

"Well, Jemel showed me . . ."

"Even so, we have to beat these knots into our own boys; we don't let them out of the women's quarters until they're perfect, but it can still take weeks. You must tell me your secret, I'll pass it on to Sherett . . ."

He was teasing, Marron thought, he knew it was no secret. He still wanted to hear Marron say it, though, *the Daughter remembers where I do not, it works my fingers for me.*

He wouldn't say that; he didn't like its implications. Instead he shook his head; Hasan sighed, slapped him on the shoulder and nudged him over to where the promised fire blazed.

"Whoever made this place," he said, sinking down onto the rug-covered floor with a sigh of relief, "they cut flues all through the rock, to keep us from smoking our own flesh. I offer prayers of gratitude for their souls every night that I am here, although I have no name to give them."

He offered more earthly gratitude to the boy who came in then, with a tray of coffee and sweetmeats. Younger than Marron, the lad was trying so hard to seem nonchalant, as though it were an everyday chore to serve Hasan, and the Ghost Walker added nothing that mattered to the tedium of the task.

Hasan spoiled it, though, not taking the cup held out to him; he took the boy's chin instead, and lifted his face into the firelight. One eye was bruised and swollen, and one lip was cut; there seemed to be toothmarks in his cheek.

"Shall I send you back to the tents, or back to the women?"

"Hasan, no . . ."

"No more of this, then, you hear me? Practise your writing, make a list . . ."

"Yes, Hasan."

That was all; a wave of the hand and the boy fled, Hasan grinning wickedly at his back.

Marron said, "You couldn't send him to your tents, the way is blocked—"

"—And the women would not have him, he's too old. He

knows that. But they fight, for the privilege of serving me. I endured it before, I did as much myself when I was young; but I won't have it now. This is no time for foolish games, they must draw up a rota and abide by it. Even the children I need fit. If Topar is so marked, imagine what the other lads must look like, the ones who didn't win. I must see them, in the morning; some might need the women truly, for their healing."

"Ask for Elisande. If she's there, she has magic in her fingers. So does her father, though, if you can't find her."

"I know; but Sherett's ointments are good enough for bleeding boys. We will have more use for the healers of Surayon, I fear. And why would I not be able to find Elisande? If Sherett had lost her, I'd simply ask for you. Someone will always know where the Ghost Walker went."

Marron shook his head. "She's not always with me."

"Is she not? I was told so."

He drew breath to deny it, foresaw the difficulties that might lead to, thought that instead he ought to tell Hasan about the djinni, which was surely more important—and then had no need to do either, as the air in one corner of the room suddenly twisted, with a glimmer that drew his eye and Hasan's also.

They watched in shared silence, while that little catch of light grew into a spinning pillar, the breeze of it tugging at their hair. Marron was breathless with tension, with a hope he dared not allow; it seemed an age before there was any further change, a tearing in the air beside the djinni, a softly golden glow with a shadow at its heart, a shadow that showed itself to be a girl as she walked forward into the room from somewhere else entirely.

The glow died, as that tear sealed itself behind her; Elisande stood blinking for a moment, then bobbed a little curtsey to Hasan and came straight to Marron.

She dropped to her knees beside him, and took both his hands in hers. She looked exhausted, her new-cropped hair matted and clinging to her scalp, but there was a feverish brightness in her bruised eyes.

"He didn't die, Marron. He didn't die . . ."

"Where is he?"

"Still there. Probably asleep, by now. He's too weak to walk, and I couldn't carry him. Esren could have brought him through, I think, but he's better there for now, so long as someone goes back to watch over him. I shouldn't have left him, really, but I wanted to tell you . . ."

He nodded and squeezed her hands in his, the best thanks that he could manage. Relief had muted him, he could find no words to say; and those few words seemed to have drained the last of her energy. She slumped beside him, rested her head against his shoulder and lapsed into silence. It was left to Hasan to fill the two cups of coffee, and to pass one to each of them.

"Drink," he said softly. "You need it, both of you. Elisande, this is the best news you could have brought; it is not only Marron who sees virtue in that young man. But you have brought another visitor with you, and I neglect it shamefully; will you introduce us?"

She drained the tiny cup, but shook her head when he moved to refill it, rousing herself with a visible effort. "Forgive me, I was distracted . . . Hasan, this is Djinni Esren Filash Tachur. I freed it from the Dead Waters, where it had been trapped by the 'ifrit; it has sworn to serve me in recompense, but I have hopes that it will be my friend, and a friend to us all . . ."

"If it has helped to save Jemel's life, it is my friend already," and Hasan rose to bow low to the spinning djinni. "Djinni Tachur, you are truly welcome here."

Its voice rang silver in that space, like the chiming of distant bells. "I never thought to find any value in the friendship of humans, but there can be surprises even for the djinn; I could see nothing when I was held in the snare of the 'ifrit, in the Waters. I have been unravelled from the spirit-weft, so this is all like being remade new. It is interesting."

Hasan bowed again. "I am glad; and doubly so, that Elisande has such a protector."

Marron stirred, glancing at her and remembering his earlier doubts. Hasan had carefully not called it a servant, but . . . "Will it protect you?" he murmured. "Have you told it to?"

"She has no need, Ghost Walker," the djinni replied, when she did not. "The djinn have their own honour. I swore to serve, and I will do that. No harm will come to her, that I can prevent."

That was good enough. Marron put his arm around Elisande, because he thought she wanted him to; as she subsided against him with a soft sigh, he said, "Tell me of Jemel, how he was, how he is now." Alive, he knew, and that had briefly been enough; now he wanted more, he wanted to share every moment that she'd spent with him and he had not.

Elisande whispered again, "He didn't die. I thought he would, for a while I thought he'd take me with him, I was so deep inside him and trying so hard; something was sucking at the pair of us and I think it was death, I think it must have been. But he's stubborn, that boy, or he's just got something worth living for," and her hand stroked his arm while her eyes flicked away from his face, to rest for a moment on the djinni. "He fought it more than I did, I don't know where he found the strength, there was none in his body; and at last it just went away. Then I could work on him, I could start to mend what was broken. He needs more, but not now; sleep is better, for a while. He will be fine, Marron, if nothing else harms him. He shouldn't be alone, though, there are 'ifrit in that world who may find him; I ought to go back . . ."

"No, not you. You should rest; I'll go. I cannot heal," *I can heal nothing,* "but I can watch him while he sleeps."

He pulled himself away from her, and saw the resignation in her face as he did so. For a moment he hesitated, but only for a moment. Hasan said briskly, "Yes, go, Marron. You can bring Jemel back when he wakes, if he seems enough recovered. Elisande, you I forbid; you need more than a cup of coffee to restore you. And I would be unhappy if you took Djinni Tachur away from me so quickly; I would like to hear both how it came to be trapped by the 'ifrit, and how you rescued it."

He clapped his hands sharply, twice; there was a scurry of steps beyond the doorway, and the same boy who'd brought the coffee appeared there, gaping soundlessly between the djinni and the unveiled girl.

"Topar, fetch a beaker of juice for the Lady Lisan, and some food; she has a starveling look. And bring her a clean robe, too. One of your own; you are much of her size, and I cannot send her back to Sherett looking like that." The robe she wore had dried in the warmth of the other world, but it was wrinkled and filthy, smelling of sweat and foul water. "If you don't object, my lady?"

"I object to this," she said, fingering the stains on her robe. "As do you; I can see your nostrils working. Thank you, Topar, I would be honoured to borrow your clothes. And a bowl of water, if you could fetch one? If you can carry so much . . . ?"

"Of course, my lady," though he'd need several more hands to do it in a single trip.

"Get help," Hasan ordered brusquely. "I'm sure there must be some other boy awake in this house. Bleeding from the nose, most likely."

Topar was struggling not to grin, as he left; Marron followed him out, not struggling at all against the bubbling elation inside him.

"Topar!"

"Yes, uh, Ghost Walker?"

"When you come back, stay with Hasan and the lady. For her honour's sake, they should have a better chaperone than the djinni. And when she leaves, remind him of his own order, that no one should be alone while the Dancer is abroad. You have heard about the Sand Dancer?"

"Yes, Ghost Walker . . ."

"Good. Hasan's safety lies in your hands, then. Lend me your knife for a moment." He had his own in his belt, and

Dard too; but he felt skittish and ridiculous, more than willing to give the boy a thrill.

Topar drew his knife and handed it to Marron hilt-first, with a puzzled frown. Marron pricked his arm delicately, gave the blade back and gestured the boy to a safe distance as the Daughter smoked up from his blood.

He opened a gateway right there in the corridor and stepped through to the other world, giving Topar a cheerful wave on the way.

HE FOUND HIMSELF standing before a cliff that was quite unmarked by any man's carving, that made a glittering match to the cliff of Rhabat. As always in this world, his arm bled more freely and the pain was greater; he closed the gateway quickly and drew the Daughter back into his wound to stifle it.

Then he ran, his feet as light and foolish as his thoughts. He coursed across the hard-packed dust, along the base of the cliff and through the winding defile beyond, where the opposite wall of this valley closed in; and so came to that same sea that he had seen before, its waters seething as though something monstrous dwelt beneath the surface. Marron spared it barely a glance; he looked along the shore, and there lay Jemel, on the same slab where he had laid him but naked now, his blood-weltered robe tossed to one side.

Elisande must have done that, he thought, approaching more slowly now. She worked best skin to skin; he pictured her lying full-length atop Jemel, her short body stretched against his, and felt a moment of stupid jealousy for her having come first to where he had never yet been. He quelled it in fury at himself—she was surely entitled if anyone was, for the pain his own desire caused her; besides, she'd lain so with him in this world, so why not with Jemel?—and walked up to stand beside his friend.

She had taken his makeshift bandage from Jemel's throat, too. Marron stared in wonder at what he could see there, the livid scar that would mark Jemel for ever now as a man who had been called back miraculously from death. It was almost a match for his own scars, though Jemel's would lose that fresh-made look soon enough, while one of Marron's never would. For the moment, at least, it made them brothers; and it was his marked arm that Marron reached out with, to lay his fingers lightly on Jemel's neck.

He could feel a pulse beneath the tender, brutalised skin, too weak to please him but he rejoiced none the less; that beat of blood was a victory in itself, against Morakh and all his kind. Marron thought he could stand there for hours, for days, only counting the rhythm of it as he gazed down at his friend's face, at the lean body below. The scar was a badge of honour, but Jemel didn't need it; his strength, his character was laid out there for Marron to read in every muscle and every showing bone.

When his eyes moved back to the face again, he saw that Jemel's eyes were open, and his mouth was smiling faintly.

"Jemel . . . How do you feel?"

He didn't really expect an answer, the question was only noise; his spirits were so running over, something had to spill out.

After a while, though, that smile moved, shaping words without ever losing its own shape. There was not much more breath in the Sharai's voice now than there had been before, when his throat was gaping open, but Marron was still caught by the marvel of there being any at all. If Jemel had been here and Marron had been back in the homelands, at the further end of the other world, he thought he'd still have heard each syllable.

"I feel tired . . . Was I dead?"

"No. Almost. Morakh tried to send you, but you wouldn't go."

"Someone pulled me back, then, I remember that . . ."

"Elisande. But she said it was you holding on, she said you saved them both, she'd have gone with you if you hadn't held on. Too stubborn to die, she said."

"Lisan. Yes. I remember her. I thought she pulled me

out." He closed his eyes for a moment, leaving Marron bereft; then they opened again, and his smile stretched. "She lay beside me. I remember the touch of her, telling me that I still had a body. I had forgotten, I think."

Marron nodded, not unhappy that he should remember that. She'd worked so hard to save Jemel, even at the risk of her own life and to the sure loss of her happiness; she deserved to have it acknowledged, by him more than anyone. By him and Marron both.

"Marron?"

"Yes?"

"Lie with me."

Marron blinked, not understanding or else refusing to understand. "What, are you cold? Your robe is here . . ."

"No, fool. But I have been in cold places, and Lisan, this world, they can only warm my body. I have been waiting for you."

"You've been sleeping."

"That's what I said. Take off your robe, and lie down with me. There is an ice-chip in my heart."

That was a thing that Marron knew about; he carried several and had thought Jemel might make another, dying for his sake, because they'd been together. Not even the living Jemel could melt those that remained, he thought, or never had thus far. But this was a new Jemel, remade—if roughly made, with his seam showing—and asking for what he never had before. Demanding, rather. This was a barrier breached, and who knew what might happen on the further side . . . ?

Marron slipped his robe off slowly, and lay down on the rock beside his friend.

It was hard and hot against his skin, but he was only distantly aware of that. Jemel was vulnerable where he was not, and Jemel was not even sweating. He moved for the first time, rolling into Marron's arms, and his skin was warm and dusty, strangely scented with the sharp dry odour of this country. His body settled languidly, as though his bones were too heavy for his own muscles to carry, though he felt strangely light to Marron; his head fell onto Marron's shoulder, and he sighed faintly.

"You are the first man who has held me so since Jazra, the first I have wanted to; but that is not so long. Do I betray his memory, and all our oaths?"

"*No!*" explosively; and then, more quietly, "I do not think the living owe very much to the dead, Jemel." *And I am the master-betrayer of us two, and my master is not even dead* . . .

"I owe him vengeance, that at least. Perhaps that's why I did not choose to follow him, if Elisande is right, that I was fighting; perhaps I have to live, to face Anton d'Escrivey and claim the death-price. Perhaps it wasn't you I came back for . . ."

But his own fingers called him a liar, tracing the patterns of Marron's bones across his skin; his lips, his tongue did the same.

"Give me your breath, Marron, to melt this ice-core that is in me . . ."

Can you do the same for me? Marron thought not; his heart was colder, reminded of Jemel's fixed purpose to slay Sieur Anton. At the same time, though, heart and body and all were quickened by Jemel's touch, heated as the rock could not heat them, nor the sun in the other world. His own hands moved in response, wary of his friend's weakness at first and then more forceful as Jemel snorted, "I am not made of glass," and proved it with fingers that were suddenly as hard as glass, teeth that seemed as sharp.

Marron broke away only briefly, levering himself up on his elbows to gain a little distance, just enough to say, "What if a djinni come by? Or an 'ifrit?"

"What if they do? The djinn do not care about men; the 'ifrit—well, I have frightened death off once already. I will pull faces over your shoulder, and the 'ifrit will go away."

And his arm curled up around Marron's neck and pulled his head down, hard.

*   *   *

NOT SO VERY tired after all, Jemel: unless he stole vigour from Marron, to turn from lazy cat to lion.

It was Marron who was indolent after, content to be a cushion to his friend against the roughness of the rock; it was Jemel who lifted his head—too soon!—to say, "Now we are both men again. And being men, we should go back to our own world where we belong."

"You should sleep," Marron protested in a mutter, meaning *let me sleep, and wake again to find you at my side.* He hadn't slept for how long? He couldn't work it out; this world was turning dark, but his own had been dark a long time before he came here. He'd thought he would never feel tired again, with the Daughter always wakeful in his blood; he'd been wrong.

"Marron, I have slept. I could sleep more, yes—but sleep is like a little death, and I have been too close to his brother to seek him out so soon. We should go back," again. "You are the Ghost Walker; you may be needed."

"Elisande can find me. She has a djinni to ride."

"I remember it, I think; there was something behind her, something she clung to as she pulled me out. Something powerful: did she say she was afraid of falling? She need not have been, it would have held her back. I thought it might have been you. But however that is, she has her duty and you have yours. And I mine: I am servant to the Ghost Walker, and will nudge him when he strays." And did, with long fingers that felt all bone now, no tender touch at all. "Come, up! Open us a door, and take us home."

Marron rose reluctantly, under the scourge of those fingers. He dressed himself, then looked at his friend and said, "Will you wear this?" He lifted Jemel's discarded robe, which was stiff and caked with blood. Even dried and dead, that touch made the Daughter wake inside him, driving down his lethargy. "Or go naked, under all men's eyes?"

Jemel laughed recklessly. "Do I care? Give it me."

He took the robe and knotted it loosely around his waist, like a kilt for decency's sake. "This will do. Now prick yourself, or shall I do it for you . . . ?"

No need for that; but he did hold Marron's hand, his left hand, while the right did the necessary knifework; and didn't let go even while the hot red smoke poured out, while the blood ran.

THEY CAME BACK to a wakeful world, the bay in shadow as it almost always was but the sea to the north running with sunlight. Marron thought the water looked a little clearer than he'd seen it before, and the air smelled a little less bad. Innate honesty forced him to confess to himself that it might simply be walking handfast with Jemel that coloured his judgement, but it was possible too that, freed of their furious captive, the Dead Waters were already beginning to recover.

There was no one to be seen on the waterfront. Jemel retrieved his weapons from where they'd been left lying when he fell, reclaimed Marron's hand determinedly and tugged him on through the gully. Here they walked under men's eyes, and Jemel at least walked with pride; Marron had to struggle against an old resurgent shame, the abiding taint of his upbringing.

One of the guards called down to them, a message from Hasan: would they please seek him out in the Chamber of Audience, where he was meeting with the sheikhs?

"You see?" Jemel said, vindicated. "We are looked for; and you would have slept through their counsels, sluggard. While I famished, for lack of food."

"If it had been urgent," Marron repeated, "he would have sent Elisande."

"Women don't carry messages."

"That one would. Or she'd have sent her djinni."

"The *djinn* don't carry *messages*!"

"That one would, if she sent it."

"Marron, has the world remade itself completely, while I slept?"

Not itself; it remade you, or she did. But he shook his head, laughing, and said, "It's the price of freedom, for the

djinni: that it serve her instead of the 'ifrit. Don't you remember?"

"Yes—but she said she wouldn't abuse it. To send a
djinni with a message, that would be an outrage . . ."

"Between the worlds, where she can't go without it? I'd
do that, Jemel. In her place, I'd do it gladly. Think how
the djinn have had her running to and fro, with no expla-
nation. I guess we know why now, they wanted her here
to free Tachur; but she's entitled to claim her price, full
measure . . ."

"No. Would you give orders to a saint, or to an angel?"

They argued as they walked, but it was all words, all su-
perficial. Deeper, Marron was delighted simply to have the
chance to waste time with Jemel, to argue pointlessly;
deeper yet, he was thinking that Elisande was exactly the
right person to have released the djinni and secured its service. She'd spent time in the desert with the tribes, enough
to know to be wary—though it had reminded her when she
slipped, and he'd been surprised; her face had shown him
just how surprised she was—but still she was Patric at
heart, she wouldn't give it the unquestioning respect it
would have drawn from Jemel, Hasan, any of the Sharai.
She would use it where its attributes were useful, whether
or not it was fitting for a djinni to be so used.

At the house of the Beni Rus, Marron veered in through
the doorway, dragging his friend with him.

"The Chamber of Audience, the message said," Jemel
protested.

"I know; but you're hungry, you said. And you're naked,
near enough. Or had you forgotten? You don't dress as a
tribesman any more, but that's no reason to dress as a beg-
gar in rags."

Jemel glanced down at his improvised kilt, and giggled.
"You're right—the sheikhs would try again to kill me, I
think, if I went before them like this. I had forgotten. I'll
find a robe, Marron, if you find the food. Enough for two,
you need to eat too."

True, he did; and if he felt hungry suddenly, Jemel must

be ravenous. Marron went scouting downstairs, where the boys slept. There if anywhere, he reasoned, he'd find food.

He found more than that, he found wide-eyed wonder and a desperate eagerness to please. There were unsuspected advantages to being the Ghost Walker, he thought, grinning privately as lads little younger than himself fell over themselves in their hurry to fetch bread and fruit and hunks of cold meat, all that was left of the morning meal. Hasan had eaten at dawn with the other men, he learned, and had then been summoned; he'd left his message here too, for Marron and Jemel to follow. There was other news to explain his urgency: three more men had died in the night despite all precautions, their throats savagely slit from behind. All were of different tribes, no one had seen their attacker.

The boys had been told to stay here in their den, and guard themselves and each other. Out of curiosity, Marron asked after Topar and was shown a heap of blankets in a corner; he could just make out a tousled head amidst the bundle, where that boy lay dead to the world, sleeping off the excitements of his night. Marron yawned, and shook his head against a sudden longing for his own bed. If the Sharai commander could go a night without sleep, as Hasan surely had, then so could the Ghost Walker . . .

He enlisted a couple of boys to carry the food and a pitcher of water back up to the hallway, where Jemel stood waiting, wet-headed and clean and decently dressed. They ate on their feet, quickly and rapaciously; then Marron calmly took the pitcher and tipped what was left in it over his own head. The boys gaped, while Jemel cackled. Marron shook water out of his ears, seized his friend's hand and led him out into the sunshine.

Small groups of men were gathered along the poolside to watch them as they went. There was no crush this morning, no intermingling of the tribes. No confrontations either, that Marron could detect: only nervousness, tension, a sullen distrust. Discipline was holding, but for how long? If Morakh wasn't found soon, some hothead would cease be-

lieving in a phantom Sand Dancer, when enemies of long
standing were all too visible and only a knife's cast
away . . .

They hadn't yet reached the doorway to the great hall
they were bound for when they saw a man go running in,
with a bow clutched in his hand.

They glanced at each other, sharing a single thought.
"All the archers should be on guard, or resting," Jemel muttered. Marron simply grunted. He wanted to run after the
man, but restrained himself with an effort; his place was
ambiguous enough already, and Jemel's was worse. Better
not to antagonise the sheikhs by bursting in unannounced,
with hot demands for news. If there was trouble, they'd
learn it soon enough . . .

And did, the simplest way: by meeting Hasan at the
doorway, as he came hurrying out with the archer trailing
him, breathless and shamefaced.

Hasan greeted them with a roar, "Where have you *been*?
No, don't answer, I know where you've been. Forgive my
impatience, but I could have wished to have you back an
hour since. Jemel, I am none the less pleased to see you on
your feet. We have Elisande to thank for that, I know. Are
you fit?"

All this without breaking stride: they had to hasten to
keep up with him.

"Fit enough," Jemel gasped, though the sudden weakness in his voice betrayed the lie. Hasan's gaze was ruthless
in response.

"You look half dead, boy. I'd send you back to the house
to rest and Elisande to tend you further, except that she is
sleeping and I may have need of you too soon." His eyes
moved to Marron, who read the message clearly: it was he
Hasan might need, but the man doubted his commitment, if
he were separated from Jemel. Even a Ghost Walker reluctant to kill might kill regardless, to protect his friend . . .

"Hasan," he demanded, "what has happened?"

"'Ifrit have been flying above the siq, and these lack-
wits," with a jerk of his head back towards the hangdog

archer, "have been loosing at them, and never thought to send a message until one was out of arrows . . ."

"We slew some," the man muttered defensively.

"Aye, and missed many, or else hit with unblessed arrows that could do no harm. They have spent all the hope we had; without an imam here, we had to preserve our few effective weapons. I *told* them that . . ."

And of course they had not listened, or had forgotten when the monstrous shadows of the 'ifrit came swooping at them out of the sky. Marron could understand both the archers and Hasan's fury. He'd heard from Jemel how an unsanctified blade would simply skitter off the creatures' armour, how it needed a pure stroke into an undefended eye to slay them. With the rare potent arrows lost, how many men would the 'ifrit pick off on the wing, how many more would die trying to make that desperate thrust when they came in to land?

That was Hasan's fear, clearly: that invulnerable monsters would destroy his nascent army before ever it had the chance to march. He was running now, abandoning any image of the good commander's unhurried self-control in his urge to see what damage, what danger faced his men.

Marron could have paced him or outpaced him all the way; Jemel, not. So Marron held his friend back when he tried to run, said, "No, be patient. Desert wisdom, Jemel—don't spend your strength."

A sidelong glance, and, "Did you learn that from her?"

"Or from you, I don't remember. You both preach desert at me, as though it were the source of all knowledge."

"All that matters, in the Sands. Important here, too. You're right, we needn't rush. I don't believe this is our day to die, but if it is the 'ifrit will wait for us."

So they walked the siq, while the sounds of running feet faded ahead of them. Straining to follow those rhythms, Marron thought that perhaps the 'ifrit were doing exactly that, were waiting; he could hear no noises else, no sounds of battle.

They caught up with Hasan at the point where the siq

was blocked, near at its end. The Sharai was pacing in the deep shadow, glaring up at a wall of loose rubble ripped from the constricting walls of rock. Men stood in an uncertain huddle, a little distance off and watching him; others—those still with some arrows left, presumably—were stationed on ledges as high as they could safely climb.

Above, above them all, what little sky Marron could see was clear blue and still, host to nothing that flew. Any birds, he thought, must have been frightened away by the 'ifrit; would be crouching probably in cracks and crevices all along the siq, the best shelter they could find. Certainly they weren't singing, any more than they were flying. There was heavy silence this side of the rockfall, broken only by the soft grate of pebbles under Hasan's restless feet.

"They are no fools, these 'ifrit," Hasan said at last, speaking to Marron but meaning to be overheard by the withering tone of his voice, meaning to be fully understood, *the 'ifrit are no fools, but these men of mine* . . . "A couple of dives to fright 'em, then they just drifted on the wind, just within bowshot. And watched, and let the arrows slip by. Counted them, maybe, if 'ifrit can count, or looked for the ones that could harm them if they can tell 'em apart. I don't know. But these dung-heads kept on shooting. They say they killed a few, but they can't show me bodies, because they fell beyond the siq. That's no matter, the 'ifrit fade from this world when they die, there would be no bodies; but they can't reclaim the arrows either.

"The only body they have shown me," with a shadowed glance towards what lay heaped beside a boulder by the path, what looked at first like a bundle of rags and no more, that reminded Marron of Topar asleep in his corner, "is the lad I left with them as a runner. They did send him, but an 'ifrit brought him back to them. They say they didn't think to send another, until Hosim here was out of arrows; I say they were all afraid, and stayed where they were safer until the 'ifrit withdrew. Marron, I need to know where the 'ifrit are now, and what they are doing. Can you find them for me?"

He could, perhaps. The rockslide was beyond climbing, even for him; but he could call up the Daughter and pass it by in the other world, come back to see beyond. He thought he might not need to, though.

"Listen," he said. "Don't you hear?"

"What? I hear nothing . . ." Hasan's voice died even as he said it, as it became untrue: as he began to hear what was already clear to Marron, the sound of stones slipping and falling, just a short way out of sight. No man could climb that treacherous heap of rock, perhaps, but it seemed that something could. From the other side, still out of sight, it was certain that something was.

Hasan gestured, and they began to fall back from the foot of the steep slope. Whatever came down, best to meet it on level ground, and not in a cloud of dust and a hail of falling scree.

Two of the men broke away, going to retrieve the body of the dead boy; Marron nodded, and stepped aside to let them pass. Little they could do in any case, with unblessed blades against 'ifrit, whatever form the creatures came in. Little any of them could do, in all honesty. Hasan's scimitar had been blessed, by Jemel's report; but he was one man, and couldn't be risked alone. He was too valuable. Without his leadership, the Sharai would splinter into factions, and their fighting strength would be dissipated.

Which Hasan knew, it seemed. He drew his blade, but made no move to set himself forward of the others. Instead he called after the men with the body, "Hurry back, and alert the tribes! Tell them to be ready, with spears where they have them. We will try to delay what comes . . ."

Delay would be the most that they could manage, Marron thought, even before he saw the creatures that breasted the height of the wall of tumbled rock before them.

They were 'ifrit, there could be no doubt of that, the glossy black armour of their bodies betrayed them; but these were 'ifrit as he had never seen nor heard of them before. Learning perhaps from the way they'd been beaten off as winged marauders, realising perhaps that flight would be useless in the warren of narrow passageways that was Rhabat, they had remade themselves in a shape designed to be more deadly.

Worms, Marron thought, *giant worms*—but these were worms with overlapping rings of impervious chitin to protect them, with their scorching red eyes buried deep behind great gaping mouths that chewed on air, that strained to chew on more solid flesh.

They rippled over the rockfall and began to slither down, dislodging vast boulders as they came, crushed rock rising in a cloud of powder all about them to speak to the tremendous mass of their new bodies.

"How did they get so heavy?" Jemel whispered. Marron had no answer for him; they'd been half hollow before, or had seemed so, by the ease they had in taking wing and their speed through the air. If these things grew wings, still they'd never fly.

It was hard to judge in all the dust and horror of their coming, but their backs stood perhaps a man's height above the ground and ran perhaps the length of a dozen men laid head to foot, before tapering to a rounded tail. Hasan was right to call for spears, Marron thought, and right too to be backing away now as all the men were, as Marron was himself. Dard was in his right hand, but his left was locked securely on Jemel's sleeve, just in case. Anyone who tried to be a hero, who flung himself forward, would meet those working mouths before ever he came within a sword's thrust of a vulnerable eye.

Retreat only delayed the inevitable, though. The 'ifrit moved slowly in this shape, but their advance was inexorable. Marron had a vision of what would happen when they broke out into Rhabat, how all the gathered men—and the women, Elisande, Julianne—would have nowhere to run. How they'd pack into the houses, and be trapped there; how those bodies would squirm in through the doorways,

how those mouths would find meat at last, while useless
weapons battered against impregnable armour . . .

"Marron!" Hasan called out. "Can you slow them, at
least, can you block the siq?"

He could try. He let go of Jemel's sleeve, trusting his
friend not to be stupid, not to waste his life; he touched
Dard's bitter edge to the wound on his forearm, and drew
the Daughter out. He shaped it into a gateway that filled the
siq from wall to wall; if the 'ifrit tried to pass through it,
they would find themselves back in the land of the djinn.

He stood waiting, while Jemel and Hasan stood with
him, while the other men massed behind. They were all
blind now, seeing nothing but the golden shimmer of another country ahead of them, encased in a crimson frame;
Marron listened, and heard something that at first he did
not understand. A slow crunching, very different from the
rumbling, scraping sounds of 'ifrit bodies dragging over
stone . . .

Uncertainly, he gestured his companions back. Neither
of them actually moved, unless Jemel came a little closer to
his side.

The noise grew steadily louder, *closer* he thought in bewilderment; it seemed to be coming from inside the rock itself, he could see wind-blown sand sift down from ledges,
little flakes of stone fall away . . .

Worms, he thought suddenly, belatedly; and thrust Jemel
behind him as he waved Dard in a frantic sweep as though
to drive Hasan away, as rock shattered and fell like a sheet
of crystal, as the great head of an 'ifrit burst out through the
wall of the siq before him.

It was so close, so dreadfully close. He could see how
the mouth was made in three parts, great beaks that opened
wide and slammed together, that opened again to reach for
him. He could see all the way into the creature's gullet,
monstrous plates that ground together, that could pulverise
rock, that would make short work of a man. Such a foul
throat ought to reek, but did not; the scent of the thing was
dry and sharp, not unpleasant—for a bizarre moment an

image of Jemel came to his mind, Jemel in the other world, scented with that golden dust . . .

He could never remember having closed the gateway, even at the time he was sure he hadn't done that; but the Daughter was suddenly there, a misty red haze hanging in the air between him and the 'ifrit. A flicker of brighter light caught his eye, and that was Jemel's sword desperately slashing over his shoulder, trying to defend him. It wasn't the blade that had the 'ifrit's mouth suddenly snapping shut, though, that drove it back into the tunnel it had chewed. It knew its own strength, as it knew its own peril; the Daughter was what it feared, and rightly so. A single thought from Marron, a momentary summoning of his will, and that frail-seeming mist would have swept forward to engulf, to destroy . . .

He did gather his will, after a moment's thought; he did send the Daughter to destroy. But he sent it upward, against the rock, backing away as he did so and dragging Jemel with him.

Where the Daughter touched, the face of the wall splintered. He drove it in more forcefully and great cracks appeared, running wide and deep; a little nudge more, and a massive slab broke away and fell crashingly to ground, blocking the hole where the 'ifrit had eaten through.

That would hold it back only briefly; but long enough, he hoped. Long enough at least for him to do the same on the other side of the siq, where another 'ifrit was breaking out of the wall.

More were coming in single file along the path, now that it was no longer blocked. They seemed hesitant, however, having once seen the Daughter. They and their brothers inside the rock stood clearly in fear of it; how long that fear would last, how long they would take to realise that it would not be wielded directly against them, Marron couldn't guess.

He moved further down the siq, to where a sharp angle took them out of sight; there he used the Daughter furiously against the rock, creating another landslip as crude and bru-

tal as the 'ifrits' own that had first closed this narrow road.
Not as effective, alas, not to creatures who could chew their
way through solid rock, but it would buy time . . .

Jemel coughed, spat out the dust of the fall and said,
"Marron, not even 'ifrit . . . ?"

"I'm sorry. Not even 'ifrit." They were living, intelligent,
never mind that they were malign; he wouldn't, couldn't
stand and slaughter again.

"To save Rhabat, and all these people?"

"There's got to be another way, Jemel. I can't do it."
With a sword he might fight if he had to—indeed he already had, to save Elisande, though he had failed with Dard
as he failed in so much—but with the Daughter, never.

As he drew it back into his body to quell the burning
pain of his arm, he heard muttered voices at his back, "He
is Patric, he wants us all dead. All but his friends, he will
take them to safety and leave us to perish . . ."

Nothing he could say against that, only prove it untrue
by staying and dying uselessly among them; he was determined suddenly to do that if he must, not to be a traitor
once more. He had betrayed his own people too often; perhaps he betrayed his enemies too by refusing to kill for
them, but he would not abandon them now.

Hasan tried to kill the talk by coming to stand with Marron, by throwing an arm about his shoulders and turning
him away from the rockfall, saying, "Come, you have done
what you can. If you had killed one, the rest would simply
have tunnelled all the way through to Rhabat; you could
not reach them inside the rock."

Even Hasan, though, had a doubtful look in his eye, a
look that said *even one dead would have been a help, and
you might have killed many before they escaped you.*

Marron couldn't dispute any of that, aloud or silently eye
to eye or even to himself, in the privacy of his own head. It
made no difference, in any case. Right or wrong, he was
what he was, what the Daughter and his life had made of
him: he was a man with a strength he dared not use, and he
thought that was worse than being weak.

It was a lot worse than being as Jemel was, treacherously hurt and nobly scarred by it, bravely come from his sickbed to face what battle there might be. It seemed strange, absurd, perverse to Marron that the hurt man should help the whole, that the exhausted should lend strength to the inexhaustible; but that's how it was. Jemel slipped his shoulder under Marron's and wrapped an arm around his waist, and it was true support he offered.

"If you come to the Sharai, you must endure gossip," he murmured. "You can feed them truth," and his mouth was so close to Marron's ear it was almost kissing, surely stoking the fires he described, "or you can listen to their lies; there are no other choices. Do what you must, don't let their whispers drive you."

Marron smiled thinly. "I will not." He could not, rather: not in this.

"One thing, though: if a man calls you a coward to your face, you must kill him, Marron. They will kill you, else; and there will be a mob of them, too many even for you unless you run to the other world, and how would I find you then?"

"I would find you," he said, *if you wanted finding, if the disgrace was not too much even for you.* "But if a man calls me coward, Jemel, I will take him to the other world—and leave him there, if his apologies aren't deep enough to please me."

Some quiet part of him was watching, listening in, gaping in astonishment that they could smile together when such danger threatened at their backs. But the 'ifrit were some little distance behind them now, still behind his rockfall, Marron thought; at least he couldn't hear any pursuit. Fear of the Daughter was delaying them, he guessed; even spirit creatures perhaps had to work, to sustain their courage against the chance of death.

So he and Jemel walked a quiet, shadowed path, two young men bound together by more than clinging arms and close-pressed heads, walking a little apart from their com-

panions; and was it really such a wonder, if their talk
drifted away from terror and towards a dreaming hope?

They came back to reality soon enough, too soon. Marron heard other voices, other footsteps coming towards
them, from around another bend in the siq. He cocked his
head to listen, and thought he could identify a couple of the
newcomers. The others quickened their pace, as they too
caught the sounds of company; Marron held Jemel back,
just a little.

By the time they reached the bend, Hasan was deep in
conversation with Rudel and the King's Shadow. Those two
had brought half a dozen men with them, each armed with
a long spear; Hasan's archers were already past those and
hurrying on, evidently anxious to be clear of this narrow
way before the 'ifrit reappeared.

"Marron, Jemel . . ." Hasan beckoned them forward, to
join the conference. "The sheikhs are organising their people, in the open ground beyond the siq; they will need time,
though, and it is our task to supply it. We must delay the
'ifrit longer, if we can."

Marron glanced up at the high walls that overhung them.
"I can block the path again, if you want me to. That slows
them down, especially if they think they might find me
waiting when they come through."

"If you destroy this path altogether," Rudel said harshly,
"then we are truly trapped, and only the 'ifrit can make a
way through."

They were trapped already, Marron thought, and had
been since the siq was first closed. He opened his mouth to
say so, and was forestalled.

"If the siq is destroyed," Hasan said, "then Rhabat will
die, whatever happens to us who are here now; and more
than the Sharai need Rhabat." He glanced at Julianne's father, who nodded his agreement.

"Thank you, Marron, but I think we need other means, if
we can find them. My own skills are no longer warlike, but
I can make shift when I must; and I have scores to settle
with these 'ifrit, for myself and for Redmond. Keep with

us, lad, but hold your hand until you have to use it. Pulling down the walls of a house is the last resort of a desperate defence."

Marron thought that their case was indeed desperate, if they were dependent on an old man who hadn't made war for forty years. Even when that old man was the King's Shadow; they were far outside the King's realm now.

Rudel was there too, though, with a grim cast to his face and any ambiguity set aside. He had his own daughter to protect, and his own close friendship with Redmond to avenge. Marron had seen him fight before, both with a sword and with fire. Swords were no use here, but whether it was craft or magic, that fire might prove a blessing.

It was Rudel and Hasan between them who decided where to make their stand, where the siq ran straight for a short way. Hasan took a spear himself; Rudel stood at his side, his hands already working in his satchel, while the other spearsmen were ranked behind. Jemel argued to take his place among them, but there was no spare weapon; Marron dragged him to the rear, to wait and watch beside Julianne's father.

They didn't have to wait long. As ever, Marron was first to hear what was coming; he warned the others, and saw them ready themselves before the first 'ifrit showed around the corner.

It heaved its rock-heavy bulk towards them, its body flexing as it came, its great mouth agape. Hasan murmured, "Wait, wait . . . Now!"

Rudel flung a ball of matter that burst into flame as it flew, flaring white against the shadow of the walls. A perfect cast, or else guided by some power the man had to control it: it soared past the open mouth and struck one of the creature's deep-set eyes.

The 'ifrit reared up, hissing, as the fire bit and clung; Hasan was already sprinting forward, the spear raised high in both hands. Marron heard more than one of the Sharai choke down a cry, and Jemel shifted anxiously, seeing how their precious leader risked himself.

Hasan was only a few paces short of the raging 'ifrit when its head crashed back to earth. He might have thrown the spear then, but did not; for certainty's sake, he plunged on and drove it into the flaming eye-socket with all the strength of his body behind his thrust.

The shaft sank in the length of a man's arm, or further. The 'ifrit shrieked; the beaks of its mouth clashed together as its head tossed blindly. Hasan hung onto the spear, seeking to work it deeper while every man who watched was willing him to jump clear and hurry back.

His feet were lifted clean off the ground as the monster reared again; he was tossed from side to side while the spear-butt bent beneath his weight; he was battered cruelly against the canyon wall, and still he clung on. At last, the 'ifrit slumped to ground again. Hasan braced his feet firmly and leaned all his weight on the spear, forcing it in further yet, until flames leaped back at him and the shaft snapped. Marron saw the red glow die in the creature's other eye. Its mouth-parts moved one final time, biting on emptiness; then its so-solid body dissolved slowly into smoke and dust, and was gone.

Hasan threw aside the charred butt of the spear, cried a challenge to the next 'ifrit that was already visible at the corner, and came running to rejoin Rudel.

"That was foolish," the older man said quietly.

"It was necessary."

"Once, perhaps. You have shown them now, that the thing can be done; remember that your people need you, we all need you if we are to survive this day."

"Should I stand back and let some other man run the risk in my place?"

"Yes," Rudel said simply. "You are the commander; you must learn to command, as well as to lead. Here comes another, but this one is not for you."

One of the spearsmen strode forward, shouldering Hasan aside. "You are a great warrior," he grunted, "but the Beni Rus may not claim all the glory. I am Shorif of the Saren; wizard, throw your fireball."

"Very well; though it is not wizardry, and I have only a little left of what is necessary. Hasan, we need another plan. Shorif, be ready, and beware—and do not linger as this madman did, after you have made your thrust. If the creature is wounded only, that may be as well; it might block its broodmates' progress, for a while."

"A wounded animal is more dangerous," Shorif said flatly.

"The 'ifrit are not animals, and wounded or whole, they are deadly. Beware!"

"I know him," Jemel murmured, as Rudel shaped to throw, Shorif to run. "He will try to kill swifter than Hasan did, for his pride's sake and his tribe."

And so would you, Marron thought, *though you have no tribe now; and so would any Sharai . . .*

The fireball soared through the air, and struck again beneath the ridge of the eye; Rudel could say what he liked, but there was wizardry for sure in his aim, if not in the ball's constitution. Like Hasan before him, Shorif was on the move almost before the ball had been thrown, and had covered the best part of the distance before it struck. He trailed the spear behind him as he ran, ready to hurl it straight-armed, direct and true. Pride indeed, Marron thought, to come so close and then to trust a cast, to stand unarmed before the creature after . . .

Where the first 'ifrit had raised its body skyward in the pain of burning, though, this one twisted aside to lash its head against the rock wall. The fire blazed on, and it whistled in its agony; but its still-seeing eye fell on Shorif. He cried out despairingly, and hurled the spear towards that eye. And missed his mark, striking only glossy armour as the massive head lunged towards him.

The spear clattered harmlessly away, and was lost; the man stood immobile for a lethal moment, and the 'ifrit's mouth closed around him.

Marron wanted to look away, and could not. He saw Shorif sucked into that appalling gullet, heard his final scream, heard it abruptly cut off as the beaks snapped together.

One more death for him to answer for, one more that he might have prevented. He wanted to push his way through to the front and plead to be allowed to bring the walls down now; he wanted to do it without permission, to save any more deaths. Delay the 'ifrit long enough, and he could save them all or try to, he could take them out of the valley's trap at least . . .

But Rudel had his wounded monster now, that unnatural fire lodged in its eye; and it was doing what he'd predicted, writhing around in its agony and blocking the path as well as any rockfall. There were other 'ifrit crowding behind, but they couldn't pass, and its lashing body prevented their attempts to mount and slide over it.

That might have been the best that the men could hope for, they might have pulled back then to join the tribes in an ordered defence of the siq's narrow mouth. Something caught Marron's attention, though, a sudden noise breaking through his bitter self-accusation. He stared wildly at one near wall and then the other; he yelled, "Back! Get back!"

The men turned slowly. There was no time to explain, and he was beyond words anyway; Dard in hand, he gestured at the rock where it closed in on both sides of the path, *there* and *there* . . .

As he pointed, so they heard it too, dull ears reacting too late and dull minds lagging even behind that. They had hardly begun to move before the 'ifrit broke through.

Marron seized the man closest to him and wrenched him away, flinging him to safety. A gleaming black beak scythed through the space where he had been and caught another, piercing his ribcage; Marron heard the shocking crunch of bone. There was no other sound; the man died without even the chance to scream his death to the heedless rock that had betrayed him.

The 'ifrit rose up, struck down, and its huge mouth engulfed another man, spear and all. The air was full of screaming now, as this and the other wreaked their terror.

By intent or lucky chance, they had divided the party; Hasan and Rudel were trapped, between them and their wounded, burning broodmate.

The path was open, at Marron's back. The man he'd saved had already fled that way; he could follow, if he chose. So could Jemel, and the King's Shadow. He turned, to tell them to run; but at that moment one of the 'ifrit turned also, its head rose like a snake's head poised to strike, and its jaws reached for Jemel.

Who did not run, of course; who stood with scimitar poised, ready to make a vain and useless thrust towards the creature's unreachable eye.

Ahead almost of Marron's thought, Dard had done the work for him. His arm was bleeding, the Daughter filled his sight. He could have hurled it in an instant, straight into the 'ifrit's mouth and down that grinding gullet; it could have torn the thing apart from within.

Could have done, and did not.

Just for an eyeblink he hesitated, a battleground of oath and instinct; of yearning and fury and self-disgust; and in that moment, the chance was lost.

Slowly, he drew the Daughter back. It was unnecessary now.

Something else had intervened, where he could not. The 'ifrit's terrible head swung from side to side, as if blindly seeking what it could not see; when it struck rock its jaws opened and began to close, and Marron could see how those three beaks carved through the stone like knives through cheese, how swiftly the creature chewed its way into the wall.

Briefly, that was all that he could look at. Then he turned his head, and saw Jemel still rooted where he was, where he had been; and found Julianne's father standing just behind him, smiling faintly.

"Thank you . . ." he whispered.

The King's Shadow shook his head a little. "A young man shouldn't get into the habit of breaking vows," he said. "You have too much to deal with already. If you kill again, you'll loathe yourself for it; but you'll also lose your fear of killing. If once, why not a dozen times more, a hundred? I would hate to see that, for the world's sake. Your friend needs your company, I think. Be swift."

Marron was swift to reach Jemel, slow to find words: "Jemel, I'm sorry . . ." *Sorry I didn't want to kill for you, even for you; I would have done, but the Shadow beat me to it, and I'm sorry for that too, that you needed anyone else to rescue you when I was there . . .*

Jemel shook his head. "An oath is an oath," he said softly. "It would be more dishonourable to break it for me than for others, now. What did he do?"

"I'm not sure. Confused the creature's mind, hid you from its senses, sent it away. The Surayonnaise can cloud a man's sight; I didn't know what the King's Shadow could do, but . . ."

"No one knows what the King's Shadow can do. Look now, see what Hasan can do . . ."

There was, of course, another 'ifrit. Marron had all but forgotten; Jemel had not. Hasan was the other side of it, unreachable.

Marron thought again of sending an 'ifrit to the other world uninvited, or of dropping a doorway beyond it, to offer the trapped men an escape; but neither was needed. For once Jemel had been swifter, to see what was happening.

Hasan had shepherded Rudel behind him, and was using his scimitar like a butcher, hacking at the 'ifrit. Beak or armour, it made no difference: where that blade touched, it cut through. Pieces of the creature fell away, to fray to nothing like smoke in a breeze.

"His sword was blessed long ago, I think," Jemel said, standing relaxed and easy, utterly untroubled now. "He is a man who plans, who thinks ahead."

That was rare among the Sharai, a part of what made Hasan the man he was, with the power that he had. Behind Rudel, the wounded 'ifrit was dying now, as that mystical fire burned ever deeper into its body. Hasan hewed, chopped, finally thrust deep; his victim thrashed and died and was gone, and the men hurried through where it had been.

"Enough," Hasan said, breathing heavily. "Well done, all. Back now, back to join our people; we can do no more here."

They had done no more than survive, Marron thought, and delay the 'ifrit a little; what more could they do in the open, where many of the creatures could come at them at once, where they were more but useful weapons were so few . . . ?

WHERE THE SIQ debouched into the valley proper, they found all the forces of Rhabat drawn up in battle array, each tribe beneath its separate banner and behind its own sheikh. That surely wouldn't have been Hasan's choice, but he had come too late. When the time came, Marron thought, the tribes would fight independently and flee independently, as they always had. His own people would never have won Outremer without that weakness in their enemy; the 'ifrit he thought would have won Rhabat regardless, but it would come easier to them now than it might have done.

Hasan was already running from sheikh to sheikh, trying and failing to persuade them to draw their men together. Rudel stood watching; sensing Marron's eye on him, he turned to say, "Their pride is their strength, and their great failure; but I think it will make no difference today. This is a battle lost before it is fought. Marron, it is stupid to blame yourself for not doing what you cannot do; but if you do no more, will you at least save Julianne, and my daughter? The King's Shadow can save himself . . ."

"I will save whoever I can," he said in reply. "You, too . . ."

"No. It is hopeless, but I think I have to stay. I have some power yet, that I can use. So too does Coren, but he is wise enough to leave at the last, I think, where I am not."

Marron could think of nothing to say; he nodded a reluctant agreement and turned to Jemel, who said, "These are my people. I want to stay, to fight . . ."

"With what? And with whom, where will you stand to die? The Saren will not have you."

"With Hasan."

"Hasan will stand with his tribe, I think, the sheikhs have denied him any other choice. The Beni Rus will not have you either, or not willingly. Jemel, if nothing else," and this was cruel to both of them, but it had to be said, "remember your oath. Your two oaths—to serve me, and to face Sieur Anton. Die here, and you fail both."

Jemel just looked at him, agonised; it was Julianne's father who saved the moment, saying, "Come with me, both of you. You too, Rudel. The Kauram and the Ib' Dharan have left such a space between them, there is plenty of room for us."

SO THEY STOOD alone in the line, four men who had no other place and perhaps no place at all in the battle to come, except that they had chosen to stand among sworn enemies against a greater evil. On every side Marron could hear the murmurs of the tribes, men bidding good luck and farewell to their brothers in arms, courage and fatalism mixed. None that he heard expected to live, they wanted only to die with honour and to have that death reported, to have someone else survive to say the *khalat* for their souls. Marron thought that might be him—but only if he could say it with his friends. If he couldn't save the girls, if he couldn't save Jemel he thought he might stay himself, and die with them. If the Daughter would let him die; he wasn't at all sure about that . . .

Like every man there they stood and waited, gazing across fifty paces of open, rocky ground to the rough cliff where the siq began. They waited longer than Marron had expected; Hasan might have had time to arrange the tribes to his own design, if the sheikhs hadn't set their men so hurriedly.

At last, though, a shadow moved through the shadows of the siq, and came out into sunlight. Many of the men were having their first sight of an 'ifrit, in any form; a hissing whisper coursed down the line.

All along the cliff-face, wiry shrubs started to shake, loose rocks fell in a hail of dust and pebbles; 'ifrit came issuing monstrously from new-made tunnels, a dozen, a score of them rippling out at once, while more came from the siq. A single voice shrieked at the sight; no one laughed.

A few desultory arrows flew; those that hit their marks bounced off. There was still Rudel's fire, but he had little left, he'd said; there was Hasan's sword, perhaps some few other blades that had been blessed. How many 'ifrit could one man kill? Or a dozen men, if there were so many? Not enough, for sure.

Someone ran forward with a spear, stabbing up towards a glowing eye; the 'ifrit swung its head almost contemptuously, broke the spear and broke the man too, Marron thought, sending him sprawling into the path of another monster. That one didn't even bother to bite; it simply rolled over the man, crushing him utterly beneath its massive weight.

The tribes were shifting in their places, muttering hoarsely and casting wild glances around. Marron wondered how long it would be now before the first spirit broke, before these bravest of men began to run.

SEVEN

After the Flood

JUST AS IT was impossible—for Julianne, at least—to look at Marron without seeing the Daughter in his blood, even when his back was turned or his eyes were closed to hide that demonic crimson cast, so she was finding it increasingly hard to look at Elisande without seeing the djinni.

It wasn't always there, at least physically, in so far as a little twist of light and dust could ever be called physical. Even in its absence, though, it seemed to lurk around her friend: a glint in Elisande's eye, an abstraction in her voice. Certainly it was never further than a spoken word away; she had only to say its name and there it was, hovering to do her bidding, the perfect servant. *Esren* she called it, though it was Djinni Tachur to Julianne and every person else.

Like an old servant it assumed privileges, though its service was less than a full day old; Julianne had already found cause to resent its elliptical rudeness. She wondered if she were perhaps becoming jealous. But no, that was absurd. Elisande had been hopelessly preoccupied with Marron for weeks, and she'd never minded that. She should be glad, if anything, that Elisande had a distraction suddenly, another focus for her thoughts now that Marron was so evidently lost to her. And such a distraction, such a servant, a guarantee of strength and security for life: she should be deeply glad of that.

And yet she was resentful, and her native honesty forced her to admit that it was more than the djinni's manner that upset her, and more too than Elisande's interest in her new companion. That was natural, inevitable, and no genuine threat. She thought that the truth lay deeper, that companionship was the key. The Daughter was no kind of comfortable companion, but Marron had Jemel now to content him, if that boy could ever be content. Elisande had lost him or given him up, but she had the djinni to occupy her in his stead, not a substitute perhaps but a clear fascination. And what did Julianne have for herself, what had she gained in this short summer? A husband forced on her, whom she had loved and lost too quickly, almost in a single day; and with the hurt of that still fresh she had found another man whom she could love, she thought. Not instead of Imber, never that, but in addition—and what an addition! Imber or Hasan, either one would make a companion to give value to a girl's life, worth a lifetime's delighted study; and the one she had taken possession of and then fled from between a night and a morning, while the other she could not have at all. Hasan's being married already to Sherett and others too, that was apparently no obstacle; but her being married—albeit in name only, and in reality for just that one desolate, abandoned night—was a fact inescapable and insurmountable. Raised in a distant country among people other than her own, with her mother dead and her father constantly away, she thought that all her life had been a search for companionship; and now she saw her friends achieving what she so deeply yearned for, and the taste of that was bitter to her. That she understood herself so well, that she resented her own ungenerous resentment, only added to her gall.

Having to be grateful to the djinni made it worse yet.
The creature's ability to transfer Elisande between the
worlds had helped to save Jemel's life, and she was of
course grateful for that; it had done both girls more immediate service, though, and she was savagely grateful for this
too.

Elisande had been deeply asleep when word came
through Sherett of the 'ifrits' attacking in the siq. Julianne
had woken her straight away with the news, and the first
thing her friend had done had been to summon the djinni
and disappear, having it convey her all around the valley
while Julianne could do nothing but stay in the confines of
the women's quarters, helping Sherett to organise salves
and bandages against a hoped-for need.

Elisande had returned to report, accurate knowledge to
offset rumour and imagination, which was gift enough.
Then the two girls had come back up to their chamber, in
hopes of watching together the progress of the battle. Their
window was firmly screened, though, as every window
was, and they hadn't been able to shift the heavy shutter. Its
ornate piercings gave them glimpses of the valley, but no
view. After a minute's struggle Elisande had pulled her
away and spoken to the djinni, "Esren, if you please . . ."

One brief touch of the little wisp that was the djinni's
visible body, and the wood had splintered, the entire screen
had fallen out.

And now they sat tightly together in the embrasure, seeing clearly; and even in her overriding anxiety Julianne
found a corner of her mind that was grateful for the chance,
and another corner that resented the source of its supply.
The djinni floated outside the room, on a level with the
window and very much in eyeshot, calmly fifty feet above
the ground. She thought it was goading her deliberately and
disdained to look directly at it, let alone to look directly
down.

Besides, Hasan was out there. From up here, they could
see all the way to the mouth of the siq if they leaned perilously out of the window, as they did. She could see how

the tribes were mustered, a small army but numbers were
unimportant, ten times as many men would make no difference if the'ifrit didn't suffer when they were struck; she
couldn't see Hasan until the last few figures came running
out of the siq. There he was, of course, the last to leave,
where else? And with him Marron and Jemel, Rudel, her
father—all of them down there and she'd forgotten that
they would be, she hadn't thought to ask Sherett; only
about Hasan, and no wonder the woman had given her another of those looks before she answered.

There they all were, though; and all safe, at least for the
moment. Saved to die under her eye, she thought grimly,
seeing how they joined the ranks of warriors, even her father who hadn't been a warrior since before she was born,
and long before.

He was a powerful man, though, he could work miracles
at will; and Rudel too, and Marron. Between them, surely,
there was something they could do . . . ?

SHE WATCHED ALMOST in hope as the first 'ifrit appeared, thinking there would be gouts of flame, perhaps,
and monsters dying. There were men who died, she saw
that, a few; and one little flare of fire from Rudel, that
seemed to madden one of the'ifrit but not to kill. It plunged
into a block of men, threshing and roaring; its cries were
thinned by distance but Julianne could hear them even so,
as she heard the screaming of the men it caught or rolled
upon. Some fled in terror, some assailed its flanks with
scimitars that might as well have been dull boughs of
wood, for all the damage they could do. She wondered if it
were better to be craven or stupidly bold, to live with crip-
pling shame or die with useless honour; she knew what
Hasan's answer would be, and dreaded to see it come.

After that, after she'd seen the banners fall and the bodies lie broken, after she'd seen how the running men infected others from other tribes, how fragile their pride and
courage were—after that, she no longer hoped for magic.

She saw those ponderous and lethal creatures, how many there were and how immune to human weapons' scratchings, and she didn't blame the men at all for running. But where could they run to? She saw how many of the monsters came bursting out of the cliff-face; if they could chew a path through rock, there would be no shelter for anyone anywhere in Rhabat.

"Cowards," Elisande muttered; dashing furious tears from her eyes. "All my life they've told me how brave they were, these damn Sharai, how they love to die in battle; and look at them . . ."

"Don't be hard, love," *though that's my Hasan they're abandoning there, as well as your Marron.* "As well try to stand against a rockfall, or a flood . . ."

Elisande stiffened abruptly, and her eyes went to the djinni. "I think the 'ifrit meant to use Esren to flood the valley, to kill us all that way, did I say?"

"No, but . . ." But she hadn't thought about the djinni; how slow could she be? She held her breath, tried not to hope, couldn't help it as Elisande spoke cautiously.

"Esren, tell me what would happen if you tried to destroy the 'ifrit, as you are."

"I would destroy myself. They have made themselves earthbound bodies, but they are still spirit within. Spirit cannot touch spirit, without a cloak for shield."

It was more than disappointment to Julianne, it was defeat, utter desolation; but not it seemed to Elisande. She said, "Take me," and squirmed to her feet in the embrasure, and stepped out into the air.

Julianne screamed and made a snatch at her, but couldn't reach. Elisande was standing on the wind beside the djinni, wind made visible, streaks of pattern and strange colour swirling around her feet.

"Julianne," frowning, absorbed, "are you *coming*? Hurry!"

"What? No, you're insane, I can't . . ."

"Oh, come on, sweet," and she held a hand out towards

the window, towards a frantic, clinging Julianne. "Esren won't let you fall. Tell her, Esren . . ."

"Daughter of the King's Shadow, I will not let you fall."

And they did not lie, and so she could believe it; and it was better protection than the other djinni had offered her, when it had made her climb so much higher than this. And Hasan, her father, people she loved were down below, in deadly danger, and still she couldn't move. Not till Elisande reached in and gripped her under the armpits, and tugged hard.

"I was scared at first," she said, hauling bodily, "but this is solid ground, or feels it. And we haven't got *time,* Julianne, people are *dying* down there . . ."

And they were, more now, too many; and somehow Julianne managed not to fight her friend, not to flail and kick. And so found herself standing on solid air; and no, it did not feel like solid ground, it had more give in it than that. It was like that floor they'd stood on or that bridge they'd climbed inside the Tower of the King's Daughter, firm underfoot but somehow yielding also. As in that place, there were colours in it that she couldn't name. She yearned for the mist that had wreathed them then, to hide her from where she stood above the world; lacking that, she screwed her eyes tight shut, and clung to Elisande.

"Elisande, what are we *doing*?"

"Going down."

"We could have used the stairs . . ."

"No time. Esren, take us to the battlefield, please. Julianne, listen. We're riding a djinni, near enough, that should attract attention; but we're only a pair of girls, we're going to have to yell at them."

"Yell what?"

"Tell them to run," Elisande said bluntly, "those that aren't already. Tell them to get up high, tell them to climb. Stairs or rocks, doesn't matter, just so long as they're out of reach . . ."

Even if the men would listen, Julianne thought, it would make no difference. Those 'ifrit ate rock; any stair too narrow for their bulk, they could chew the walls wider. Any pinnacle too steep, they could chew the base away until it fell.

Elisande was determined, though. At a word from her, the djinni took them swooping down towards the battle; wind whipped at Julianne's face. She squeaked, and tightened her grip on her friend.

"Julianne, I can't breathe . . ."

"Neither can I."

She did slacken her hold, though, just a little. As the noise of the wind died in her ears, she heard instead the sounds of fighting—or the sounds of failure, rather, the sounds of defeat and death. She cracked her eyes open and saw the gleaming body of an 'ifrit heaving itself along directly below; it held one man skewered in its jaws, while others fled before it.

Something like silence fell among the tribes, as they saw two women floating on a cloud of colour, it must seem to them, with a djinni spinning alongside.

Hasan's voice cried loud, against that hush: "Back, all! Back to the houses, and we will try to defend the doors! We can do no good here . . ."

Him they would listen to. Elisande added her own voice, even as men began to turn and run. "Not the doors—climb higher, as high as you can! Climb high, and trust . . ."

Julianne didn't need to say a word; nor did she have time, as Elisande ordered, "To the Dead Waters now, Esren."

They flew away, skimming above the heads of the fleeing men; Julianne wanted to close her eyes again, against that dizzying landscape. She loved speed, but not like this, with nothing beneath her and nothing to hold to except her tense, excited friend. People were not made to go so fast, she thought, with so little support.

Elisande was screwing her head around, trying to make out what was happening behind them even as the scene dwindled. "Will they listen, will they do as I said?"

"I don't know. You gave them no reason . . ."

"The 'ifrit would have heard too. I'd trust Hasan, but I don't know if he'll trust me . . ."

Julianne couldn't answer that; she knew her man too little, less well perhaps than Elisande, who at least understood the Sharai.

The djinni soared above the narrow gully, giving them a view of the bare, sere heights which Julianne quickly turned her face away from. Elisande was gazing forward, her eyes fixed on the Waters.

"Well, they must trust and so must we," she said, "we dare not linger. Esren, set us down here."

Here was the cliff-edge, high above the storage-caverns and the waterfront, with no way down. Julianne didn't protest, she was only too glad to have good rock beneath her feet again; she slumped rather than sat, hugging her knees to save herself from hugging the ground. Every muscle in her body was shaking; it was an effort even to lift her head, to watch her friend. She didn't understand at all what Elisande meant to do, or why she had had them brought to this place. They were safe from the 'ifrit, true, unless there were any left a-wing, which there didn't seem to be; the sky was clear from one horizon to the other. But she couldn't have meant only to see them safe, she wouldn't have abandoned everyone else . . .

"Esren, do what the 'ifrit would have had you do. Draw up the Dead Waters, as much as you can take, and make a flood to wash the valley clean."

"Lisan, I could take it all."

Amazingly, she laughed. "Well, not that much, perhaps; I don't want to drown my friends. Take enough, though. Make a waterspout, make a storm. And tell me you can kill the 'ifrit that way . . ."

"I can kill the 'ifrit that way," it said, echoing the rhythms of her own voice mockingly.

"Good. Then go and do it."

The djinni dropped from Julianne's sight, down below the edge of the cliff. Elisande beckoned, "Come and see. It's all right, I won't let you fall."

"Elisande, I *climbed* a cliff, remember? Higher than this, it was . . ."

And it hadn't cured her fear, whatever she might pretend, only taught her that fear could be overcome under a pressing need, that her will could be stronger than her terror. And so it was now, under no stronger need than her friend's urging and her own curiosity; she came slowly to her feet and stood beside Elisande, gripping her hand tightly as she looked down.

She was only just in time to find the djinni, a distant glint of light that she lost quickly among the glints of sunlight on water. There was a momentary eddy, where it must have insinuated itself beneath the surface; then there was nothing but the vast sea. She wondered briefly how it must be feeling, returning to its age-old prison; but she didn't know if the djinn did feel things that way, and she had more urgent questions anyway.

"Elisande, I don't understand. The 'ifrit can grow wings, and fly . . ."

"Not now. At least, I don't think so. You saw them; they've changed, become huge, and they've been eating rock. That ought to weigh them down. What kind of wingspan would they need, to lift those bodies? I'm sure they can't do it in time . . ."

She didn't sound sure at all, but the djinni had. It still didn't make sense to Julianne.

"Well, perhaps not—but they can live in water, we know that too."

"Yes—but again, they'd need to change from what they are. I don't think they'll have time. And if I'm right, they won't drown anyway. They'll be crushed. Remember what Esren said, spirit can't touch spirit—but they've made themselves those bodies, and it can do the same, it can make itself a body from the water. When they meet—well, I wouldn't like to be an 'ifrit. That djinni hates them, Julianne. Watch, and trust . . ."

She found it hard, but there was nothing more that she could do. She thrust her doubts aside, and did watch; and saw something greater than an eddy build within the water, saw the surface sucked down into a giant whirlpool. Out of its centre a pillar rose, a massive spinning cone, balanced on its point. It grew broader and higher, sucking up the dark water until the bay below was quite dry, its murky floor exposed; then it moved. It went smashing into the wharf, shattering stone. Julianne didn't see it disappear into the gully, even with her new-found courage she wouldn't lean over as far as Elisande was leaning; but she did see how it pulled more water in its train in a great surge, a wave that battered at the cliff so hard that she swore she could feel it shake the rock she stood on.

A moment later the sound of that meeting rolled up and rolled over her, carried her physically back from the edge and sat her down, hard. That was how it felt, at least: a sound more solid than anything she'd encountered in her life, a sound like a wave itself, felt rather than heard, thudding deep into her bones; the impact of it was impossible to withstand. It passed on, and left utter silence behind it, as though it had stolen all the sound there was. She blinked around, and was meanly glad to see Elisande sprawled in the dust at her side.

Elisande was gaping like a stranded fish, her mouth opening and closing, saying nothing. It took a moment for Julianne to recognise shapes on her friend's lips, to realise she was trying to speak. She laughed—and couldn't hear herself laughing, could only feel it in her throat. Slowly, it dawned on her that she was deaf.

Elisande had made the same discovery, by the way she was poking fingers into her ears and waggling them about. She looked absurd, but Julianne was far from laughing now. She pressed her hands against her own ears, and found that they hurt. Elisande was looking at her fingertips; she raised them to show Julianne the wet red stains of blood.

Julianne pushed herself to her feet and staggered unexpectedly, couldn't catch her balance, had to sit down again in a hurry. She stared wildly at Elisande, and mouthed, *what's happened to us?*

Elisande shrugged, and got cautiously to her knees. She reached across to take Julianne's hands, gripping tightly. They stood up together, supporting each other when they wobbled; it felt like a victory simply to be upright in a strangely dizzying world.

Walking was harder, but they managed it in a slow and unsteady fashion, arms linked like two drunkards, each a prop to the other. At Elisande's tugging insistence, they headed towards the gully.

Julianne wouldn't go close to the edge, she felt too unsafe; even from a little distance, though, they could see dark and turbulent water frothing white as it raced through the narrow canyon. It must have been reaching halfway up those high walls, perhaps more.

Staring down into that hectic moil, she felt as giddy as she had before, when it had been she who was rushing in the djinni's immaterial grasp. She needed to close her eyes again; better yet, she needed to sit down again, and did.

And lay back on good firm rock, and kept her eyes closed against the sun, and felt entirely alone, cut off; and thought it was not so bad, she could live like this. For a short time, for an hour, say. A lifetime might be harder. But her life would be grim in any case, and at least she'd be spared recriminations. She thought Imber would keep her out of kindness now, so she would at least have him to look at. And no need to make dreary, meaningless conversation with other women to pass their time or hers, no need to twist and spy for her father's manipulative schemes . . .

She lay and baked in her isolation, even Elisande left her alone, and she was almost content. Picturing a future in Elessi—*the poor deaf baroness, struck down in the midst of her own folly, such a goodness of the baron to take her back*—she managed almost not to think about Hasan, almost not to wonder what had happened in the valley: whether the men had reached safety in time, because for sure there had not been much time given them; whether they would have climbed high enough, because they'd had no real warning and that water was monstrously deep; whether Hasan had taken the time or trouble to save himself, because he would certainly have been last to leave the field to the 'ifrit and last to set his foot on a flight of steps, herding all his men before him.

Well, it didn't matter. Living or dead, she had to give him up. Perhaps she should be practising now to be a good Elessan hereafter: perhaps she should be hoping that the gathered Sharai were all drowned, and Hasan most particularly so, as he was the only man who could make an army of them. Perhaps—but she was suddenly tired of it all, and too drained to try. She lay and baked, and managed almost not to think at all.

SLOWLY, SLOWLY THE world came back to find her.

It came first as a white hissing, that she took a little time to notice and a little longer to identify as sound. It seemed to be entirely inside her head, and she wondered if this were common among the deaf, that they should hear noises of their own to compensate for losing any other.

It grew louder, though, too loud to live with, surely; perhaps this was what happened to mad people, she thought, that their heads filled with sounds that they could not abide. This was a rushing, thundering noise, that she thought would lift and float her and carry her off, it was so deep and so intense; and even then, it took her a foolishly long time to understand. Memory did it for her in the end, a triggered snatch of a similar roaring and a picture with it: of course, the great falls in the river at Marasson. Water in a dreadful hurry, pounding at rock in its haste. What she was hearing was the sea still gushing through the gorge as the djinni pulled it, still flooding into Rhabat and *oh, let Hasan have climbed high, high . . .*

There was something else she could hear, apart from water. She could hear voices, though she couldn't make out their words.

She opened her eyes, squinted into the light, saw Elisande sitting cross-legged and talking: talking as much with her hands as with her voice, admittedly, but she was at least talking.

The man she was talking to was Julianne's father. She could only see his back and the shadow it cast, but that was plenty. The King's Shadow they called him, but the one he carried was his alone.

She sat up cautiously, finding the world steadier than it had been, or else herself steadier within it. If Elisande said anything about her, she didn't hear it; if one of those expansive hands paused to make a smaller gesture, *your daughter's awake,* she didn't see it. Perhaps he simply knew. At any rate he turned, he smiled and beckoned, and she crawled uncertainly to his side as she had not since she was a child, and a small child at that.

He put a hand out and stroked her hair, tangling his fingers in it, as he had not since she was a child. "Can you hear me, little one?"

She could, though he sounded not quiet but strangely distant yet, and muffled by the constant roar of water; she was glad to be watching his face, to read what his lips said while she listened.

She nodded, and tried a word in answer; but her first "yes" seemed to come out silent, and her second was a bellow that made him flinch, that rang unpleasantly inside her own head.

Elisande laughed, came to her side and cupped her hands over Julianne's ears for a moment.

She felt warmth, an intimate touch that spread all through her, mind and body; and when Elisande took her hands away, the world seemed back in balance. The only trouble that she had in hearing was the way the water's surge overrode all noises else, drowning normal voices . . .

She didn't want to think about drowning. But the question was so very much there in her head, she had to ask it. "How was it in the valley when the waters came, father? Did you have time to see everyone safe?"

He smiled wryly. "I think the waters came as a relief after the djinni, Julianne—at least to the 'ifrit. But no, we couldn't get everyone to safety. I had half an idea what Elisande meant to do, and Hasan took his cue from me; even so, though, there were too many sheikhs with their own ideas, and too much confusion. There were still men milling about on the valley floor; the djinni avoided them, but the water did not. I saw some men go under. I had to, ah, walk to safety myself, in the end; my boots are wet."

She understood him perfectly. He meant that he had stayed to usher or command as many men as possible out of the water's reach, he had lingered too long too far from safety, he had been forced to use his magic to convey himself out of danger as the flood lapped at his heels.

"What of the others?" she asked. "Rudel, Marron? Jemel?"

He smiled; she thought perhaps he understood her just as perfectly. "Rudel I last saw bullying a number of the sheikhs up onto a ledge above the water's rise; I think they will be marooned there for some time, and I think he will not stop talking until the flood recedes. It is probably a waste of breath, but breath is cheap and I can't think of a finer way to waste it. Marron had his arm cut even before the water came; he had the Daughter dancing attendance on him, while he waited for Jemel to be ready to be rescued. I think you need not be concerned about those two."

"And Hasan?"

"Ah, now Hasan was more stubborn, he didn't want to move till all his men were safe, which they never would have been. In the end I had to drag him along with me. He's standing behind you, girl."

She gaped; Elisande giggled, and let her gaze flick past Julianne's shoulder. Something in her face suggested she'd been fighting the desire for a while now.

Julianne wished she could have turned round like a lady and stood up like the baroness she was, with dignity and poise; she feared that she had turned like a child demanding gratification, and then scrambled to her feet like a hoyden.

A whip of wind brought her hair wildly across her face, the only veil she could pretend to.

It didn't matter. He was there, standing in profile to her as he gazed towards the valley, a commander snatched away from his war; but he turned to face her as she rose, and was just a man whom she couldn't believe that she wanted, nor that he wanted her. They were two utterly different disbeliefs, utterly opposed to each other; and the one burned shame into her cheeks, while the other was simply refuted in the avid look in his eyes.

She yearned to respond to that, to hurtle into his arms. But now when she wanted it least, all her father's training came back to her under his eyes; she sank into a ridiculous curtsey, and said, "I am glad to see you safe, my lord. I had been afraid for your welfare."

"And I for yours," he returned. "Lady."

Oh, every inch the lady now, when she ached to be otherwise; she thought he was teasing her, though, as well as speaking true. She managed to find a little acid under her tongue to answer him with, as she whispered, "Prince . . ."

He smiled, and held his hands out to her. Nothing could have held her back then: not her father's disapproving eye, not her friend's fascination, not the brutal, lashing memory of Imber's face, the echo of his voice, the shadow of his fingers' touch on hers.

Still, she thought she would only grip Hasan's hands and exchange barbed courtesies, no more. What more could they do? This was no time for dalliance, it would be absurd . . .

Neither did he dally. He seized her wrists, so that she could feel her own pulse against his fingers' pressure; she could have counted its racing beat, but that she seemed to have forgotten how to count. In his closeness he absorbed her, he made her stupid, senseless, a thing of body and desire and nothing else: no thought at all, no history.

This was his strength, to steal heart and mind together; and other men's wives too, seemingly, where he chose. She had no choice in this, or else she had made it already, and days ago. He drew her close and she did hurtle that last little distance between them, a very long way.

His arms received her and claimed her, while his mouth possessed her. For the first time in her life she tasted passion, and returned it. If a quiet voice somewhere in her head whispered Imber's name again, it was soon lost in the tumult of her body's hunger, and his response.

When at last her arms recalled their duty, uncoiled themselves from his neck and pushed him back—and they had to work to achieve that, against his obstinacy—it was bizarrely not her husband whom she offered as excuse.

"If," she gasped, "if Sherett were to see us, or hear about this—"

"—She would be shocked by your shamelessness, but not surprised at either one of us. Be easy, little one, Julianne," and there was something in the mere way he named her that made her shudder, unless it was his hands' grip around her waist, "lady. The first time I saw you I said that I would marry you, remember? Sherett knows. She will welcome you to my household."

"You did say that, prince. And I said that I was married already . . ."

"You lied. You are no more married than your friend there, Lisan. She told me how it was. They forced you to it, in the absence of your father; they said their words over you, but your man refused you on your wedding night, and you have not been with him since. By our laws, that is no marriage."

When had that happened, when had Elisande betrayed her? She'd find out; but in the meantime, she was bereft of words. He was right, of course. Even by the laws of her own people, a marriage unconsummated could be annulled without stigma, and both parties would be free to marry again. She hated the thought of her Imber—*hers!*—being wed to any woman else; and yet, and yet . . . She had fled him, and now she loved another. Loved them both, she thought, husband and new man too; but could not have them both, and Imber might renounce her in any case, might have done so already, word of it might be chasing her across the desert. Better surely to have one than neither . . .

She temporised; said, "You must speak to my father, prince . . ."

"Lady, I have done so already. He has no quarrel with me over this."

What, had all her world conspired behind her back? She could have been angry, if she hadn't so wanted to weep over her lost boy, *oh, Imber, I'm sorry . . .*

"Then you must allow me to speak to him," she said stiffly, hoping that he would think her angry, would not see how she was fighting tears.

"Lady, I would allow you the world if it were mine to give. Go, speak with him, he is there . . ."

She hadn't meant right this minute; she needed time, and he wasn't allowing her any. She said, "Prince, you were in the midst of a battle, before my father plucked you out. Should you not be concerned with that, rather than with adding another woman to your harem?"

He didn't so much as wince, though she had meant that to bite deep. He said, "Lady, I should be, and I will be. But I saw the djinni come, which you did not. I saw how it assailed the 'ifrit, ahead of the flood; I do not believe that it left one living. You are right, I should go and see, to be sure; but I will not move one step from this place, until I have my answer. Julianne, enough delay. Will you wed me, or no?"

Again, her name in his voice melted her entirely. She pined for Imber, but still said, "Hasan, if my father permit it, I will."

He smiled, and kissed her again: lightly this time, a fleeting warmth that still whispered of the fires that had scorched her before. Then he released her and turned away, as if knowing that she could not move before he did.

Ignoring Elisande's wide grin, she walked back to where her father stood watching and said, "What do you mean to do now, old man—reclaim me from Elessi, in favour of a better offer elsewhere?"

The bitterness in her voice was deliberate, because he would have done exactly that against her own wishes, if he had seen advantage in it; or else he would have forbidden it despite patent desire in her, if it ran contrary to the best interests of his scheming. She was all too conscious of being trade goods in a marketplace. She had been raised to understand that, and had long since schooled herself to acceptance. Even so, she didn't feel inclined to make it too easy for her father. At least no easier than she had already, unwittingly, under the web of that dark, hypnotic spider who had snared her. Having shown how deep she was entangled, she had small chance of persuading him that a protest was anything more than token. She felt like a woman offered diamonds, protesting at the mine; it could hardly carry conviction. But oh, she did wish sometimes to find some poniard sharp enough to pierce all his layers of disguise and dig its way through to the small twisted leathery heart of him, just to test whether it truly had any feeling at all . . .

He looked at her in that neutral manner that had always greeted her temper, that used when she was a child to make her angrier than she had been before; it spoiled all the fun of a tantrum, to see its monumental lack of effect. This time, though, it wasn't his own detachment he offered her; he was only quoting.

"Go where you are sent, Julianne, and marry where you must."

That robbed her of any intent of her own, as so often he had before; this time she was robbed almost of breath, for a moment. "Do you think, do you think that's what the djinni meant . . . ?"

"Child, who can know what a djinni means? If Elisande spends too much time with her Djinni Tachur, she may learn something of what drives it, or what it seeks to achieve; if she does, though, it will have been too much time, and she will be the lesser for the expense of it."

"Your prophecies are more oblique than the djinni's," she grumbled.

"But more accurate. It sees clearly what might happen; I see only vaguely, but what I see is certain. Shall we make your djinni happy, Julianne, shall we say that you must marry again, marry here, marry Hasan?"

"You're not seriously offering me the choice?"

"I am hoping that you would choose what I can offer. I think the evidence supports my hope. Child, do you want that man or not?"

"Yes," she said, on a sigh. "May the God forgive me," *and Imber, somehow, sometime,* "but I do. Even a part-share, I'll share him with Sherett." *He'll be sharing me, after all, some part of me will always yearn elsewhere.* "Can I truly have him?"

"Your marriage to the heir of Elessi would have brought you major influence, perhaps in twenty years, if that young baron doesn't get himself killed meanwhile; it was a prize worth the play. Your marriage to Hasan of the Beni Rus may bring peace between our peoples. Not immediately— I'm afraid that Hasan must have his war, there is nothing we can do now to prevent it—but sooner than it would otherwise have come. You may prevent his razing Outremer. Julianne, you can have him, yes. I think that you must."

Which was what she had known all along. She nodded, a compact concluded. So small a gesture, and yet it meant so much: a rift irreparable torn between herself and her own country—how would this be seen, back in Elessi? That she fled her new-made husband and ran to the arms of a Sharai; and she could dispute nothing in that hard summary—and herself a sacrifice again, for that country's good. A willing sacrifice, to be sure, but she must go under the knife none the less. For once she appreciated her father's foresight in raising her in a far-off land, although it wasn't this that he'd foreseen. She was at least accustomed to living among strangers, and she wouldn't lose friendships by that cutting-off; she had none in Outremer.

Except Elisande, of course. That one she would not lose,

come what might. Though she still might scarify her for
sharing with Hasan what should have been kept private, the
secrets of a desolate wedding-night . . .

Julianne turned to find her, perhaps to confront her; and
found herself forestalled by the simplest of tactics, a kiss on
the cheek and an anxious, "Will you be happy, Julianne? I
think you could be . . ."

"So do I," she said on a sigh. If anyone could ever be
happy, with a constant blade in their heart. Perhaps that was
only the adult condition, though: they were all acquiring
them, Elisande and Marron, Jemel, herself . . . "You
shouldn't have told him, though, Elisande."

"Should I not? He only asked me for confirmation; he'd
guessed already, from something that you said before. And
if my betraying a confidence is the price of your happiness,
sweet, it's worth the paying."

*I could have been as happy otherwise, I could have been
happy with Imber too . . .* But Elisande might never have
guessed at that. She'd known all Julianne's doubts before
they'd met the baron, she'd helped her try to evade that
meeting and try to escape afterwards, try again and succeed
at last. The verity of Imber, the way he'd snared Julianne's
soul at her first sight of him—that had never been confessed, and Elisande might simply not have seen it. Hasan
had done the same, but publicly, for all to see.

Julianne wondered if she would always be a wanton, de-
siring one new man after another. She couldn't quite believe it of herself; but perhaps every girl expected to be
chaste, before discovering the reality of men. Well, however wayward her character should prove, she thought she
could depend on Hasan and Sherett between them to keep
her modest in body, if not in mind . . .

"One thing," Elisande murmured, slipping an arm
around her waist. "I think you can be sure with that man,
that he won't be leaving you to sleep with me tonight . . ."

"Elisande!" Her heart seemed to skitter frenziedly at the
words, the image, the anticipation—and better Hasan than
Imber, perhaps, better a man than an inexperienced boy?—

so that it took her mind a little while to catch up with the full import of what her friend had said. "Tonight? What do you mean, tonight?"

"Oh, I think you're in for another hasty marriage, sweet. Don't you? Look at them."

To be sure, Hasan and her father had their heads locked together in talk; but, "They might as easily be making plans for next month, or next year . . ."

Elisande shook her head. "These things happen quickly; the Sharai do not linger. Life is too uncertain to delay. And they're nomads, remember. Who knows when two wandering families might meet again? Besides, your father's as unpredictable as Hasan. He has to be there, as head of your family; that's more than custom, it's the law. Him or his representative, male and blood," which meant it had to be him, she had none other. "Will he still be here tomorrow, even, can you swear to that? Can he?"

No, of course he couldn't, and neither could she. If the King summoned him again, he would go on the instant and without a word.

He glanced round then, sensing their eyes on him, perhaps; he said, "Elisande, can you tell your djinni that it has done enough, and that we would be grateful if it would put the sea to bed again?"

Elisande nodded, her eyes bright with pleasure at his phrasing. She spoke the djinni's name, quietly but firmly, "Esren!" and it was there, dancing attendance in the air.

"Esren, turn the waters around now."

"I have done so already," it said, its voice chiming coldly in Julianne's ears. "The 'ifrit are no more, and the siq has been cleared of its rockfalls. Some of the water went that way; what remains is running back. I have removed the bodies of the dead men, and set them together in a place that I found, that seemed fitting. I will not have those waters corrupted further."

"Esren, you're a marvel."

"I am a djinni," it said simply, "and so marvellous to you, who are less than I. To my own kind I must be a mockery, for having been snared so by the 'ifrit, who are greater than you but still less than we. Any one of the djinn could have freed me at any time, and they would not."

That was interesting, Julianne thought. It served to explain both the djinni's sour disposition and the service it offered to her friend, over and above the terms of its promise. If it felt betrayed by its own, it must feel a corresponding gratitude to her, and might prove a better companion even than Julianne had hoped.

"I would not say that the 'ifrit are greater than humans," Elisande growled, in high indignation.

"Nevertheless, it is true. They are spirit; you are flesh. They demean themselves by taking form in this world, and so I could destroy them when I did the same; your bodies demean you with every moment that you wear them, and yet you cannot let them slip."

"We have spirit," Julianne suggested, "as well as flesh."

"If that were so, the two should be divisible. I have taken many bodies from the water; leave them where they are or set them otherwise, they will still rot. I do not believe they are uninhabited houses, whose owners have moved elsewhere."

"That is what we are taught."

"It may be that you are taught lies or ignorance, daughter of the King's Shadow. I travelled widely between the worlds, before I was penned in; I never found a human spirit that thrived beyond its body."

"It may be that the djinn do not know all that there is to know," Elisande said snappishly, "or go everywhere that there is to go. I have been in two worlds, yours and ours; perhaps when I leave this body, I will find that there is another yet, and that you are still bound to my service."

"That would be an interesting lesson, Lisan, for both of us. I do not foresee its happening, however."

Do you foresee her death? The question hung in the air, unasked by either girl but very present; Julianne was glad when her father's voice cut through their silence, before

Elisande could yield to the temptation of finding another way to phrase it.

"Children, haven't you learned yet not to debate philosophy with the djinn? It is a thankless exercise. Like fathers, they assume a higher wisdom, and cannot be shaken from it. Julianne, a word with you."

MORE THAN ONE word, in fact, but yet not many: remarkably few, to change utterly the course of a girl's life.

As Elisande had predicted, the wedding was to be that night. "Before the sheikhs can recover from the shocks of the day," her father said, "and seek to forbid it."

"Would they do that?"

"Some might try. They see too much that is Patric already, what with Rudel's and my invasion of their council, and Marron's misappropriation of their prophecy. That in particular is a great confusion to them. If their war leader marry a Patric girl—and not just any girl, not a nameless captive taken in a raid but the daughter of the King's Shadow, no less—they may feel they are being consciously acted against. As they are, in truth; but Hasan will have you, and I will not pass up that opportunity. Even at the cost of another feast," he added heavily, "and this time one that I must pay for."

She surprised herself by laughing, feeling a wash of genuine merriment overtake her. "Even Yaman and Sherett together couldn't make a feast in an afternoon," she consoled him, "even if the kitchens weren't flooded, which they must be."

"Mmm. I don't know if the djinni will have left them so. Perhaps; it has a peculiar affinity with water, and may not see the problem. But a feast there must be, even if it's only stale bread seasoned with good wishes and a little affection. That would certainly be cheaper. The Sharai are generous to their guests, but rapacious in business . . . Ah, don't worry, girl," seeing her expression, "it won't be as you think. Its people may have survived, but this has been a

disaster for Rhabat. Most of the stores were in cellars; the
crops are lost and the land has been drenched with salt
water, much of the livestock will have drowned. We'll all
be on desert commons tonight, and for nights to come.
Whatever the women can conjure up—and it may seriously
be little more than bread and dried fruit—we will call a
feast, and I will pay them handsomely for it. But everyone
will share the same, you'll see. The sheikhs will eat with
their men, and all the tribes will eat with me. And see you
married to Hasan, and who knows? Some at least may see
Outremer married to Sharai, and get to thinking. We can
help them a little, perhaps, by the way we dress you. I must
speak to Sherett . . ."

"Then you'll have to wait," she said, "at least a little, unless you want to swim. The djinni may have turned the
water round, but listen, it's pouring yet."

He smiled at her, a little wearily, as he always had done
when she was being particularly stupid. "Julianne, I could
walk dry-shod and directly into Sherett's private chamber;
I've done it before. You know that. Or Elisande's djinni
could carry us down in glory, to the general amazement of
all. But I'd rather not draw any more attention than we
need just now; we've given the sheikhs cause to be grateful
to us, or rather Elisande has, and that's humiliation enough.
Patrics and guests, and we protected them where they were
helpless . . . Better not to make a public display of talents,
after that. Not if we want to ease this marriage past them
unprotested. Hasan will have trouble with them after, mind;
but you shelter behind your veil, shelter behind Sherett and
the most trouble you'll have will be with their wives.
Though that's trouble enough, I grant you . . ."

"I can take it. I practically grew up in the Emperor's
harem back in Marasson, remember."

"Did you? I thought I forbade you even to visit that
house?"

"Of course you did. So of course I went there as often as
I could—which meant often, with you being away so
much. They made such a fuss of me, sweets and kisses and

all the gossip, it was wonderful. I used to carry messages for the new girls sometimes, to a soldier or a lordling who'd caught their eye."

"Julianne! That's a capital offence, for the messenger as much as the girl . . ."

"Not for me. I was daughter of the King's Shadow, the Emperor himself wouldn't risk your anger by beheading your only child—and besides, I wasn't stupid even then. Even if the girl could write, I wouldn't take a paper. Just a message I could remember, and a token—a scented handkerchief, a flower, anything that might have been my own."

"And if you'd been betrayed, by a soldier or a lordling . . . ?"

"It would have meant their heads too; they wouldn't be so foolish. And why spoil the game, in any case? That court thrives on intrigue, and the girls' affairs are the least part of it. It was the older women I watched more, they were much more interesting. I was a child, but you taught me well—I could see how they fought for influence, how they undermined each other, how they manipulated every whisper that came their way. They were like a collective mother to me," she said, smiling at him brightly. "I learned from them as much as I did from you. So I'm fairly sure I can survive the scheming in the women's quarters, even if it's all turned against me. It won't last long, anyway; whatever happens, whether they go to war or back to their tents, the tribes won't linger here."

INDEED THEY WOULDN'T. Couldn't, rather: Rhabat could not sustain them. Julianne had heard what her father said about stores and crops, but her mind had been on marriage—on marriages, rather, on hope forsaken and hope cautiously reborn—and she hadn't given any thought to the reality of what he'd been describing. She had seen floods before, she had pictures in her memory to call on; but she'd been a child then, and it was only ever the poor who suffered in Marasson. She'd gaped from rooftops at dark rivers flowing through what used to be streets, and had been too young to feel anything other than the thrilling wonder of it all.

Now, though—now she stood high and vulnerable and exposed on the plateau above Rhabat, gazed down on turbulent waters and could see nothing but the devastation they had wrought.

As the djinni had promised, the sea was receding, back to its own bed again; as she had heard, it was not yet gone, and not yet finished doing damage.

They followed a goat-path that tracked along beside the rift. Where it was narrow, the water-level had dropped far enough that she couldn't see it without going right to the edge; Elisande did that, she did not. Enough that she could hear it, still roaring and echoing within the confines of the gully.

Where the rift broadened, where there had been that first quiet pool amid its stand of trees, the flood was quieter but inescapable, a seething mass that ran from wall to wall. A few surviving trees stil showed their tops above the surface, bent and straining; as she watched, one more was swept away, tumbling in the water to show how it had not broken but been plucked up, roots and all. Wiser to be weak, she thought, to snap at the trunk and lose all your topgrowth and still have at least the hope of growing again.

She followed the tree out of sight, seeing how it broke too late against the rock, how currents ripped it asunder; then she moved her gaze effortfully against the flow, to where the gully walls closed in again. A cataract was gushing there, driven by the weight of so much water at its back. Julianne's eyes were drawn further, though, to her first sight of the valley beyond.

It lay open and empty before her, as she had never seen it before and had never thought to see it. The waters were retreating like a slow tide; some of the higher terraces on the far side were visible, stripped of their crops and washed down to bedrock in places. Where some soil still clung, even from this distance she could see white streaks of salt against its sodden black, and knew it would be barren for generations.

She could also see a charnel-heap of drowned horses, camels, other animals. That must have been the djinni's work, plucking them from the water in an excess of tidiness. She remembered that it had done the same for the dead men, but had set them somewhere else in a rare gesture of courtesy. Briefly she wondered where, as it had not said; but momentary curiosity was drowned itself by a sudden pang of distress for little Tezra and Sildana too, who must surely have been trapped in the stables, and so died in that overwhelming flood. Rubon had been lucky to escape it, if he hadn't met some worse fate instead, out in the desert . . .

All else in the valley was still inundated under a sheet of dark, reflective water. Smooth as silk it appeared from this height, drawn tight and creased where it funnelled into the gully, only a little lacy along its lapping edges. All the high doorways in the cliff-face were still submerged; a stain on the rose-pink rock above showed the extent of the flood's reach. There was movement at some of the upper windows, Julianne saw, faces showing. For the first time in years she was glad to be up high and not contained down there, where the stink of the water must be dreadful within the houses. There would be no escape, until the flood had retreated a great deal further.

"Perhaps," she heard her father say musingly to Hasan, "this is not such a good night to hold a wedding?"

"It is the best night possible," came the swift reply. "We must move tomorrow, and no one can say when we will come together again at Rhabat; we have lost this place, for a while. How better to bid it farewell, than with a wedding? And one that does not set the tribes at each other's throats for jealousy, that it was one girl and not another who was chosen . . ."

"It may set all the tribes together at your throat."

"No," Hasan laughed. "I am Hasan; they will forgive me

this. Besides, they have all seen your daughter, they will understand."

"And envy you?"

"What man could not? She is a treasure. But a foreign treasure, so it will not be a case of knives. We fight only over our own. And truly, Coren, we need this. We have won a victory, true—but at a cost greater than the victory was worth. We don't even know what we were fighting for. Why would the 'ifrit want Rhabat, what use would it be to them when they have their own country? They are malicious, dangerous—but never like this, never organised, never an army. We have kept them out, but driven ourselves out too in the doing of it; the siq will be choked with rubble despite the djinni's efforts, I doubt we'll be able to walk out without climbing, and this ground will not yield again in my lifetime. We have lost the heart of our land, or at least seen it grievously hurt. And we have lost friends too, many animals, and much pride. We fought and died; it was a girl and a djinni had to save us. If we give the tribes nothing more to talk about tonight, they will talk about all of this, and victory will become defeat. If we give them a wedding and call their rations a feast, they will dance all night and look to a new morning."

"And when that morning come, they'll be too tired to move before noon. I have been to Sharai weddings. But you're right, of course. Let me talk a little with my daughter . . ."

He took Julianne by the elbow and led her aside. Sharp eyes followed them, and not only Hasan's; Elisande was interested, and Julianne wondered how good a djinni's hearing might be. Perfect, very likely. It could probably hear a whisper from the wrong side of a thunderstorm, if it chose. No point warning her father, then. Besides, she had no secrets from Elisande, except the one.

"So it begins," her father said. "Hasan means every word of what he says—and yet he is also looking ahead, pursuing his dream. If Rhabat is closed to the Sharai, all the more reason for them to seek Ascariel. He will work that image into their heads tonight, the golden city won to replace the rosen that has been lost. If the tribes scatter back to their own lands, then he loses all he's achieved and more; this was their only neutral territory, and the sheikhs won't come again if they go away thinking this a disaster.

"If he can keep these men together as the kernel of his army, if he can give them a vision, something to fight for that they understand—then he wins, and he will in the end win Outremer. You might help to prevent that. At such a marriage, at such a time, you may be privileged to sit with the sheikhs. No point your preaching against the war, you are a woman and would not be listened to; besides, it would be seen as deep disloyalty, to argue against your husband. Bad enough at any time, it is not done among these people, and you'd best find a curb for your wilfulness, daughter; Hasan may grant you some leeway, but Sherett will not. In public, on your wedding-night, even he would be outraged. Still, what you can legitimately do, you can play on their attachment to Rhabat. Stress its beauty, remind them of its importance as a place of trade and conference, plead with them not to abandon it. That would be more than fitting, it would be quite winning in a girl newly married into their culture. The land here will not support them as it used to do; but they can bring in fresh stores, and men to clear the siq of what rubble the floods have left. Give them this as a project, and they will be less keen to go to war; they may lose sight of Ascariel altogether, at least for a time. Or if they're quarrelsome—and they may well be so, tribal loyalties could be resurgent after a battle that's left them nothing to count but their losses—you might quietly feed their tempers, to encourage an open break and dispersal in the morning. You know how to do that with subtlety. Anything, to counter Hasan's keeping them united and focused on Outremer."

"You're asking me to act against my husband," she said, spelling it out forcefully, brutally, "from the very moment that we're married?"

"Yes. Of course. For the sake of both our peoples, Julianne, his and ours. That's why I agreed to this match."

She knew that, none better; but still resented his easy assumption of her compliance. If she were going to marry Hasan—and she was, she really was, though she couldn't quite believe it yet—she wouldn't willingly do it as a spy or a secret enemy. Hasan had chosen her for her own sake, and that was what she wanted to give him: herself, uncomplicated by her father's plots.

And yet he was right, any influence she had she must use, and quickly. Loyalties struggled within her, loyalties to two peoples she hardly knew, two lands she had hardly seen. In theory it was simple and obvious to decide for peace and against war; in practice it meant beginning this new marriage, this new life in dishonesty and guile, where she wanted to bring only trust and wonder and an eager, aching desire.

"Father, if it must be done—will you leave me to do it my own way?" *And not beginning tonight, please, let me have just one night . . .*

"You won't have such an opportunity again, to work on the sheikhs of all the tribes together. And don't think you can lure Hasan out of his intent with sweets, child; he has conceived a passion for you, true, but his other passion burns hotter and deeper by far. That one will not prove vulnerable to soft entreaty, even to please you."

No. That she believed . . . She sighed, and said, "Well, Rhabat was wonderful, and should be so again. And the Sharai do need it. That much I may do with honour, if I can. The rest—we'll see how things fall out tonight."

"Good enough. Don't forget, though, this is what I trained you for, Julianne. Use the skills you have, don't make a waste of all those years."

Well, she was determined not to do that. But she was determined too to be more than a tool of her father's making, as she was to be more than her husband's plaything, his junior wife. She hoped to show them both, these strong men, that she had strengths of her own, and ideas too. She had seen her friends develop strangely, grow into an uncertain independence; she would not willingly give herself into another's possession now. After this night she would be a girl no longer; she intended to be a woman of character, a figure who commanded respect . . .

THEY LINGERED ON the height there, speaking little as they watched the waters dwindle. Eventually they saw movement below, men wading knee-deep between the houses; for appearance's sake they waited longer, until the last of the flood had drained away.

Then, "No hidden stairs down from here, Hasan?" Elisande enquired.

"None that I know of. We are on the wrong side of the ravine to use that passage we descended by before; and I would not take you that way in any case. Marron found an 'ifrit at the tunnel's head, and it may be there yet. Your djinni will not have reached so high with its waterplay."

"If it's there yet, my djinni could deal with it; but no, that's a long and a dull way down. Will you ride with me, Hasan, or walk with the King's Shadow? Julianne will walk, I think . . ."

"Julianne will walk, you know," she said immediately. "Hasan, come with us? If she wants to float about in midair, let her do that; but let her do it alone, she deserves no better company."

He smiled, and shook his head. "Go you with your father, Julianne, this last time before you are mine. If I let Lisan carry me—or the Djinni Tachur, rather—I may at least prevent her making too wild a show of herself."

For a moment, Julianne thought her friend was going to pull a face at him; instead she drew herself up haughtily, at least as high as she could manage, and tried to wither him with a glare.

"How if I make a show of you, though, Hasan? A much-married man on the eve of another wedding, skidding around the sky with a girl, unchaperoned . . . ?"

"Hardly that, with a djinni in attendance. And who knows what mischief you might not get up to, if I let you go alone and unattended? I am with you, Lisan, never doubt it."

Listening to them banter, Julianne thought how much tidier things would have been if it were Elisande he meant to marry tonight. For all of them: Hasan would have acquired a woman of power and a wicked companion, while Julianne's father would still have had his spy; Elisande would have had someone to look to beyond Marron, an end to pining and a meaningful role, while she—she could have stayed half-married to her delightful boy, with the promise of that other half to come when at last she found her way back to him again. No divided loyalties, no private agony of doubt . . .

But life had lost its tidiness, long ago it seemed; even her smooth father could be ruffled sometimes. As when he took her hand and led her through a golden nimbus into the discreet shadows of the gully below—and found himself standing ankle-deep in sticky, stinking mud.

She could have laughed at the disgusted expression on his face, the way he sought too late to lift his clothes above the clinging muck; she could have gagged at the smell of it herself, or shuddered at its chilly touch as it oozed through the seams of her boots. Instead she seized the moment and said, "Father, I know this marriage is politically convenient to you, and you've taken care already to say how you want me to behave, how I should use all the skills you've given me. There's only one thing missing now."

"Is there?" he murmured distractedly, as he picked his way fastidiously through the mud. "What's that?"

"You haven't wished me happy." *And I'm your only child and you're treating me exactly like a tool, a thing you made for a specific purpose; and I should be used to it by now, but I just don't believe that you care . . .*

"Oh, Julianne." He stopped, turned, stared up at her. "Have I not? I'm so sorry. Blame it on the confusions of the day; I've been too caught up in trying to see through this

tangled web of events and consequences. I yearn so much
for a djinni's sight of what may come, sometimes I forget
what I am, a man and a father . . ."

It was a gracious apology, and she might almost have believed it earnest if she hadn't known him too well, if she
couldn't see him already working out what effect this moment might have in the future. She'd never thought of it
that way before, but he was entirely right: he would kill,
she thought, for the foreknowledge of the djinn, unreliable
though it was. Or for anything that would gift him a greater
understanding, that would make him a better servant to his
King. She'd never doubted that he held her in affection; she
was sure that he would wish her happy, so long as that happiness didn't come at the expense of his wider goals. If the
survival of Outremer depended upon her utter misery she
was certain that she knew which way his choice would
fall . . .

Still, she tried not to show that in her smile; and she
would have welcomed his hug, his kiss for they were meant
to be, signs of a love that was quite genuine, if they had
come. That they were interrupted by the djinni's abrupt de-
scent was no injury. The intent had been there, and that was
what mattered. She had touched as deep within her father
as she could reach, and the block she'd encountered was
nothing new and carried no blame.

She watched them come down, her friend and her
husband-to-be, seeming to stand alone on a platform of air
turned solid, while the djinni was only a shimmer in the
dusky light; she was half inclined to suggest that she and
her father join them, that they all be wafted through to Rhabat above the invasive mud. Discretion was all very well,
but the price of it here was vile.

Hasan forestalled her, though, jumping down onto none-
too-solid ground. She heard the squelch as his bare feet
landed, and had to fight to suppress a giggle. She was perhaps none too successful; the look he gave her was imperi-
ous and intended to be crushing. Except that she refused to
be crushed, could not be crushed by him. She returned his

gaze undaunted, and heard the smile in his voice as he
turned to give his hand to Elisande.

"Be careful, Lisan, this is slippery. Ill footing for a lady, I
fear . . ."

Fit for Julianne, he was implying meanly, and her soul
rejoiced. She didn't need her father's good wishes, nor a
djinni's foresight; she needed nothing more than him. Even
the ache of Imber's loss she could bear, so long as she had
Hasan.

ELISANDE DISMISSED THE djinni, discretion again, before
they waded through the mud into the open valley. Hasan
was greeted with joy, by men who'd thought him lost; Julianne could sense how quickly the news would travel between the tribes, *Hasan is safe, we have our leader still . . .*

He stayed with them, though, all the way to the door of
the women's house. She'd been wondering whom he would
tell first, about his intentions for that night; and was answered when Sherett came out to greet them, when he took
her elbow and spoke privately to her.

She knew her man, clearly, or else they had discussed
this already; there was no surprise on her face as she
glanced across. No caution either, no disapproval, if not exactly the welcome that Julianne was hoping for. She looked
harassed more than anything, a woman with burdens
enough already being confronted with something more.

Julianne steeled herself, and hastened over to join them.

"Sherett, it was not my idea to have this happen
tonight . . ." Or at all, if she were honest: it had only been
a dream of desire, that she'd never thought could possibly
turn real.

Sherett's veil hid her mouth, but not her eyes; the sudden
smile was easy to read, as she gripped Julianne's hands and
said, "That I could have guessed. It is this man who has no
patience, who must see everything done at once. It means
that the hall must be cleaned, and Yaman must somehow
gather food enough for a feast, although we have no

kitchens and no stores; but what is that to him? He has decided, he will wed tonight, and so we women must scrub
and clean. Go, then," to her husband, whose mouth was
twitching against his evident iron control, "show those fool
men you are still breathing, for what use that is, and give
them something else to shout about." And more soberly,
"Visit the wounded, Hasan. We carried them up to the
gallery when the waters came; there are few enough survived that far, and I doubt if any will live the night."

"I will," he said, "and thank you, Sherett. You are a
jewel."

"Aye, and I must make another shine tonight. Come
then, girl," with a sharp tug on Julianne's wrists, "we have
a great deal to do, and little enough time for it. Besides
everything else, I will be blamed if you do not look your
part tonight."

Absurdly, Julianne hesitated. "Uh, my feet are filthy, I
don't want to trek mud through the house . . ."

Sherett laughed shortly. "Julianne, there is mud through
half the house already. And the baths are unusable, and we
have no fires and no clean water to waste. We must make
shift somehow. Will you *come* . . . ?"

THEY MADE SHIFT in an upper room, with wet cloths and
ungenerous ewers of cool water that Elisande ferried from a
cistern, she said, that collected the rare rainwater when it
fell on the plateau above. The channels didn't extend as far
as the ravine where they'd been standing earlier to look
down on the valley, but she said there was an intricate net-
work cut into the rock, funnelling the runoff away before
the returning sun could steal it. Every house had its cistern,
water stored against a sudden need; Julianne would be surprised, she said, how much rain the system gathered in a
year . . .

Julianne was surprised that the system existed at all. She
asked how long it had taken the Sharai to create it.

Sherett snorted; Elisande said, "The Sharai do not build,

sweet. Neither do they dig. They just use what they can find or seize."

"What God brings us," Sherett said firmly.

"It's the same thing. Isn't it? God set this in my path, for me to find; God gave my enemy into my hand, so that I might seize what he had. Anyway, Julianne, whoever built Rhabat built the water-system above it. A small people they must have been, unless they used their children for the work. The brats here have a game, where they wriggle into the ducts to sneak from house to house. They get lost, or get stuck in some tight angle, and have to yell for help; and it's always the girls who are sent in to look for them. Boys get too big to fit."

"Not true," from Sherett. "The main channels, at least, a man can squeeze along; they have done so, trying to find their way here. We do send the girls in after lost children, and to keep the channels clear; but that is partly to prevent boys learning what we would prefer men not to know."

"Does any man ever make it this far?" Elisande wanted to know.

"It has happened," Sherett said primly. And said no more; Julianne wondered if Hasan had ever squirmed his way damp and breathless through the dark, to court her privately. Or some other man, perhaps, before Hasan . . . ? She would ask, she thought; but not yet. After the ceremony, perhaps, when they were bonded wife and wife to the same husband . . .

The idea of that ought to seem so strange, she thought; and yet it did not. It had never been her people's custom for a man to take more than one wife, but she'd grown up among people whose custom it was; she'd never for a moment imagined that she would marry within that custom, but she found herself quite comfortable with the thought. Possessiveness had always been a puzzle to her. She could share Hasan with this woman, and not feel jealous or deprived. There were other wives too, older, but they seemed to be of little account; they were not in Rhabat, and she hadn't even heard their names yet. Perhaps it was only the smugness of the new favourite, but she thought she could discount them. Sherett never, but there would never be the need. She hoped . . .

"Tell me about the ceremony," she said, realising suddenly that she knew nothing about the wedding-rites of the Sharai. "Will you be there?"

"Of course. Everyone will be there. And how could I not? That's my husband you're marrying. I must present you, ready for his taking—and you will be presentable, girl, if I have to scrub every inch of skin off and drench you with orangewater after. Lisan, there is still mud beneath those toenails."

"I know it. I can smell it, too—unless that's coming from my own feet. Hold still, Julianne, this pick is sharp, and you can't get blood on your wedding-dress. It's supposed to be bad luck. Symbolic, I suppose . . ."

"Indeed you cannot," Sherett confirmed. "Silly girls have been known to cut themselves deliberately, to delay a match they do not want. In the Sands, within the tribe, very silly girls have been married naked; the men lose patience with such games."

Well, at least she wasn't silly, or not in that way; she'd sooner hasten than delay. She was nervous, of course, but it was anticipation and not nervousness that made her skin shiver. She thought Sherett knew that, from the thoughtful glances that those shivers drew.

She had a silly question, though, knew its foolishness before she asked it; the answer should have been obvious and was not, or not to her.

"If there are no priests, no imams in Rhabat, how can we be married? Who conducts the service?"

Sherett had taken a rough comb of bone to her wet hair, to tease out tangles that the wind had made; she paused in her work now, and her voice sounded genuinely bewildered as she said, "What have imams to do with a marriage?"

Julianne was too stunned to offer any answer. Elisande had to rescue them both, sitting back on her heels to say, "Julianne, sweet, this is not Outremer. It's not even a Catari town, where the imams might hold sway. The Sharai rarely see a priest from one year's end to the next; they say their own prayers in their own way, and deal with God on their own terms. He doesn't have much of a place in wedding arrangements. There's nothing that happens in the Sands— or in Rhabat, or anywhere the Sharai pitch their tents or lay their blankets out—that needs an imam's endorsement."

"Indeed not," Sherett affirmed with vigour. "Why would there be? They are fat men; they know little of our lives, and nothing that is useful."

They know how to make a weapon proof against 'ifrit, Julianne thought. But she was wise enough to know an insult when she heard it, and to recognise prejudice when it was backed by bile; she said mildly, "How is the ceremony conducted, then, if not by a priest, as ours are?" *And how are we married, if not before the God and under His law, as I was . . . ?*

"It's a marketplace," Elisande said cheerfully. "They are much more honest here, they don't disguise the true nature of the event. Sherett and I will make you look as precious as we can, then hide your worst disfigurements behind a veil and disguise your earthy odours with a bucket or two of perfume. Your father hands you over to Hasan, who gives him the price agreed, which is certainly not what you've cost him to rear; the crowd sucks air through its teeth and shakes its head and agrees with itself that poor Hasan's been monstrously overcharged. They have a really nice time, and so do you, because both sides give you presents. In return you give your father his freedom from you, which can't come a moment too soon for any man with an expensive daughter. What you give to Hasan, of course, is your own affair . . ."

Julianne snorted in indignation, put a foot on her friend's shoulder and sent her sprawling across the floor, where she lay curled up and cackling in high delight with herself.

"Stop it, the pair of you!" Sherett ordered, snapping a wet cloth at them that stung where it struck. "We don't have time for childishness. Julianne, I will tell you how the wedding will be. Your part is not difficult, but it must be done perfectly or you will shame me and your father both. And what shames me shames Hasan, what shames Hasan before the tribes shames all the Beni Rus . . ."

Julianne sighed. "Teach me, then, Sherett." She thought that this would become a familiar cry, that some considerable part of their life together might be devoted to Sherett's teaching her how not to shame their husband. She would try to be a dutiful wife and sister-wife, as she had tried to be a dutiful daughter; and if she must break out and be wild sometimes—and she would, she thought, as she always had—she would be wild with Hasan and perhaps with Sherett too, they could all be wild together. If those two had forgotten how, well, she'd just have to teach them . . .

JULIANNE DID FEEL something like an animal being prepared for market, before Sherett was content with her. Nor was Elisande spared, despite her grumbles; even her rough-hewn hair had to be trimmed into respectability, although her head would be decently covered for the feast.

As soon as they were both approved, they were taken to the store of fine clothes that was hoarded here, that the flood had not reached. Julianne's father could have had no chance to speak to Sherett, as he had promised, but it wasn't necessary; their thoughts echoed each other's, unless long tradition simply overruled any other factors.

"You are not of our people, Julianne, but you should dress as we do now, and go barefoot to your wedding. A bride may wear silk, but it must be of our own colour, to honour God's choice of us; the tribes will be glad to see you respect our customs."

Julianne was nothing loath. The gown Sherett picked out for her was deepest blue, so dark it looked almost black except where it sheened in the lamplight; it was simply but beautifully cut, slipping like oil over her skin to hug her tall slender figure. Even without a mirror, she knew she looked well in it. She didn't need Elisande's silent applause, though she smiled her gratitude for it.

Elisande would have her own role in the ceremony—"as you have neither mother nor sister to stand with you, Julianne, you may have your friend"—but was left free to choose her own robe, while Sherett slipped away to supervise the preparations.

She made a dressing-up game of it, trying on a dozen different gowns and parading them for Julianne's approval, each one more exotic than the last. When she had her friend reduced to a state of helpless giggles, she shrugged off the skimpy satin that had induced it and said, "That's better, you were looking altogether too solemnly blue. The dress suits you, Julianne, but the mood does not. Help me now, find something quiet. It's you the men must be looking at tonight . . ."

Between them they chose a crimson gown of watered silk, fine enough to satisfy even Julianne's pampered tastes and dark enough to meet Elisande's insistence that she not outshine the bride. "I'll catch no eyes in this," she said, stroking her palms over the fabric. "I'll feel wonderful, but no man will come close enough to know it. Not like you, sweet. Your Hasan will be hard pressed to keep his hands off you, even under Sherett's eye. Later, though . . ."

"Don't joke, Elisande."

"I'm not joking. It's what you want, isn't it?"

"Oh, yes. It's what I want," more even than she had wanted it before, when Imber had refused her, that dreadful night of misunderstanding. "But I don't want to talk about it. No secret, but it should be left private even so."

"Sorry," her friend said, grinning insouciantly and looking not sorry at all. "I wonder where they'll put you? He can't come here, but I'm not sure you can go to him either, a woman alone in a house of men. We never had a wedding, the times I was here. Perhaps they have a special place—or perhaps you will go to the Beni Rus but Sherett will come with you and sleep across your doorway like a page-boy. She'd keep you private, that one, the men must

be terrified of her. I know I am. I pity Hasan, caught between the two of you; not to mention his other pair, back in
his tents. No one ever does mention them, have you noticed? I expect they're busy doing what good wives do,
raising children. Sherett's given him a couple already, did
you know? She told me that. He'll expect them from you,
too. And soon. Tonight you can enjoy yourselves, but it'll
turn earnest soon enough . . ."

"Elisande, stop. No more. Please? Whatever happens,
it'll be according to custom. That's good enough for me.
And—Elisande, there'll be a man for you too, if you want
one. I'm sure there will."

"Perhaps—but not the one I want. Still," smiling slyly,
mercurial as ever, "at least Rudel won't choose my man for
me, eh? That much I can be sure of. We don't do that in
Surayon; and even if we did, he knows I'd refuse, just to
spite him."

"Oh, your poor father. Elisande, my love, isn't it time for
you two to make some peace between you? It's cruel, the
way you treat him, when you're all the family that he
has . . ."

"Cruel, is it? It was more cruel, the way he treated my
mother. He abandoned her, and she died. I watched her *die*,
Julianne . . ."

"He didn't know. He'd have come back, if he'd known."

"He should have known, he should have seen it in her.
He had time enough to realise what it did to her, every time
he went away. Don't ask me to forgive him, Julianne. I
can't."

"Yes, you can. And I do ask it. He hurts, Elisande, as
badly as you do. He mourns her just as much."

"What, has he told you? Have you been talking about
me? Or her?"

"No," or only a little, "but I've heard his song. It needs no
more. Elisande, for my sake, then, if not your own? Please?"

Elisande only shook her head, but there was perhaps
doubt in her eyes, the moment before she hid them.

Julianne could say no more; it was a blessing, she

thought, that Sherett chose that moment to come back, before the silence could grow oppressive.

BOTH GIRLS WERE coached rigorously in what would be expected of them at the ceremony. That turned out to be a blessing also, even if it didn't seem so at the time. Julianne had thought that getting married would be easy; she'd done it before, after all, and had found it simple enough. It was the being married after that had been hard on her.

This time, though—this time it was more than a girl's natural nervousness in front of strangers that dragged at her heels, slowing her steps as she walked towards what she wanted. It was more than Imber also, though he would be a chain she must carry for a long time, she thought, and possibly for ever: first love brutally betrayed, wilfully betrayed again and again without ever losing its sense of aching wonder.

It was more than two people who were to marry here, it was two cultures that were or likely would be shortly at war, and she had duties that went far beyond making a success of the marriage. She had her father at the one side to remind her of that; she had Elisande at the other to remind her unwittingly of the last time, of Imber; she had Sherett ahead to lead her, to remind her of how alien these people were to whom she was giving herself.

Small wonder if she walked slowly, heavily towards her future, she could forgive herself that. She found it harder to accept her trembling fingers, the greater shudders that seized her body and shortened her breath. They were nothing to do with the political situation or her particular, peculiar circumstances, and all to do with Hasan: just the thought, the anticipation of him and this night to come. He was a man, she reminded herself furiously, no more than that. He was a man and she was a girl, it was natural and inevitable that they should join together in the dark, as thousands did and had done each night since the beginning; and still she couldn't stop the shivers coming. She wanted to take hold of Elisande's hand, to see if that warm grip could suppress them, but her friend might think her fearful. She was not afraid, not that, and would not be thought so.

Her father had decreed that this time—"to save your pretty dresses, children"—they didn't need to wade through the crusting mud ouside. He was the King's Shadow, after all, famous for appearing out of nowhere, and she was his daughter; drama would be expected, the tribes disappointed if it were denied them. This once, they must play to their audience.

Even so, he had asked Elisande not to summon her djinni tonight. That was unnecessary—she'd already made it plain to Julianne that she would do nothing to steal any glory from her friend—but she'd accepted the admonition with a nod and no protest. How they made their entrance was in his hands, and his alone.

His arrival in the women's quarters had raised not an eyebrow between the three of them; his smile as he arranged them in their proper order, as he gestured to Sherett to lead them off along the corridor, suggested that more than eyebrows would be raised shortly among the men of the Sharai where they were gathered in the Chamber of Audience.

They walked—slowly, oh so slowly, as Julianne struggled under her many burdens—and a golden light enveloped them as they went. The walls that had been so close about them were lost in the dark beyond that light, but not merely hidden: taken away, Julianne thought, removed, or else she and her companions had been removed from within the walls.

Briefly they seemed to be nowhere, in a space that had no place in any world. The light they walked in her father had brought with him, be it created or stolen from elsewhere; it wasn't native here. Nothing was, or could be. There was no ground that she could feel beneath her feet, no taste of air, no touch of wind; again she wanted to grope for Elisande's hand. And did not, and was glad a moment later when the smaller girl's fingers touched hers, touched and clung.

"Now," her father's voice sounded strange, thin and muffled though he stood almost shoulder to shoulder with her, "try not to startle, as we come through. Concentrate on startling the men. Grace and elegance, Julianne, and trust me. I'd have walked through fire, to wed your mother; would you do less, to achieve the man you want?"

The darkness faded to shadow, and grew form; sounds of voices swelled up all around them. But there were noises closer, hisses and sharp cracks from beneath their feet, it seemed; and the darkness left them but the light did not, it grew brighter if anything, flickered and flared about them as they walked.

And as they walked, those voices went away again, fell silent one by one. Julianne could see little through the fierce walls of light that encompassed her, but she could feel the weight of many men's stares upon her.

And stiffened her shoulders against them, raised her head; and so perhaps took a little longer than Elisande to realise quite where they were.

In the Chamber of Audience, of course, that much she knew; but there were pillars on all sides, men on all sides, no wall on either hand; her father had brought them into the middle of the hall, then, spurning discretion altogether.

But, the middle of the hall—not an open floor, no . . .

In the middle of the hall was a firepit, and they were walking through it.

ALL THE LENGTH of the firepit they walked, perhaps the length of three tall men laid head to foot, with boots and helmets too; and the fire licked about them all the way, and not a hair was singed, not a bare foot was blistered or even scuffed with ash.

It was all illusion, Julianne thought, just a conjuring-trick. If they were truly walking in the fire she should be treading on shifting logs and cinders, and was not. If she looked down, she thought she'd see her feet walking on a cloudy light, that same soft nimbus that had brought them here, that she could still see like a pale swathe around Sherett ahead of her. The flames would hide it from the staring men, perhaps; or if they caught some glimpse, it could only add to the legend of this moment, *the firelight wrapped itself about them, and would not let them burn . . .*

They came to the end of the firepit, and stepped out onto solid floor; Julianne felt a sudden heat at her back and wanted to hurry now, but was restrained by her father's hand on her elbow.

Seeing the hall clearly for the first time, she saw how crowded it was, packed with men sitting, men standing behind, all gaping. The only clear space was where they were, where the sheikhs sat in a group before them.

On his feet in the centre of that group was Hasan. She let out a soft, slow breath, and stopped walking; stopped thinking almost, focused eyes and mind entirely on him.

He hadn't looked at her, not yet. He'd said something to Sherett, but she had missed it; she heard his wife's response, though, ringing strongly through the silence.

"Husband, as you commanded me, I have brought you the girl of your desire."

"Wife, you bring me more than ever I could deserve."

He set his hands on Sherett's shoulders, and kissed her brow; she stepped aside and beckoned Julianne forward, with her supporters.

And now it was easy, thanks to Sherett's careful rehearsal. She could never have improvised her way through a ceremony like this, it was so at variance with every wedding she'd ever sat through, and she would probably never have kept her temper. She knew what was coming, though, phase by phase and almost moment by moment. She could stand—much like a prize cow at market, yes, but it didn't matter—and keep her eyes fixed on Hasan, as his were fixed on her. No touching yet, but that didn't matter either. The very air between them throbbed with a tension unresolved. Her body shivered in response, and he must have

seen, her gown hugged her skin so closely. Well, let him
see, let him know; there would come a time for touching
later, when he would learn more intimately the effect that
he had on her. No hope of disguising it then, so why worry
now?

She stood proud and silent while he and her father bick-
ered over her value. It was all show, all ritual; the true price
was already agreed, and everyone present knew it. She
stood—still proud, still silent—while the inevitable objection was raised, that she was married already. That was
Elisande's cue to testify that she was virgin still, that her
supposed marriage was a mockery. Her friend played the
part to perfection; her father confirmed that the wedding
had been performed in haste and in his absence. She didn't
have to say a word. Imber—*oh, Imber*—was dismissed
with grunts and shrugs, all the divorce that she needed.

Only once did she depart from what had been drilled into
her, and only in a small way, though it meant much to her.
It was her one chance to speak, and Sherett had told her
that she could say what she liked; it was good form for the
girl to weep and wail and plead, to seem reluctant to leave
her father's care. She wouldn't do that, but when at last—
after she had already been bought and sold, all terms
agreed—Hasan turned to her and said, "Will it please you,
then, to be my wife?" she had her answer ready.

"If it please you. Prince."

Just the one unexpected word, added to a dutiful text; it
made him blink none the less, and add a few words of his
own.

"It pleases me very much. Lady."

And he took her shoulders and kissed her on the forehead, as he had done with Sherett; her skin burned so at his
touch, she hardly heard the great shout that went up all
around, hardly realised that she was again a married
woman.

Her father left her, to join the sheikhs; Elisande and
Sherett took her to one side, to where they would be permitted this once to sit and eat with the men. Among the

men, at least—not close enough to speak with any of them. *Sorry, father . . .*

"Well," Elisande murmured, ever sharp, "do you feel wed?"

She shook her head. "Not without a priest's say-so, how could I?"

"You will," Sherett assured her, and she struggled to suppress another shudder, for fear that they should misunderstand it.

AS HOST, HER father made a clever little speech, praising all present for their valour against the 'ifrit before ever he praised his daughter or her new-made husband. He added that in honour of the occasion, city girl wedded to desert lord, they would eat only desert food tonight, "to give her a taste for it."

A ripple of laughter ran around the hall. No one was deceived, they all knew the true reason, but they were glad to hear him make a joke of it.

In fact, the feast was not so sparse as he'd suggested. There was meat in plenty, though they must have slaughtered half the surviving herds to supply it; there was fresh-baked bread for all, though Yaman must have begged flour from every careful man who carried his own supply, and Julianne couldn't imagine what she'd done for an oven. No grit in it, and no charring: it was far from desert bread.

And there was fruit and toasted almonds, plenty enough for a feast even without the flasks of *jereth* that were passed from hand to hand to give a touch of splendour to the occasion. The women were brought their own, with beakers to drink from. Julianne had eaten little, as befitted a new bride, but she sipped gladly and eyed Hasan over the brim of her cup. She couldn't take her eyes from him; she had tried, but they kept drifting back of their own accord. It was manifest that Sherett approved; it was, she supposed, inevitable that Elisande would tease.

"Look your fill, girl. He'll be too close for seeing soon, and the lights'll be out."

Julianne wished she'd been trained to control her blushing as well as her tongue. As the one was impossible, though, she decided to let the other loose. "Oh, and I suppose you've not been looking for Marron, in all this scrimmage?"

Elisande just glowered at her. Instantly sorry, Julianne changed tack rapidly. "Anyway, I thought you said there'd be presents for me?"

"That's right."

"So where are they, then?"

"A man cannot give presents to another's wife," Sherett said, sounding genuinely shocked. "After the meal, Hasan will receive the bride-gifts on your behalf."

"Oh. Yes, of course he would. And what, he gives them to me later?"

"No. He gives them into my charge, as the senior wife present. You are a girl yet, Julianne, and girls should be modest; a young wife should not flaunt gold before her elders. I will decide when you are ready to receive your gifts. In the meantime, they will be stowed with our other treasures."

"Oh," again. But yes, that sounded truly Sharai: to hoard wealth, rather than display it. "Um, do I actually have a chance to see them, before you lock them away?"

Sherett laughed. "Greedy child. Yes, you do. They will be brought to your room tonight, and you may play to your heart's content until the morning."

Somehow, she had made that sound implicitly plural, and inherently lewd. Julianne's cheeks were on fire again, goaded by Elisande's speaking silence. Ah, well. They might guess, but they couldn't possibly know. For once she blessed the secrecy of the veil.

NONE OF THE men made any approach to them during the meal; it would be improper, Julianne supposed, to ad-

dress a woman in her husband's presence. She saw Rudel
suddenly, sitting among the sheikhs where she was sure he
had not been before. He might legitimately have come
across to speak to his daughter—but of course he would not
do that, nor would Elisande welcome it if he did.

One of the serving-women came with a tray, to clear
their dishes away; as she knelt to her work, she said, "I
have a message for you, Julianne. From the bearded
Patric."

"Rudel?"

"Yes. He asks me to tell you that the Ghost Walker has
returned, with the tribeless one. That one is sick still from
his wound, and Rudel has treated him. He sleeps now, and
the Ghost Walker stays with him."

That wasn't a message for Julianne. She glanced aside,
to be sure that Elisande had heard, and caught her staring at
her father. If there were a message in the look, Julianne
couldn't read it.

She sighed, and turned her eyes back to Hasan.

AS WITH MOST feasts Julianne had attended in her life, it
was hard to say exactly when the meal was over; the bread
and meat were long gone, but men still nibbled from bowls
of nuts and candied fruits. She had no appetite even to nib-
ble; she did peel an orange by touch, but set it aside un-
eaten as she saw the sheikhs lean over to Hasan one by one,
passing him small things that gleamed and sometimes
sparkled in the light. He thanked each man formally, and
gave the gift courteous attention before placing it on a tray
before him and turning to receive the next.

"This will take a long time," Sherett said, "and it is not
good for you to watch. You are too acquisitive, Julianne.
Come, we will leave now and see you to your chamber."

Was she acquisitive? She didn't think so—except in the
matter of husbands, of course. Talking about the presents
had been a distraction, no more. She didn't want to go, but
that had nothing to do with the increasing mound of gifts.

She stood, though, practising obedience, and looked back only once as Sherett led them out. She couldn't catch Hasan's eye, but her father looked up and blew her a rare kiss. That warmed her heart, though it did not quell its fluttering.

THIS TIME THEY did have to brave the mud outside, as Elisande was still honouring her promise not to call for the djinni. A path of sorts had been cleared alongside the foul and stinking pool, but their feet and the hems of their dresses were still filthy before they came to the house of the Beni Rus.

There were guards at the doorway as ever, but they bowed the women through. Well, that answered one question, at least; she would spend her wedding-night in the house of her husband. Perhaps it should never have been a question. Would Sherett stay, would Elisande? Surely not; the Sharai might conduct their marriages like a cattle-mart, but they had a strong sense of what was decent. Privacy must be vital, in a world of tents . . .

Some effort had clearly been made to clean the hallway; Sherett dabbled her bare feet in a bowl set there for the purpose, and instructed the other two to do the same.

This house was plainer by far than the women's; there were no rugs in the passageways, and no hangings on the walls. That gave her a better chance to admire the architecture, she supposed, which was magnificent; but she really wasn't in the mood to gawp at elaborate mouldings or wonder how they'd worked the rock so finely. Besides, Sherett was unlikely to encourage dawdling . . .

Indeed, she hurried the girls up several flights of stairs, and so into a high room where a dull fire and the dim light of a single oil-lamp in the window were barely enough to show them how simple the furnishings were. Rugs on the floor, and a fur-covered pallet; a low table with folding legs with a plain stool set beside it, one large chest with an intricate lock, on which stood another bowl of water with towels beside. Julianne guessed that Hasan's tent would look a lot like this inside.

"Good," Sherett said. "Lift that bowl down, Lisan, and help Julianne to wash her feet properly; she must be clean, to greet Hasan when he comes."

They did as they were told. When they were finished, Julianne gazed uncertainly at the murky water and said, "Should I ask for another bowl, for Hasan?"

"You cannot give orders in this house, girl. Our husband will ask for water if he needs it; and you will wash his feet."

Rebellion stirred momentarily, pride warring with obedience. Thinking about it, though, she gave a submissive nod, which served also to hide her expression from the sharp eyes of her companions. She thought she might find some fun in washing Hasan's feet, as a preliminary . . .

"Now, out of that robe, Julianne. It is dirty; and besides, silk is for public show, not for the bedchamber."

"Oh? And how then shall I greet our husband, when he comes?"

"In your bride-gifts, of course," Elisande suggested wickedly. Julianne's temper flared for a moment, and was lost in a sudden surge of giggles as she pictured herself clad in gold and jewellery and nothing else. Shyness had no place between husband and wife, between Hasan and her tonight; but even so . . .

Sherett simply snorted, threw up the lid of the chest and drew out a simple woollen robe, Sharai blue of course.

"You will greet him as a modest maiden, dressed in the style of your own tribe and his. Lisan can teach you the ties."

She knew them already. Her fingers were unaccountably clumsy tonight, but Sherett watched closely, and finally nodded her satisfaction.

"Now the veil, so. You need not hood your hair in your husband's house, but it is his privilege to reveal your face. Well, we are done. Be good, girl; give him pleasure, and he will give it you a hundredfold. I know my man. Ours." Surprisingly she kissed her then, as Hasan had done, formally on the forehead. "You will have a wait; use it to prepare yourself, in peace. We will leave you now."

"What, all unchaperoned in a house of men?" Julianne was fighting to keep her voice light, but a quaver betrayed her.

"In your husband's house, you need none. What, do you suppose I bring a chaperone when I come to the Beni Rus? Every man here would die for you tonight, Julianne. Be easy."

She hadn't actually been nervous of the men, but she said no more. Elisande hugged her fiercely, pushed both their veils aside for a warmer kiss than Sherett's had been, and then rearranged Julianne's for her with fingers that fumbled just a little.

"Julianne . . ." She sounded suddenly more tearful than teasing. "Enjoy him, and be happy. I will miss you . . ."

It only struck Julianne then that their paths must part here, tonight; she would follow her husband in the morning, and Elisande—she didn't know what Elisande would do, or where go.

Her friend hurried out of the room, though, before she could ask questions. Likely Elisande had no answers, and feared to be asked. Her choices must be few. She could trail Marron like a dog, perhaps, and be miserable; or travel with her father and be worse than miserable, snared in that old and weary passion that twisted both of them out of their true character . . .

TIME PASSED. SHE explored the room from corner to corner, and found nothing in it that she had not already seen; she explored the trunk and found nothing in it but clothing, all dull to her fingers and drab to her eyes.

She gazed out of the window, and saw all the valley dark; she twisted her head to look up at the stars for a while, but that made her neck ache and taught her nothing. She had no talent to read the future in the constellations, nor in anything else. Like her father, she briefly longed for a djinni's foresight; but it had been a djinni's foresight that had brought her to this, and she was still uncertain whether she had gained or lost by it.

SHE HAD GAINED trinkets, at least, when she was allowed them. It took two men to carry the great tray of wedding-gifts into the room; they set it down on the chest, bowed to her Sharai-style, with graceful hands, and said they would stand guard outside the door until Hasan should come.

Oh, let him hurry, she thought, kneeling beside the chest to toy with the heaped adornments.

Necklets, armlets, anklets, chains of heavy gold; other work that was more ornate, tiny boxes of finest filigree studded with gems and strung on a delicate chain to be worn at the waist, if she were ever permitted to wear them . . .

She tried on some pretty bangles despite Sherett's injunction, and admired the look and feel of them on her arms. And thought, *nomads wear their wealth—except for the Sharai, who store it in secret. As they will store me, veiled and hidden from the world. Hasan has bought me—and paid too much, the fool!—and will keep me as a treasure, one of his several treasures . . .*

She let the bangles slip, listened to their clatter as they fell back onto the pile, watched one tumble onto the carpet and reached out to retrieve it.

And then, just then heard the soft hiss of a man's breath at her back; and thought Hasan had come for her at last, at long last, and had found her unprepared, weltering in misery.

And took a moment before she turned to greet him, trying to have a smile ready for when he lifted back her veil—

—AND IN THAT moment felt a hand close like iron on her throat, and heard a sour voice whisper, "You think he has you, and you him? No, you are wrong, girl. I have you now . . ."

The room was growing darker yet, as her mind grew dizzy. She opened her mouth to scream, and found no breath to do it with; she wrenched her head around in a desperate effort, and saw Morakh's face too close to hers, far too close but the walls it seemed were closer and the ceiling was coming down so fast, and suddenly there was no floor beneath her and nothing she could do but fall, and oh, she was so afraid of falling . . .